DECONSTRUCTED

SHARON K. ANGELICI

©2025

Write with Light Publications Colorado, USA

Paperback ISBN: 978-1-7378158-9-1
Hardcover ISBN: 978-1-970289-03-9

Library of Congress Number:

Dedication

To the author community, thank you for understanding and sharing the language of the indie author world with me. Jen, Donna, Alaina, Alicia, Charlie, Jamie, SWBC and many more GCLS authors, you are proof an introvert like me can overcome her fears. Thank you for your support and for your friendship.

To Whitney, thank you for inspiring sobriety in my storytelling. You matter and so does Ostrichized.

Kathy, thank you for Write With Light and for all the support as we publish the twelfth book together.

Hill, thank you for being here. I'm proud of you.

Mom, the new normal without you in it sucks ass. I wish you were here for every book I've published in the seven years you've been gone. You would have loved Morgan and Ella, and I think you'd have liked the rest of my work. They're all a part of my queer little heart and I wish you'd have known this part of me.

Michelle, Isa, Peg and Paula, I can never thank you four enough for the support and for the early read-throughs of very very rough drafts. Thank you for always showing up for me. I am grateful for the space you've made for me in your lives. Isa, my LEGO wife, I cherish every scoop of pieces and scatter of parts. Let's never stop feeding that inner child; the 'research' never stops, and neither should the slushies.

Rach, none of this happens without the courage of an eighteen year old young woman. Everything changed the day your feet hit the ground in our home.

Roz, you are so much more than my favorite editor. You challenge me to be better and to kill my darlings. Thank you.

Rach and Roz, my creative co-conspirators. Your talent and patience make it possible for the rest of the world to read my work. I'm honored to share this earth with our growing family. Mamaw kisses to K & A.

David, Victoria and David, the gratitude is too immense for me to express in this dedication. Know that I cannot share the worlds in my imagination without your support and creativity. Thank you for all the adventures, even as adulthood takes hold. Never lose the joy of play.

To my readers,

Please know that the characters in Deconstructed go through crisis involving injury, conversations of suicide, emergency situations and trauma.

DE
CON
STRUCTED

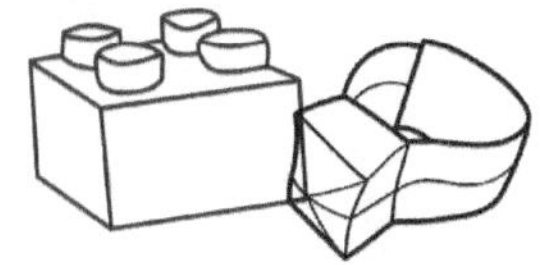

** This story embraces the world of Lego collecting. A world the author adores. With respect to the brand and copyright, the characters in *Deconstructed* experience the same world known as the Briick world.

1.

The Absolutely Not

Ella fidgeted, rolling and tipping the velvet box in her hand. This moment was supposed to be magical, memorable. The culmination of countless thoughts and plans.

The flower petals danced around her foot as she froze. She saw lips moving, heard the words but the flavor left a bitter taste.

"No?" Ella repeated. She was down on one knee, dressed in her perfectly pressed formal uniform, the tips of her polished boots reflecting the sun's light. She'd planned everything. The flowers in painted pots, assembled, not cut. The meticulously selected music playing through the sound system from their loft. The candles lit on the rooftop patio table flickering from the light breeze. The fizzy drinks bubbling in the fluted glasses to celebrate the beginning of forever.

'No' was not the answer she'd expected. It wasn't the dream come true. It was the implosion of a future she didn't know she wanted until she'd fallen for Morgan Elise Hail.

Why, after eight years, could all of this lead to the answer 'no'?

2.

Months Earlier

The Calendar

"Are you ready for this?" Ella leaned against the boxes stacked on the wheeled cart.

"Am I ready to watch you sign boobs and flex with gym chicks?" Lester unfolded the collapsible table and kicked it into the upright position. "Yeah, Cinder. I'm ready."

Ella considered his summary of the last few calendar sale sessions. "There were two chicks from the gym, you jerk and they're my boobs I'm signing." She adjusted the table's location, pushing it in line with the others, before unloading the boxes of firefighter calendars.

"Cinder, I've seen you all kinds of ways, but I never guessed it'd be sideways." He unfolded the calendar until it flipped to the image of Ella in her February cupid costume.

"Morgan loves my calendar page this year." She flashed a cheeky grin.

"She would." He tossed the calendar on the table. "If you keep this up they'll be able to do an entire twelve months." He fanned his hands in the air, as if displaying a title across a marquee. "Ella Eastman, Lady Firefighter."

"Cut the shit, Soot Boy." Ella did a quick count in her head. "You are right, though. A few more and I won't need the rest of you bums to show up for signings." The comment was lighthearted but still provoked groans from the rest of the guys casually setting up their prearranged positions for the afternoon signing session.

They were Station Eight-Eighteen and as close to family as any professionals could be. She'd been with them for as long as she hadn't: nearly eighteen years. A lifetime, if she considered the innocent she had been as a probationary member of the team. Fast approaching forty, Ella had big future decisions to make. She had an incredible life outside the station. A life with the woman who'd stolen her heart. Two separate but important worlds growing impossible to hold apart on many occasions. *Morgan*, she thought, *She's the most important person in my world.*

"You've got that look." Les bumped her shoulder.

"What look?" She knew she'd been caught again. Why did thinking of Morgan reduce her to a gooey pile of partner mush.

"That 'I love my girlfriend' look," he teased.

She combed through the lengths of hair, twisting it into a sloppy top bun. "Stuff it." She shoved him away, knowing without a doubt she did in fact have that look on her face, that tingle in her heart and desire coursing through her blood. She loved Morgan more today than the day before and there were times she questioned how she'd ever gained such extraordinary luck.

"Sooo…" he teased, drawing out the word dramatically. "Did you figure out how you're going to ask her yet?" He planted his elbows on the tabletop, resting his chin in his hands with fluttering lashes. "Did ya, did ya?"

"Don't be such a child," Ella said. She was evading, and they both knew it. She was struggling to put together a single solid idea for the perfect proposal.

"Come on, Cinder." He cut the cello tape on the box and passed a handful of firefighter calendars to Ella. "You know she'll say yes. There's no other answer, and you also know she's waiting for *you* to be ready."

"It's a big deal, Soot."

He chuckled. "The big deal was when she showed up for that." He pointed at her forearm scar with the corner of his calendar.

Ella rubbed the jagged mark on her skin, a permanent reminder of one of the worst arson fire events of her career. "Hell yeah, she was somethin' wasn't she." The pride in Ella's eyes punctuated her admiration for the small but mighty woman she loved.

"She sure the hell was, and is," Les emphasized. "So ask her already."

"I want it to be perfect."

"Ah, hell Cinder. Nothing's perfect," Lester said. "You should know that by now." He slid onto the metal folding chair beside hers. "Just ask."

"Don't worry. I will when everything feels right." It wasn't easy to let go of her need to make it perfect. Morgan was more than special; she was hope and joy, comfort and pleasure, and it was the pleasure that was unexpected when they'd met more than eight years before.

Ella wasn't a player, but she played. Her athletic body drew the attention of all genders, but the moment Morgan waved her disapproving glance up and down Ella's Arsonist cosplay costume, something long-buried inside the firefighter came to life. Yes, the proposal needed to be big; Morgan deserved a story to tell for the rest of their lives.

Ella was ready, mostly. She had long ago sold her house, and she and Morgan were making things work. She was balancing a demanding career with a supportive partner, but she couldn't explain why the next big step hinged on a perfect proposal moment.

Their eight-year anniversary had arrived, and wasn't that the leaping off point? What more could they need before taking the next step? The answer was perfection; somehow she had to give Morgan everything, and that included a perfect proposal.

~~~~~~~~~~

"How many does that make?" Lester tapped the small appliance with the toe of his boot.

Every time one of the countertop ovens appeared, Ella was quick to hide it beneath the table.The joke, now long running, was at the very least embarrassing.

Roger, another member of the department, chaffed as he leaned forward to add, "Are you asking how many in general, or just for today?"

Ella crossed over her table to see beyond Lester's torso. "Bite me, Rog." She tossed a marker at him.

"Will I get a toaster oven if I do?" He grabbed the pen and tossed it back.

Lester chuckled, but because Roger had terrible aim the marker hit him instead. "Hey!" He feigned injury. "Let me take cover before you launch next time."

"Suck it up, Soot boy," Ella said. "Stand in the target zone and you're bound to take a hit."

Lester didn't want to suck it up so he made a show of looking under the table. "That's the second one today." He nudged Roger.

Roger kicked back in his chair, happy to keep Lester between him and Ella's aim. She had more than a dozen
~~~~~~~~~~

marking pens on the table in front of her. "Damn, Eastman, leave some ladies for the rest of us."

"You two are the worst, but you straight white guys will never compete with this." She flexed the bicep of her right arm. "So sit down and watch me work."

And they did watch the crowd grow in front of her table, for hours. Ella talked and listened to stories about any and everything. She was an inspirational representation of women in emergency services.

"Ella!" a curly-haired child screamed as she raced across the firehouse floor. There was an echo in the unusually empty space three hours into their calendar signing and fundraising event. It was obvious by the girl's excited squeal that she wasn't there to see trucks and equipment; it was the sight of the woman at the end of the table making her run. The girl dodged between the clusters of lingering people, cutting through the crowd of twenty to get to firefighter Ella Eastman. The child's rubber boots clopped and slapped her calves, her pale blue sateen cape seeming to cause enough drag to prevent her from a full-out run.

"Here comes a little fan," Lester leaned in to whisper.

"You know, 'little fans' are my favorite." Ella flexed the fatigued fingers on her signing hand. It was near the end of the designated time for meet and greets, and all Ella wanted was to kick up her feet and relax with her lady. She and Morgan had a date tonight, one that under any other circumstance would be considered romantic enough for the big proposal. What pulls the heartstrings together better than rewatching the final episode of the sixth season of their favorite show, *The Blasphemers*?

A proposal idea came to her halfway through the calendar signing. Maybe she'd get on one knee as the commercial break hit, before the big dramatic moment when The Bruiser dives down the water-filled drain pipe. The heightened emotions would catch Morgan off guard. But there was one element missing—a big one in Ella's mind—she didn't have the perfect ring for the perfect proposal, so tonight she'd have to wait.

She stood to stretch her long legs and heard her name again.

"Ella!" the child squealed, hitting her at full speed. The collision set the girl bouncing off the firefighter's solid body causing the short length of the glistening cape to blanket the child's face.

"Oof." Ella caught her before she hit the floor. "Hey there, little one. Slow down." She pushed the cape aside to reveal a sweet, smiling face.

"I can't slow down," the girl huffed. "I've been waiting all day to see you and I didn't want to miss you, and I want you to sign my cape," she explained in a single breath as she thrust the fabric forward. "And my trading card." The plastic sleeve holding Ella's image fell to the floor. "I mean, my trading card of you."

Ella grinned as she stood up from the table to retrieve the plastic enveloped card. She loved meeting people in the Station Eight-Eighteen neighborhood, and the popularity of her February page was exciting, but this little girl was here for a very different reason. As Ella knelt, the girl reached forward, grabbing hold to keep the firefighter still.

The child traced the long scar on Ella's arm. "You are really brave," she whispered, barely loud enough for the firefighter to hear.

Ella knelt on the concrete floor of the firehouse. She wanted to give the typical 'all firefighters have to be brave' response but she could see something different in this child's eyes. There was a connection and it went much further than hero worship.

"Thank you," Ella said, at the same time noticing the compression gloves over burn scars on the child's fingers and hands. "I think you were brave, too."

The child's brown eyes filled with tears as she stared at Ella. "I tried to be, but it hurts sometimes."

Ella didn't turn away like many people would. She understood scars—the deep ones worn inside and out—and what this child needed most was someone to affirm that she wasn't alone.

"What's your name?" Ella asked.

"Addison." The girl smiled.

"Well, Addison, what if you and I go over here so we can take a picture and you can sign my calendar."

Addison giggled. "That's silly. You're sa-pos-ta sign mine." She held her calendar up to make sure Ella understood her role.

"I'll sign yours, but my calendar is full of brave people just like you." Ella pointed at the girl. "And it will be twice as special once your name is on it."

Ella pivoted to stand as a woman approached, and from the look in Addison's eyes this grown-up belonged to her.

"Addie," the woman said.

"It's okay, Gramma. Ella wants my name for her calendar. She says it'll make it special."

Grandma? Ella thought as she stretched to her full six-foot height. *How is the woman standing beside this child a grandmother?* "Ella Eastman." She stretched a hand forward.

"Bridget Kelling." They shook hands. "What's this about a signature? Please tell me she isn't bothering you."

"Oh, no, she's amazing and the two of us were talking about how brave we are."

"Yeah, Gramma, Ella says she has a special calendar for brave people like me." Addison poked her thumb against the velcro closure of her cape to point at herself.

Ella led them to the table where she'd spent the last few days meeting and greeting people for the most recent firehouse calendar release. Decked out with bright-red hearts and velvet-covered cupid arrows, her face and physique were representing this year's month of February. It wasn't the colorful Pride month photo from eight years prior, but the cupid-like image was setting hearts ablaze across her social media platforms.

"What does a brave people calendar mean?" Bridget asked, pointing to the logo of a fire helmet merged with a disability symbol.

Ella sat in a folding chair and Addison leaned close. "My firefighter brother was injured a few years ago and we started this project to help him and so many others like him." She was trying to be discreet about Sebastian Wilson, and the near fatal injuries that occurred during the fire that left the scar on her arm. She touched the pile on the table. This was not the firefighter calendar that Addison was holding, it was the special fundraising calendar focusing on Wilson's newly-discovered passion for graphic design.

"This is Project Lifeline." Ella opened the front cover. "January is all about Jeremy Pleth," she explained. "He makes prosthetics." She paused, waiting for Bridget to look and decipher what little Addison might not understand.

"I know what those are." Addison's eyes brightened. "My friend Adam has an arm like that." She pointed at the image where Jeremy stood surrounded by the pieces he'd personalized with superhero artwork and colorful patterns. He specialized in customizing children's prosthetics.

"That's right," Bridget said as her eyes met Ella's.

"If we turn to the month of August, you'll see Analise Philips." Ella flipped the page. "She works with scars like mine." She laid her arm across the page to point at her own pebbled skin. The surgeon who'd mended Ella was talented but after reopening the initial wound to remove infected tissue, it hadn't healed as they'd expected, and an obvious scar remained.

"And maybe like mine." Addison laid her hand beside Ella's.

"Yes," Ella said, "and that's why you should sign on this one." She shook the gold acrylic paint pen before handing it to the child.

"Where should I put it?" Addison asked, using all of her strength to uncap the marker.

"Wherever you want."

"I'm gonna sign Addie, since that's what everyone calls me." Her little tongue jetted to the side of her mouth as she concentrated on scrawling the letters of her name on the page.

Ella smiled at the backward E. "It's perfect."

Addie capped the pen before imitating the shaking motion. "Now you have to sign mine." She pushed her calendar forward and turned it to the Valentine's Day page.

"You want me to write it on the red heart?" Ella asked.

"Yep."

"Yes, please," her grandmother corrected.

"Yes, please," the child repeated with a short huff.

'Stay strong, little sister,' Ella wrote and drew tiny hearts before and after her name. She blew across the ink to help it dry faster.

"Can you sign my trading card, too?" Addie cuddled the calendar to her chest.

Ella was slightly embarrassed to sign the card as the glossy, body-oiled image of her with the sledge hammer draped over her shoulders was slightly more suggestive. Ella wrote her name in similar fashion across her pencil-sketched abs. The image made her think of Morgan, who'd drawn it, and she couldn't prevent the smile that grew.

"There you go." Ella waved the card so the ink could dry, then slipped it back into the protective sleeve. Embarrassingly, it was not the first time she'd signed her Station Eight-Eighteen trading card.

"Thank you," Addie said as she spun around to show off her cape. "Could you sign this, too?"

Ella read the Blacktree Burn Center title with the children's hospital logo on the back, along with the phrase 'Not all heroes wear capes, but this one does.' She was definitely signing Addie's cape.

"Come stand right here," Ella said as she made space behind the table, "and I'll sign it on the shoulder. That way I'll be right beside you. Okay?"

"Okay." Addie leaned closer.

Ella placed her hand beneath the fabric and signed her name. "You're my hero," Ella whispered.

"There are a lot of heroes in this room," Addie's grandmother said, lowering a hand for the child to hold. "You're just as kind as everyone says you are."

"I appreciate that." Ella smiled as she watched them leave. It was sweet the way the other guests and friends of the department waited for this very personal one-on-one conversation, but the firefighter was definitely ready to cap her pens for the day.

"Grandmother?" Lester leaned in and whispered through gritted teeth.

Ella chuckled at her friend. "Seriously! How's that possible?"

Lester slapped her shoulder. "Another time and place I'd..."

"You'd what?" Ella shook her head. "You're all talk, Soot Boy."

"I thought best friends were supposed to build each other up?" He frowned.

Best friend. She let the term rest in her head. Lester was definitely her friend, but after so many years fighting fires together, he was so much more. Les would always be family. "Build you up. Like some kind of kid's toy?"

"I could be her toy."

"Dude." Ella held her palm up. "Don't say another word. I don't want to hear your granny fantasy thoughts."

"At least she wasn't carrying a toaster oven," Roger chimed in.

Ella glared and Lester stepped between them. "Cool down, Cinder. All in good fun."

Ella kicked the cardboard box holding the toaster ovens.

"You have to admit, she was a beautiful woman," Les said.

He was right. "I still don't want to hear about your granny dreams. Seriously, any filter you had has disintegrated since your divorce."

"The kid called her Grandma, not Granny," he defended. "There's a difference."

"I'll take your word for it." Ella collected the markers from her spot at the signing table. Thinking about divorce made her terribly sad—the end of something that was once the beginning. She was at the beginning of forever with Morgan; well, as 'at the beginning' you could get after eight years. But endings came, she thought as she placed the Project Lifeline calendar in the box.

Seb's smile on the calendar's back cover was real, but so was the truth that his career ended before it truly began. She thought about her time, about the years she had left in Station Eight-Eighteen. Was twenty years enough? Twenty-five? What came after? She'd only ever been a firefighter.

The lingering crowd had thinned to station house family and friends of the crew, and she'd stayed well past her slotted time.

"You taking off?" Lester asked as he relaxed against the metal folding chair.

Ella looked at her watch. "Yep. In an ironic turn of events, Morgan is facilitating a rage room divorce celebration."

"That's really taking off?" Lester asked.

"Nothing pairs better with divorce than sledge hammers, an hour or two with your bestie, and a blood red rage room," she said.

Lester tossed his calendar pile on top of Ella's. "Don't I know it." He pushed the cardboard box with his foot. "Don't forget your rewards."

Ella picked up the box of toaster ovens. "Thanks, I'd hate to leave them behind."

3.

The Divorce

Ella watched the monitor displaying the rage room Morgan was currently in. To her disappointment, she'd arrived a few minutes after Morgan had led the two women into the Exes Wreck room.

A few weeks earlier, they'd painted the walls a color that Morgan's business partner, Beatrice, referred to as 'blood-of-my-enemies red', and the title seemed to please many of the recently divorced who came to rage. In contrast to the intense customers' energy, her girlfriend was adorable in her full-length skirt, with a clipboard tucked beneath her arm as she spun the mini sledge hammer in her opposite hand.

Ella hadn't personally experienced this pre-rage room speech from her girlfriend, but she'd respected the safety lesson when she heard it from Beatrice eight years before.

"Another one?" Beatrice asked as Ella slapped the cardboard box on the counter.

"Oh, no, it was two today. It's a big fucking station-house joke now." Ella unfolded the flaps, removing two very battered and clearly-used toaster ovens.

Beatrice laughed. "You keep doing those calendars and converting the masses," she teased, "they'll bring on the small appliances. Haven't you ever heard 'If you build something they will come'?"

"Seriously, it isn't funny." Ella dropped the used toaster ovens onto the utility cart before flattening the cardboard box. "I swear the rest of the team is going to start, and they'll come out of the woodwork."

"Lesbians or toaster ovens?"

"Ugh." Ella considered the question. "Yes and yes."

"What a horrible dilemma," Beatrice teased. "I could use a lesbian or even a bisexual right now."

Ella's eyebrow raised. "Use?"

"You know what I mean," Beatrice corrected. "I'm open like that."

"Uh huh," Ella replied snarkily. "If my team gets any smart ideas I'm going to start smashing those things at the station." She side-eyed the monitor screen, scrutinizing the two women Morgan was instructing.

Beatrice followed Ella's glance. "The redhead is pissed with a capital P," she said as she adjusted the sound-system controls.

Ella chuckled. "Divorce can do that to a person."

"Oh, no… the redhead, she's the best friend." Beatrice pushed the intercom button. "Sound check. Can you hear me, Morgan?"

Morgan gave a thumb's up. The shout-out wasn't only to relay that the audio setup was active, it was also a heads-up that the room was being monitored.

"No shit," Ella said. "If the best friend is that mad, how is the recently divorced?"

"In a word—" Beatrice chuckled, "ready."

"I can't ever imagine divorcing her," Ella said, her attention returning to Morgan.

"Pfft," Beatrice spat. "You'd actually have to work up the nerve to propose, Hot Stuff."

"I've got the nerve. I'm figuring out the perfect plan."

Beatrice shrugged. "Words, Hot Stuff. I hear the words but I don't see the actual plan."

"Has she said something to you?" Ella asked, never taking her attention from the monitor.

"She says a lot to me, duh. We work together."

Beatrice was possibly the most frustrating person Ella had acquired in her relationship with Morgan. From day one, the feisty accountant had reduced Ella to 'hot stuff,' 'hot firefighter,' 'muscle mama' and dozens of other reductive but also semi-accurate pet names. Ella wasn't always annoyed by it, like she had been in the first few years—this playful, sarcastic nicknaming was Beatrice's love language—but occasionally it felt out of step.

"You're a bean counter." Ella watched Morgan exit the rage room, and moved closer to open the door to the office for her.

"By day," Beatrice protested.

Ella looked at her watch. "It's two-thirty."

"By appointment only," Beatrice hissed. "Anyway, without me you'd have to retire and work the R.A.T.S. front desk." She used her middle finger to point at the Rage Against The System logo on the window.

"Finger," Morgan interrupted, grabbing hold of the digit, reprimanding Beatrice before tipping up onto her toes to give Ella a kiss. "Why are you using the finger?" she questioned her best friend.

"Ask your partner," Beatrice said as she yanked her hand free.

Ella gave her best 'shut your mouth' glare. Beatrice read it loud and clear, silencing herself about the proposal conversation and that it had yet to occur.

"Why is my business partner flipping off my life partner?" Morgan patted Ella's cheek.

Ella leaned into the touch. "Would you believe me if I said she pushed the wrong button?"

"Yes." Morgan smiled as she tossed her clipboard on the desk.

"Hey," Beatrice squawked. "I did no such thing. It's not my fault your muscle mama can't make a decision."

"What exactly are we talking about?" Motion on the monitor caught Morgan's attention. "What the heck? I told her she can't hit the cart. Damn it!" She tapped the intercom and flashed the overhead lights. "You need to stop," she yelled, and hurried back to the rage room.

"Can you please not blow the proposal for me?" Ella was serious. "I only get to do this once. I want her to cherish the moment and I want it to be a surprise."

"That's really sweet," Beatrice said, momentarily sincere. "I swear I'll keep my mouth shut."

Ella leaned close to the monitor, watching the brunette divorcee bundle her hair in a messy top bun while Morgan gave her a proper scolding. "That woman is something."

Beatrice tugged the waiver form from the clipboard. "I'd say. Look at the aggressive penmanship. I'm not sure what her settlement was, but I don't think she won."

Ella watched the animated conversation taking place in the Exes Wreck room. "She knows how to rule a crowd."

Beatrice stared, confused, until she realized Ella wasn't talking about the divorcee but her best friend. "You've got it bad, Hot Stuff."

"Don't I know it," Ella said.

Morgan returned to the front desk, scrutinizing her people closely. "What are the two of you plotting?"

"Dinner," Ella said.

"The future," Beatrice said.

Morgan shook her head. "Do you need a minute to get your stories straight?"

Ella chuckled. "No. I was admiring you on the monitor, and your friend had the gall to harass me for loving you."

"It was hardly harassment," Beatrice said defensively.

Morgan tugged Ella's hand, guiding her down for a kiss. "Hi, again."

"Hi," Ella whispered across soft lips.

"Gross," Beatrice said, excusing herself from the room. "I think I have beans to count."

"See you later and thanks for helping," Morgan said as she led Ella behind the counter. After the stern warning to her clients, she wanted to keep a closer eye on the monitor.

Ella winced as the baseball bat smashed the thirteen-inch tube television's base. "Divorce rage, damn."

"It's the worst case scenario. She said he got everything."

"That sucks," Ella said.

"Her best friend has a mouth." Morgan chuckled. "Apparently she went after the ex with a shovel when they were moving her things, and that's how they ended up here."

"A shovel?" Ella wasn't surprised. She leaned against the counter watching the women swing, alternating the sledgehammer and bat combination, as they pounded the television like railway workers setting a spike on the track.

"Never mess with the best friend," Morgan said as she slid into the space of Ella's legs.

"Duly noted." Ella wrapped Morgan in her arms while they continued to watch. "How long is their session?" she asked.

"An hour."

"They look like they'll probably need two," Ella teased.

"Funny you should say that. They booked Friday night for a group of four." Morgan shrugged. "She said she's bringing the people who were in her bridal party."

"We're gonna need to expand."

Morgan turned in the embrace, looking up at her lover. "Are we?"

Ella swallowed hard. "Uh huh."

"I like the sound of that."

"Me too." Ella snuggled tight as Morgan relaxed against her. They stood for a long moment, Ella's eyes on the monitor as her lover squeezed their bodies closer.

"Two toaster ovens." Morgan tried not to laugh.

"Not you, too." Ella released her hold only to have Morgan cling on to keep her there. "One of the toaster ovens doesn't even have a cord," Ella said. "Is it bad luck if they bring you a broken toaster oven?"

"It's not, I'm sure. Think about it, they probably don't even make them anymore," Morgan explained.

"Good, then they'll run out soon."

"Oh, sweetie, I don't think so." Morgan pulled Ella's arms tighter. "It is kinda adorable. Cute, really, in the big picture."

Ella whispered, "Sure."

"A lot like you," Morgan said.

"Cute?" Ella pointed to herself, offended. "Uh uh."

"Don't worry, baby. I promise not to tell anyone." Morgan's stomach rumbled.

"Hungry, love?"

The rumble grew louder. "Maybe."

"Sounds more like definitely," Ella teased. "Why don't I go upstairs, take a shower and make us some food, and when you're finished we can eat?"

"Sounds heavenly. What are you cooking?"

Ella pushed the cart aside. "Not sure yet, but it definitely isn't going to include toast."

~~~~~~~~~~

"Hi honey, I'm home," Morgan teased as the elevator passed the floor before lurching to a stop. Ella was there,
~~~~~~~~~~

tugging the steel jaw-like safety gate open to help Morgan out. It was an old-style industrial lift that looked more like the mouth of a monster gobbling up its passengers, but it functioned well and Morgan loved using it on long, labor-intense days.

Morgan greeted Ella with an adoring glance, but the kiss between them was quick as Morgan held her far enough away to admire her from head to toe. The firefighter was quite casual, wearing her 'Hot Stuff coming through' apron. It was a playful gift given to her by Beatrice that she pretended to hate but genuinely cherished. From the backside, Morgan admired the very short boxers and workout tank.

"The front of your outfit is doing a wonderful job of matching the back." Morgan tugged at the lace holding the apron in place. "Hot Stuff."

"Uh uhh." Ella held the desperate fingers. "We'll nourish one hunger at a time, Ms Hail."

Morgan moistened her lips. "Can I choose what appetite to satisfy first?"

Ella stopped. "Baby, everyone knows if you're going to rev an engine for hours you need to fuel it first."

"Hours?" Morgan smiled.

"Many," Ella affirmed. She took the bag from Morgan's shoulder. "Did you bring some rocks? What's in here?"

"I have a project." Morgan flipped her bag open.

Ella raised the bag, imitating a free-weight curl. "It looks like you have a library card problem?"

"Oh, no, I have a library card solution," Morgan joked as she removed four paperbacks and three hardcover books. "Beatrice and I are finally going to start a book club for the rage room."

"Really?" Ella was intrigued. This wasn't the first conversation about a book club, but it was the first sign of progress toward organizing one. "Are these the first selections?"

Morgan tucked the books to her chest. "Maybe. I have to read them and then we will make a no, maybe and yes pile."

"And what kind of literature will your club be reading?" Ella tipped the books for a closer look.

"Romance, obviously." Morgan flashed the cover art.

"Is it obvious?" Ella questioned. "I guess I thought a rage room book club would have non-fiction or thrillers and murder stories. You know, all ragey and aggressive."

"Well, since B and I don't enjoy those genres, and we get enough ragey and aggressive by day, we get to choose, and romance wins!"

Ella pumped a fist in celebration. "Yay, romance." She turned toward the kitchen, remembering she still had food on the cooktop. "Why don't you come tell me all about your winning genre while I finish making dinner?"

"Right, you said something about satisfying an appetite."

"Or two." Ella winked.

They ate, and as Ella questioned Morgan about the reading choices she and Beatrice were considering, Morgan asked about the signing session at the station house earlier that day.

"She sounds so darling," Morgan said about Ella's interaction with the young girl. "What was her name?"

"Addison, and she was really adorable." Ella passed the plate across the counter as Morgan washed the dishes. "I had no idea what a difference these events would make when we started doing the calendar, and now, after Sebastian, I don't think we will ever be able to stop."

"That's a good thing, right?"

Ella shrugged as she leaned against the counter. "It is, mostly."

With her hands covered in suds, Morgan tossed a towel at Ella. "Dry the dishes, and confess."

Ella snickered. "So bossy."

"So evasive." Morgan sensed the emotional wall.

"There's a lot going on," Ella said. "Things are changing."

"What things are changing, love?" Morgan's question was gentle, soothing, to coax Ella's thoughts.

"West Side flower shop closed." Ella swiped a tear.

This was no small thing, not to Ella. "The shop where you bought Kay's flowers," Morgan whispered.

Ella's nod was no mask for the heartbreak. "She's gone for real now. That place was the only connection. The last one…" Her best friend Kay had been gone for nearly fifteen years, but the loss for Ella was a wound that never healed, not fully. They were more than best friends—they were sister-buddies with plans to charge through life together. But depression and suicide changed everything.

"Oh, love." Morgan opened her arms and Ella moved to fit inside.

"I have to find another place to buy her flowers." Unable to carry the weight a moment longer, Ella slid to the floor, sobbing.

Morgan tried her best to carry them down but the thud was not gentle. "You can find another place."

"Uh huh," Ella mumbled into Morgan's shoulder. "But it's just one more thing I…"

"Tell me," Morgan said. "I know this is more than flowers and flower shops."

The loft was quiet for the longest time as Ella struggled to her feet. This wasn't the way she wanted to tell Morgan about how the fifteenth anniversary of Kay's death was affecting her or how other big decisions were weighing on her heart.

Morgan was patient as the conversation cycled from toaster ovens to rage room expansion until Ella finally got to the serious topic she wanted to avoid.

"You're really thinking about retiring?" Morgan asked, her voice breaking on the final word.

Ella stopped in the doorway to their room, her fingertips curling around the trim. She felt the stretch in her shoulders and also appreciated the lingering gaze as Morgan admired her body. "I'll have given the station twenty years," she said.

Morgan swiped at a tear. "That's a long time." The subject of Ella's retirement was her secret dream, a reality she'd hoped for since the accident that left the scar on Ella's arm and another etched across Morgan's heart.

"It would be less dangerous. Less worry for you if I retired."

Morgan patted the side of their bed. "Come here and sit."

Ella didn't move; she couldn't. She needed the harsh edge of the doorway against her fingertips to anchor her. She also knew that tenderness from Morgan's touch wasn't what she wanted as she processed the difficult feelings. "I need to get this out before you get all soft and loving," she explained. "It hit me today as I was signing autographs. We do a job that people call heroic."

"Ella," Morgan said softly.

"Just… let me say what's been going around in my head." Ella's shoulders flexed as she gripped the doorframe tighter. "You know Les, he couldn't keep his life together, and Seb… there's only so much you can give away before there's nothing left, you know."

Morgan nodded.

"And I have you." Ella smiled. "And sometimes the thought of not having you is so overwhelming. The idea that I won't come back or that I'll come back less." She paused to take a breath. "I don't want you to live our life without me in it." She turned her head to catch the tears with the shoulder of her t-shirt. When she turned back, Morgan was there. Her slender arms came around Ella, and for a brief moment the firefighter stopped fighting.

"I love you." Morgan looked up at her. "What you do is heroic, and messy and emotional. It also doesn't end when you take your uniform off."

Ella's arms eased around her girlfriend. "Yes," she whispered. It was true; in uniform or out she was a caregiver, sacrificing daily, giving little pieces of herself away for the greater good. But at what cost to her emotional health?

"Let's get more comfortable." Morgan stepped backward, guiding them to the bed. "You need to sleep and I think I need to hold you for a while."

Ella didn't fight her. "I'm tired," she whispered as she pulled her shirt off.

"I know, love." Morgan folded the comforter back, guiding Ella to her side of the bed. She made the safest space, the home Ella craved but thought she'd never find.

"I love you," Ella whispered.

Morgan pushed Ella to her side, her smaller body spooning around to blanket her through the emotional storm. "I know you do, love, and I love you right back."

4.

The Books

"**D**arlin'," Ella called as she stumbled over the stack of books beside the bed. "Morg, sweetheart, you have to move these to a shelf… Or you have to stop gobbling up these novels." It wasn't uncommon for Ella to return from her days at the station to find her lady relaxing on the couch or snuggled in bed reading a book. With the full operation of an online booking schedule at the rage rooms, Morgan could enjoy breaks throughout the day, and the elevator to their second-floor loft made it convenient to haul the mini library of books she was acquiring, but they had to have chosen a book-club read by now.

Morgan clutched the current book to her chest. "Did you just suggest that I should stop reading my books?" She was five chapters deep into her third romance of the week, sometimes finding it simpler to listen to audio as she staged breakables in the rage rooms, but also needing the weight of a book in her lap when it was time to relax. "I'll never stop. Do you know how many of these books I haven't read yet?"

There were stacks: what was next to read and the three sorted piles of yes, maybe and no way. Morgan had a system to her search for the first book-club read, even if it had grown to resemble something chaotic.

Ella chuckled as she leaned in for a kiss. "By the looks of the stack I tripped over, I'd have thought you'd read an entire library by now."

Morgan tugged at the drawstring on Ella's hooded sweatshirt, coaxing her back for a second, deeper and longer-lingering kiss. "Ella, my love, you have so much to learn about a 'to-be-read' pile."

Ella smiled. "And you're going to teach me what that means, right?"

Morgan released the strings. "I am, but you make a good point about the piles. We could use another bookcase." She scratched her chin, thoughtfully. "I wonder if I know anyone who might have a tool belt and some hard wood."

Ella righted her ruffled sweatshirt, puffing her chest, feeling the confidence of her competence with a belt full of tools but not necessarily having a vast supply of wood, soft or hard.

"I'll give Lil a call," Morgan said.

Ella guffawed. "Lily Flower? You're going to ask Lily Flower?"

"You shouldn't use that nickname," Morgan chastised. "You know she hates it."

"But…," Ella defended, "but you want *her* to build your shelves and not me?"

Morgan appreciated the huff and the tiny pout forming from Ella's lips. "You're a firefighter, honey. She's a general contractor. Plus she still claims she owes me a favor."

Ella didn't like the way this plan was unfolding. She was more than capable of building the perfect shelves to hold all the books stacked on the floor and then a few more. "Lily Flower owes you a favor?" She opened the cabinet under Morgan's worktable to find her tools. "What's the favor for?"

"Preventing Cove and Lil from homelessness."

Ella dropped her hammer, confused about the situation with their friends. "Wait, wasn't that a long time ago?" Years before, when Lil and Cove shared an apartment, they realized quickly that their extreme personalities meant they wouldn't live well together. When Cove came to Morgan for help, Lil took it personally—words were said and feelings were hurt.

"You remember their drama with the landlord?"

"It was kinda hard to forget when Beatrice brought it up almost weekly," Ella said. "But that's very past tense."

"It is, but who mended the fence with the creepy landlord so Cove and Lil didn't get thrown out onto the street?" Morgan pointed both thumbs to her chest. "This woman, right here."

"Does Lil really owe you for something like that?"

"According to her, yes. I never really needed anything right after and I've always had you."

"Hell yes, you have," Ella interrupted. "And all your needs were met."

Morgan chuckled. "Yes, baby. You've met all my needs… until now."

Ella plopped down on the couch beside Morgan, holding onto her hammer and the not-so-worn tool belt. "I don't even like the way 'until now' sounded coming out of your mouth." She dropped her tools on the cushion and pulled Morgan's feet across her lap.

"Let's just give Lil a call and see what she can do," Morgan suggested. "Plus you know how she is when she gets an idea in her head."

"I want to help her," Ella insisted.

Morgan wriggled her sock-covered toes, poking Ella's abdomen. "Of course you will."

"Promise you won't let her do it while I'm working."

"I promise." Morgan marked the page she was on and tossed her book on the floor. "Do we still have a date tonight?" she asked.

Ella smiled. "Popcorn and flamethrowers."

"Stop it," Morgan teased. "You're gonna make me lose all self control."

Ella tickled Morgan's toes before sliding her fingertips up the loose fit of her pants. "You are aware we can pause play whenever the excitement strikes." The ragged-cut fabric brushed Ella's hand and the origin of Morgan's favorite sweats brought a smile.

"I'm very aware of the pause button." Ella's wandering hand was warm against Morgan's shin. "I'm particularly fond of play, though." The tease brought the reaction Morgan wanted. "What's that giant smile for?" she asked.

Ella didn't even try to hide her grin. "Just having a U-HAUL moment."

Morgan knew what she meant, knew it was the memory sparked from the knit fabric climbing closer to her knee. The couple had a history with the faded thread-bare pants Ella had cut to accommodate Morgan's short stature. They were hardly dating at the time, but the firefighter's attention to Morgan's insecurity broke down barriers, and it was when they finally knew that being loved could also make you feel safe.

"You made me fall in love with you in these," Morgan whispered.

"You've said that before." Ella's hand moved higher up the inside of the loose-fitting sweats.

"That's because it's true." Morgan's breath hitched from the tenderness of Ella's touch.

"You've said *that* before, too."

Morgan closed her eyes, her head falling back as Ella's fingertips traveled to the sensitive hollow behind her knee. The firefighter knew her body, adored her body, and Morgan never wanted the explorations to stop. "You made me feel..." she gasped, the delicate fingertip dance delighting her inner thigh as they traveled through the baggy fit of her pants.

"Feel?" Ella questioned, teasing as she leaned closer to navigate her lover's body. "What do you feel, Morgan?" Her hand paused as it grazed bare skin. "No panties?"

Morgan's stare was wicked. "You've fallen into my trap, haven't you, firefighter?"

Ella's hand paused. "You vixen."

"You like it and you know it."

"Oh, no," Ella pulled her hand away, angling to hover above her lover. "I fucking love it."

~~~~~~~~~~

"Do you think they're setting the stage for the cute barista to couple-up with the florist?" Morgan plucked a piece of popcorn from her shirt. They'd finished the episode, using the pause and play buttons more than once. Morgan was wearing Ella's fire department t-shirt. Her sweatpants lay crumpled on the floor, replaced with a pair of dinosaur spandex boxers.

Ella paused to admire her outfit before sitting down with the freshly popped corn. "The florist and the barista?" she asked.

Morgan's legs parted, welcoming Ella to sit between them. "It's cute, right? He's super flirty and always has a gardening pun to share."

"Puns can be dangerous though."

Morgan chuckled. "Ooh, deadly punning." She reached for some popcorn. "It could be a superpower?"

"Wait." Ella turned. "Do you think the barista could be the season eight Big Bad?"

Morgan considered the idea. "What's the best way to fight a florist?"

"For a barista? Really hot coffee?" Ella guessed. The chuckle that followed nearly shook the bowl of popcorn off her lap.
~~~~~~~~~~

"He's a computer genius, honey. What's the barista gonna do, spill hot liquid on his keyboard?"

"But he's a florist, too," Ella reminded her.

"Right, but the Big Bad wouldn't go after the florist, they'd go after the super-hacking computer wiz, not knowing he's the florist." Morgan perked up. "That's the best setup for romance and it's super gay. I think he needs a love interest after seven seasons."

Ella released her handful of popcorn and set the bowl on the table. "So that means it'll never happen."

Morgan could feel the shift in excitement and hear it in her lover's tone. She coaxed Ella back in between her thighs. "It's not network television, so it could happen."

"Maybe." Ella relaxed into the embrace, settling Morgan's legs against her hips.

"Besides, we don't even know that's the direction they're going in."

Ella grinned as the fabric of her shirt inched up, exposing her abdomen. The move was slow and could have been unintentional until she felt an icy cold finger dip into the muscular definition. "And what direction might it be going in?" A clipped moan escaped as she arched into the touch.

"You like that?" Morgan asked.

"You know I do," Ella hissed as her head fell back against her lover's shoulder.

It was a mismatch of size as the muscled body flexed atop the petite woman's thighs and torso. Morgan played her like a finely-tuned instrument—fingertips dancing across ribs, caressing sensitive goose-pebbled skin, tickling hair just below the band of her *The Blasphemer* fangirl boxer briefs. She knew what power she had in this moment, how she could wind her lover tight and make her go.

The touch was light as a feather across her body and Ella felt it everywhere. "Mor… gan," she moaned.

"Yes, love." Morgan delighted in her arousal, caressing Ella's chest, lingering to circle a hardening nipple. Morgan loved every part of this woman's body: her mind, her heart, their soulful connection. But it was this, the way she acquiesced when Morgan adored her, that made their lonely nights apart worth it.

"Oh…" Ella moaned. "I don't think…"

Morgan whispered, "That's good. I don't want you to think. I only want you to feel me touching you and nothing else." Her hand slid beneath the elastic of her boxers and Ella's shoulders flexed. Morgan lived for these moments of surrender, after years together, easily predictable for the woman writhing against her. Ella was controlled and purposeful, rarely fully relaxed except during intimate moments like this.

"I love you, Firefighter," Morgan whispered as fingers slid beneath her boxers. Ella's body braced against her wrist and forearm.

"Yes," Ella gasped. "Don't stop."

There was music in this loving touch. Morgan whispered against Ella's ear, "Tell me what you need?" She knew her lover was already so close.

"Slow, baby. Go slow."

Ella's hushed words empowered Morgan. "Yeah?" The single word slid from her lips with the same drawn out intention of her moving hand. Ella relaxed into the motion as Morgan pulled them tight together to grind against Ella's hard ass. "Is that what you want?"

"Yes…" Ella hissed. "Morgan, yes." Her back arched.

Morgan felt muscles strain against her as her lover reached her peak. "Don't hold back. Let me love you." Pleasuring Ella was everything. It was all Morgan needed to hear as the woman gasped in her arms.

"Yes," Ella screamed.

"You're so beautiful," Morgan said as her hand was slow to still.

Ella gripped Morgan's wrist before she could pull away. "Stay, keep it. Just wait there a little longer."

Morgan smiled, before closing her eyes.

~~~~~~~~~~~

Hours later, Ella woke, Morgan's hand resting on the hem of her printed boxers. The bowl of popcorn was half strewn between the couch and the floor. A grin stretched across her face as she rolled to watch Morgan sleep. The woman was beautiful. She admired the faded freckles on her cheeks and the tiny lines around her mouth, evidence of the happiness they shared.

"You deserve perfection," Ella whispered, vowing in that moment to make their proposal a once-in-a-lifetime memory.
~~~~~~~~~~~

5.

The Shopkeeper

Toni, or Antoinette Peterson to the local shopkeepers' guild, sat at the desk behind the sales counter of her flower shop, staring at the line of text highlighted in grey on her screen. "Screw you!" she screamed for what felt like the thousandth time. The color grey was somehow a metaphor for how the day was unfolding. "Screw you, Mandy!" she yelled louder at the computer monitor in front of her.

She'd waited for hours to hear from her girlfriend, knowing for the last few weeks that their almost two-year relationship was hanging on by an unraveling thread. With a few harsh words in an instant message, those fragile tendrils broke terminally free.

She blinked hard, her brown eyes resolved as she adjusted to the flashing cursor focusing in on the word: 'over'. The use of triple exclamation marks was a hurtful gut-punch, but no tears fell as her heartless ex-girlfriend used this note to cut the final ties.

"Who breaks up with someone by text message?" she asked aloud, though there was no one in the room. "And right before an anniversary?" She rubbed her hands together, fighting the stiffness that came without warning and lingered far too long. She flicked the red paper flower in the colorful origami bouquet she'd folded to celebrate.

She wanted to crawl home to bed and curl up in a ball of grief, but the bell on her front door jingled the presence of a customer. It was the last Friday of the month, according to the deliciously sapphic image on her firefighter calendar. Usually she adored the end of a week when happy lovers bought sappy sentiment in the shape of a bouquet. For Toni, it kept the hopeful romantic alive inside her. She closed the screen of the laptop and spun around to greet her latest customer. Perhaps someone else's romance story could brighten her day.

"Good morning." Toni grinned at the backside of a nearly six-foot-tall person, appreciating the pile of long, dark hair bundled in a messy bun, and the fit of tight jeans. The woman turned, and Toni couldn't miss the firefighter-emblemed shirt stretched across a very tight chest.

"How can I help… you?" The last word squeaked out as she tried to process what or who was in front of her. She stumbled against the utility cart holding a fresh array of potted plants.

"I have two things, really," the firefighter said. "I have a special order request, and I'm looking for something out of the ordinary for my partner." She found herself playing with the folded paper cat face sitting beside the greeting cards.

Toni was always practicing origami folds and kept the art on display throughout the shop. What started as an accidental and forgetful misplacement of a paper crane had become low-key signature shop decor. It was ridiculously sentimental and cutesy but also a way to keep her hands dextrous, plus the art form made her happy.

Toni noticed the scar on the firefighter's arm and tried to play it cool. This was the firefighter calendar woman, she was certain—the gorgeous model from the ripped-out pages she had hanging on the wall only a few feet away. She tried to keep focus and not act like a kid meeting their idol, but her mouth wasn't listening to her brain and the question burst out. "Are you Ella Eastman, the firefighter?"

Ella chuckled. "Maybe." She shrugged. It had been years since the news report about her bravery and even longer since the fire that nearly ended her career, yet Ella couldn't escape being recognized even in a city the size of Blacktree. She wondered if the simple quest to buy graveside flowers for Kay and plants for Morgan was about to get weird.

Toni waved her hands, fanning herself, "Oh gosh, I'm not going to fangirl, I'm not going to fangirl," she chanted as she stepped around the counter to remove something from the desk cubby behind Ella. She laid the new calendar on the countertop, still pristine in the cellophane wrapping. "Okay, maybe I am going to fangirl, but only a little bit."

Ella laughed quietly as she recognized a few odd but not uncommon things on the wall behind the shopkeeper. It was the image of herself in rainbow suspenders and a crop-top proudly representing June for Pride month from the eight-year-old calendar. What struck her most was the overlap on last year's calendar paper-clipped in place. It was obvious the shopkeeper didn't display the firefighter calendar to know what day it was. She grinned. "That kinda looks like mine at home." She pointed at the cork board holding the glossy images in place. "My partner likes that picture, too."

"Would you sign the new calendar for my..." Toni stopped mid-sentence, remembering that as of fifteen minutes ago she no longer had a girlfriend. "Would you sign the new one for me?"

"I'd love to," Ella teased, "but only if you'll help me with a special bouquet and the perfect gift for my partner. She doesn't like cut flowers very much. The bouquet is for a cemetery visit. I had an arrangement with another florist I've used for years but they lost their lease and chose to retire so I'm hoping you can be their replacement."

"Was that Eveline at West Side Flowers?" Toni asked.

"It was." Ella wasn't surprised this person knew the other florist.

"We tried to help negotiate a new lease with the landlord," Toni explained.

"We?" Ella wondered if the shopkeeper was somehow related to her favorite florist.

"My girl—my ex-girlfriend and I," Toni summarized. "She's an attorney upstate and I asked her to intervene. It didn't work out."

"That's terrible." Ella meant it. She'd used West Side Flowers since her best friend's death. They knew her, and understood the significance of the anniversary, and she was terribly disappointed when the shop closed without her knowledge.

"Sometimes we don't win the big fight no matter how hard we try," Toni whispered, and seemed to disappear into the thought. "Anyway, let's see what we can do to make up for the loss. You said you wanted potted plants for your partner."

"I do," Ella said as she plucked a marker from the counter's pen cup. Holding it up, she asked,"This okay to sign with?"

Toni nodded. "Yep."

"I'll have to open your calendar to do that." She tapped the cellophane wrapper.

Toni slid her finger along the folded plastic. "I guess you will."

Ella uncapped the pen, poised to scrawl her best and well-practiced signature across her image. "Where would you like it signed?" She grinned, knowing exactly where most women-who-fancied-women wanted her autograph.

Toni blushed.

"Across the chest?" Ella watched the flush of red move over the woman's face and down her neck.

"Is that weird?" Toni asked.

Ella made a swirling letter as she scrawled the first word. "Not weird at all. It's pretty common, actually."

"I'm not surprised." Toni wanted to add that there was definitely enough surface for the way Ella wrote her name, but she could already feel the burning sensation of the blush tinting her throat and spreading across her own chest.

"There you go." Ella capped the marker.

"Thank you." Toni fanned the ink. "You have no idea how much this makes me smile after a kinda crappy day."

Ella shrugged and the shop fell silent, suddenly awkward as Toni didn't know if she should hang it up or leave it on the counter. Ella dropped the pen in the cup and the sound snapped Toni from her fangirl haze. She waved toward the open doorway. "Right." She clapped, switching to professional shop owner mode. "Let's take a walk in the greenhouse." She led Ella toward the back door that exited to the greenhouse. The gravel-covered lot behind her shop made the perfect space for the framed glass structure.

Ella followed. As they passed the display of wind chimes and sun catchers, a colorful sign reading, "Support STEM," caught her attention. "What are these?" There was a lightness in her voice as she realized the flowers weren't actually flowers, but building blocks put together to look like flowers.

"Oh, funny, right?" Toni said. "These are the new Briick sets, from the Gardening collection. They've become very popular with my 'plant killers'." She held up her fingers to make hovering quotation marks before picking up the assembled plastic snapdragons.

"I haven't played with Briick sets for years." Ella sorted through the boxed flower choices. "Seven hundred pieces. These might be fun to build together."

"Is your partner a plant killer?" Toni asked.

Ella chuckled. "She is anything but a plant killer. In fact, she's fairly amazing at bringing things to life."

"That's sweet."

Ella dismissed the comment. No one needed to tell her how sweet her partner was. "Can I get the snapdragons and the larger potted arrangement of exotic blooms?" She stacked the boxes together.

"You sure?" Toni asked. It was disappointing to think she'd lost a sale of potted live plants to the construction sets her ex-girlfriend insisted they sell in the shop. Yes, she was an occasional Briick set builder, and supporting STEM was important to her, but toy flowers could never replace the room-enhancing energy of a live plant.

"I'm absolutely sure about the Briick sets, but I will need something she can pour water over, too."

Toni took the boxes from Ella and set them beside the register. Ella Eastman, firefighter from Station Eight-Eighteen, was a thoughtful partner. As they entered the greenhouse, she wondered how she could find a woman like her.

"Tell me about the bouquet?" Toni asked, thinking she would make quick work of the request.

"This is gonna seem weird, but I order these flowers once a year." Ella began the long story of Kay, losing her to suicide and the grief that still hit her unexpectedly but always when the anniversary came around.

"This is a beautiful way to honor her and to grieve her," Toni said. "I'll have these ready for you on the date we discussed, and every year until something changes."

"Thank you," Ella said.

"It's what we do." Toni opened the sliding door of the greenhouse. "Now let's talk about potted plants for your partner."

~~~~~~~~~~~

Toni knocked fast and continuously against the apartment door. The hallway was as quiet as the lobby where
~~~~~~~~~~~

she was too nervous to wait for the elevator. After climbing the three flights, she was catching her breath when the door swung open. "You'll never believe who came into the shop," she said before her friend could offer a greeting.

Cove stood in the doorway, blocking Toni's entry, their tattered hockey jersey tucked into equally battered cargo shorts. Their hair was messily coiffed, an obvious attempt to make a twenty-minute styling look like they'd only rolled from bed to answer the door. "Wait, no hello or how are you?" they asked. "No love for me?" They slapped their palm against their chest, feigning devastation.

"Shit, I'm sorry," Toni said. "Hi Cove." She gave them a brief hug as she stepped inside the apartment. "I love you and you are the bestest of best friends in the whole wide world, and you're never going to guess who spent nearly two hundred bucks in the shop today."

"Okay, I'll play." Cove chuckled. "And come on in; you look like my elevator is out of order again and you're about to drop." They closed the door and followed Toni inside. Cove was accustomed to Toni's outrageous highs and lows. Although the highs were entertaining, they were often chased by unbearable-to-witness lows.

"She came into the shop," Toni blurted.

"Toni, slow down," Cove said. "What the hell are you talking about?"

"Not what." Toni grinned as she dropped her backpack to the floor. The pocket's zipper snagged on a loose string as she tried to force it open. "Shit, this zipper is such an awkward steam-stealer." She tugged a few more times before pausing to clench her fingers. Her grip was strained, almost killing the moment. Almost. "I'm still in shock, I think."

Cove dropped to a knee, taking charge to fix the sticky zipper situation. "There ya go." They opened the bag for her.

Toni planted a quick peck on her friend's forehead. "You're the best of all besties. Now look!" She removed the plastic sleeve containing the signed calendar page.

Cove's eyes went wide as they recognized the image adorned with a scrawling signature that read, *'Toni, you're the tops. Ella Eastman.'* Cove was almost speechless. "Seriously, really?"

"I KNOW, right!" Toni was nearly overcome with excitement. Her fingertip traced the firefighter's personalization. "I'm her top."

"That's not what it says," Cove pointed out. "You're the tops. That doesn't mean what you think it does."

"Leave me alone and let me have my dream."

Cove shook their head, "You do realize, T, I dated that woman's girlfriend's best friend."

"Yeah, the accountant, Betty, or whatever."

"Beatrice," they corrected.

Toni shook off the dizziness of the statement. "Sure, but at best that's triple-removed friendship and until today my calendar wasn't signed, smarty pants, and now it is and I... MET... HER!"

"Did you touch her?" Cove teased, and retracted the humor.

Toni's face squinted abashedly. "Absolutely not without consent."

"You made a fool of yourself, didn't you?"

Toni shook her head. "Maybe I did, and maybe I earned a new and loyal customer."

"You said two hundred bucks. What did you sell her?" Cove asked.

"Well, Ella and I got to know each other's needs pretty well."

Cove pushed Toni's shoulder. "Bullshit."

"NO, I'm not kidding." Toni flopped into the chair, tossing her leg over the rounded armrest. "She gets an annual memorial arrangement. We set that up. She's also celebrating some anniversary with her girlfriend, and can you believe she's with someone who doesn't appreciate cut flowers?"

"I've known a few." Cove opened the refrigerator. "Did you hydrate after the marathon firefighter experience? I'm assuming by the fidgeting that my elevator was out again."

"Hit me with a coconut water." Toni held a hand up to receive it. "And the elevator was taking too long."

Cove reached in the back of the fridge. "Wow, coconut water. You really did take it all on."

"I'm telling you, her shop visit was life altering."

"Are you gonna dump me for a hot firefighter as your new bestie?" Cove dropped the dew-covered can on Toni's belly.

Toni grabbed her friend's wrist. "Never. I'm never, ever giving up my BFF."

"Cool, I guess you're standing by those *Fs*."

"You know I am, forever friend. Not gonna change."

Cove dropped into the chair beside Toni. "Okay, start from the beginning and don't leave out a single detail."

"I was actually having a really shitty day."

Cove's brow furrowed. "Shitty how?"

"Mandy cut the cord."

"Finally!"

"Hey," Toni barked. "That's my heart you just heard breaking."

"Breaking, really?" Cove argued.

"I'm sad, Co," Toni admitted. "Two years is a long time."

"I know, I've had to listen to your misery for half of it," they said. "One of you needed to end that relationship last year."

"It's hard when—"

They interrupted. "I get it. I'm not trying to hurt you. I just want you to know this isn't a surprise."

"It still hurts," Toni said, not convinced it truly hurt as much as she'd expected. Perhaps she'd let go already and was rooted firmly in a hazy loop of self-deprecation and denial.

"I'm sad that you're hurting, but not sad that Mandy took a hike." Cove patted their friend's leg. "So tell me all the good parts about today?"

Toni smiled. "Ella Eastman is more incredible in the flesh."

Their eyebrow peaked. "How much flesh?"

"Stop it, jerk." Toni swatted. "Don't tumble down the firefighter rabbit hole just yet."

"Alright, alright," Cove ceded, relaxing against their seat back. "Take a big sip of that water and tell me about your day."

~~~~~~~~~~~

Cove flipped the flyer over, excited about the prospect of smashing anything to pieces. "We should go."

Toni shook her head. "It's a little stalker-y don't you think?"

Cove hit the promotional flyer with a quick fingertip flick. "She gave it to you."

Toni tried to pluck the card but Cove was too fast. "Yes, but I'm sure she didn't really mean it."

They read the top of the card as it was written, chuckling at the wording which had probably been suggested by Beatrice. "Why else would Ella Eastman give you a thirty minute 'Exes Wrecks' rage-smash-for-two coupon?"

Toni shrugged. "Probably because I started to whimper about my breakup."

They waved, encouraging Toni to continue. "And."

"The best way to get over someone is to smash things with a bat."
~~~~~~~~~~~

Cove laughed. "O-kay, not where I was going but that sounds good, too."

"Won't it be weird?" Toni asked.

"Because of Beatrice?" Cove replied.

"Yes, I know you still have feelings."

"My feelings can handle B." They dropped the card on the table. "And it's a free pass, dork. Ella made it appropriately un-weird. So we should go."

Toni tucked the card back inside her bag. "Maybe we can go in the future. Today, I think I'll bask in the glory of being her top."

Cove groaned, "Seriously, T… that's not what it means."

6.

The Briickhead

The drive to the construction site was quieter than most mornings. Usually, by the time Lil pulled into the parking area, the Briick mini character dangling from her rearview mirror was spinning and jerking from the stops and starts in traffic. Today, as she shifted the truck into park, her assembled Briick mini contractor had only a slight sway.

Lil was a typical Briickhead: that person who attended conventions to trade for a discontinued set or someone who had a designated space in their home only for builds. Briicks were more than a part-time hobby, and were probably the reason her construction company rarely felt like work.

The cellphone's buzzing in her pocket was not going to be good news, she thought as she slapped the door of her truck, closing it harder than intended. Forgetting the messy flop of hair atop her head, she attempted to fit her hardhat in place, mumbling as the tangle of blonde hair caught the adjusting strap. The sun was barely peeking over the horizon and already she wished she could go back to bed.

With rigid long-legged strides she walked around her vehicle, dropping the hardhat through the window so she could collect her hair into a sad excuse of a stubby ponytail.

She paused, staring at the three red-block letters of her shortened name on the back of her hat, in sharp contrast to the tradesperson yellow of the hard plastic.

It was seven in the morning and she could almost appreciate the sunrise breaking through the tree line along the construction site's property, as she anticipated the conversation she was about to have. *This is the life*, she thought as she answered, recognizing the number on her phone. "Yep, this is Lil," she said.

"It's not good, boss." Max's grumbly voice crackled without the niceties of a greeting.

"Don't give me excuses." Frustrated, she rubbed the stubbled hair beneath the blonde ponytail, wondering why she hadn't shaved her entire head. "Give me solutions."

He mumbled something she couldn't decipher before saying, "I'll call again."

Inspection delays and supply chain issues had stretched her patience from the moment her company broke ground on this project. She'd barely had five minutes to calculate who would go home early when her phone rang again. She didn't waste time on greetings when the logistics director's name displayed on her screen again. "What have you got for me?"

"Noon," he said. "It'll be there by noon."

"That's more like it." She tapped a pen to the material's list on her drawing, making a tiny slash beside today's date. "Good job, Max."

"Thanks boss." He said before ending the call.

Lil checked the time on her watch before dialing her cell again. Truth was, the rush of her morning had as much to do with the shipment as it did with organizing everything so she could spend the next two hours waiting in a digital queue for an improbable surprise.

The funky beat of the synthesized 80s hold music was entertaining for the first ten minutes, and as much as she wanted to slip in an earbud she worried the call would cut out and she'd lose her place in line.

~~~~~~~~~~~

"Hey, Lil." Marshal, the muscular manager of the Sage Lounge, greeted her as she stood in the entry. "Lunch or business?" he asked. It was his job as manager of the restaurant-by-day and queer-club-by-night to get to know his regulars by name.

"Business, mostly," Lil said. "Brooke and I need to discuss a few things. Can we sit up top?"

"Sure, Crumbly is up there but no one else this time of the day." They followed him toward the staircase.

"Great, I haven't seen Morgan in ages," Lil said as the trio climbed to the second floor. Marshal grinned as they approached the table where Morgan sat erasing lines on her current pencil sketch.

Lil took a few seconds to admire Morgan's work before the artist realized they were there. She was talented, and Lil, as skilled as she was at building, never made art like Morgan. "Hey Crumbly," Lil joked as the trio paused in front of her corner table.

"Lil!" Morgan slid around to give her friend a hug. "What a great surprise. How's life?"

"So good to bump into you… and life is life, you know. Taking it as it comes right now." Lil hitched her thumb toward the person behind her. "You remember Brooke, my brickmason?"

Morgan did remember the brickmason; in fact after their initial meeting months ago they'd established a friendship based on smashing things with job-site recycle. "Hi Brooke."

"Hey." Brooke made a fist and Morgan bumped it. "How's that stack from the Maple Street demolition working out?"
~~~~~~~~~~~

"It's great," Morgan said. "There's something very satisfying about throwing a brick or two into a panel of tempered glass."

Brooke was shy around most people, a true introvert until she was in the presence of the artist. "We are just about to sit down and discuss another project and we're earmarking all the good junk for you. There are some great glass bricks I thought you'd like."

"Oh, speaking of good junk, I've got a few scraps of corrugated roof deck and a blown glass chandelier with a huge crack. You interested?" Lil asked.

"You two sure know how to keep a lady happy," Marshal teased. "Look at her, she's practically salivating."

Morgan grinned. "A lady's got to stay in business, and yes to whatever you can bring to the rage rooms."

"Is there a contractor in this town that you don't know?" Marshal asked with a goofy grin.

"I'm sure there is," Morgan said. "Do the two of you want to join me or are you working?"

"We're working right now but I'll stop by after." Lil gave her friend a hug. "I've got a surprise to show you."

"Ooh, a surprise. I'm intrigued," Morgan said.

"You're really going to like this one," Lil added, walking backward as she followed Marshal and Brooke to the opposite side of the balcony dining area. "Chicks and Briicks. Five stars." She waved her finger guns.

"What the heck does that mean?" Morgan asked, suspecting her friend was up to no good.

"Don't leave til I come back."

"Stayin' right here." Morgan patted the table in front of her sketch pad.

"See you in a bit," Lil called as she crossed the room.

~~~~~~~~~~
~~~~~~~~~~

"Take a look at this." Lil pulled out the chair beside Morgan and the artist jumped, startled by the sudden break in focus as Lil set her tablet on the table between them.

There was no greeting, just the gruff contractor sliding onto the seat next to her. Morgan was scraping eraser crumbs into a little pile in front of her. This charming quirk was a signature behavior and also why more than ten years ago Marshal nicknamed her *Crumbly*.

"Is this my surprise?" Morgan scooted the pile onto the plate left for collecting the mess.

"It is, and it's going to blow Ella's mind." The screen lit with the logo of *The Blasphemer* television show, but it looked different. The characters weren't the typical cast photos but miniature figures made from plastic bricks. Lil smiled as the show title was assembled brick by brick across the screen.

"They—are—not!" Morgan gaped. "How did I not know? How did Ella not know?"

"I have no idea but I didn't make this up. And it gets better because the launch for a five-set series is going to be at the Briick Briick-tacular convention in a few months." Lil's expression was animated, resembling a child let loose in a candy store with a pocket full of cash as she swiped the screen to scroll through the close-up views of the building sets.

"Wait," Morgan said as she reached to stop Lil's hand. "That's the Arsonist with a tiny little flamethrower."

"Cool, right?"

"And Bruiser." Morgan pinched and separated her fingers to zoom in. "He's got a crochet hook and a little Briick blanket."

"And look, they gave the Florist a tiny blue flower."

"Forget me not," they said in unison, repeating the final words from the season three finale.

"Ella's going to scream when she sees this."

"I got tickets for all of us." Lil grinned.

"You did what?"

"I was on hold for hours. It sold out fast and the super VIP ticket comes with the exclusive pre-release set." Lil smirked as she showed her the picture of the Briick set.

"We can't let you do that." Morgan rested against her seat-back. "That's way too much."

"Consider it payment for everything the two of you have done for me." Lil crossed her arms, essentially taking the fight out of the debate.

"We haven't done that much. At least not enough to cover the cost of our two VIP tickets," Morgan argued.

"You want me to break it down for you?" Lil asked, and before Morgan could respond she ticked off the list. "You and your beautiful butchy beefcake have saved my ass many times. Do I even have to mention Cove? Or the time Ella unloaded an entire shipment of roofing materials saving me from forking out two days' rental on another damn delivery truck. She handled that skid steer like a pro and this is the super bonus that entitled you to the partner ticket, she nailed the shit out of the second-story framing at my Fifth Street walkup."

"She didn't do it to get paid," Morgan said.

"That's the best part about it, about her." Lil rubbed the stubble on the back of her head. "She never asks for a thing. So it's up to you to convince her."

"Up to me?" Morgan patted her heart. "Uh uh, no way. It's up to you. You'll have to sell her on the trade."

"Done." Lil chuckled.

"She's not that easy, you know." Morgan slid her sketchbook into her shoulder bag.

"She'll go." Lil stood. "I know how much she loves the Arsonist. Once she sees that little Briick figure she'll be racing to the front of the line."

"I guess we'll have to wait and see." Morgan's phone vibrated on the table where the image of Ella's smiling face was grinning at her. "Speaking of hot firefighters." She hit the answer button.

"Were we?" Lil joked as the duo walked toward the staircase.

"Hi beautiful," Morgan said as she raised the messenger bag to her shoulder.

Lil reached for the bag. "I'll take it down the stairs so you can hold the handrail," she whispered.

Morgan paused. It was sweet the way Lil paid attention to Morgan's needs, so much like the way Ella did. They were similar, she observed many times in their friendship, not only in body type and butch presentation, but in the way they made a person feel protected and safe. She used to hate the need for help, but being loved by Ella changed Morgan. Her kindness and trust made it easier to accept help from the people in her life. Today was a good day, physically, but going down stairs and flexing the limited mobility from the scars on her legs was occasionally a struggle.

"You still at Marshy's?" Ella asked.

"I am. I bumped into Lil and we had a nice talk." Morgan transferred the phone to her opposite hand so she could steady herself with the handrail. "You finish the errand?"

"All wrapped up and out the door," Ella joked. Her surprises weren't wrapped, or even constructed, but she was very excited and a little impatient to see Morgan's reaction.

Morgan could picture Ella's smile. She knew every tiny line on her face and the brightness in her eyes when something excited the firefighter. "Are you still going to help me set up for the big bashing party?"

"Biceps are ready," Ella teased.

"Oh, I love it when you're all pumped up."

"I know you do," Ella said.

Lil paused, looking over her shoulder at Morgan. The artist tipped her head, not even attempting to feign embarrassment.

7.

The Surprise

Ella heard the hum of the elevator motor. She'd sent it to the ground floor expecting Morgan any moment but for some reason it felt like the climb was taking forever.

"Happy 'I love you and you're the best partner' day!" Ella was standing in the space between the kitchen and living room of their open-air loft apartment. Her red, sleeveless, cropped shirt was almost invisible behind the two Briick set boxes she held strategically in front of her chest.

Morgan's eyes went wide, her casual grin stretching into an appreciative smile as she stood stunned by the sight of the nearly-naked, muscled firefighter. "Ell-a!" Morgan squealed. Remembering Lil was standing behind her, she turned to cover Lil's eyes.

"Not so fast, little lady. You've gotta be quicker than that," Lil joked. "I already saw Miss December, a little bit more of Miss June and quite a bit extra of Mzz February." She buzzed the last with an eyebrow wiggle.

"Aw, fuck. Come on, Lily Flower." Ella spun around to set the boxes on the counter, revealing the rest of her skimpy outfit.

"Jeeze, Eastman. Put some pants on."

Ella grumbled, "You're ruining my surprise."

Morgan dropped her messenger bag on the chair. "She isn't ruining anything." Her glance traveled the length of Ella's muscled body, lingering longer in her favorite places. It was accurate to say that years in the gym left Ella perfectly sculpted. "From where I'm standing, nothing is in ruins." Morgan tipped onto her toes, stretching to kiss her girlfriend.

"Hello, beautiful." Ella's hands circled Morgan's hips as she raised her for a kiss.

"Hi yourself." Morgan smiled as she wrapped her arms around Ella's neck. "You know 'I love you and you're the best partner day' isn't a real holiday, right?"

"Yes." Ella chuckled. "But it should be." She spun Morgan around and raised her to sit on the counter. "It should always be, because you are the best thing that's ever happened to me." She fit herself between her partner's legs and kissed her, this time with more intimacy than their guest needed to experience.

Lil coughed. "Uh, maybe I should come back later?"

Ella groaned as her forehead fell against Morgan's. "Lily Flower is still here."

"Yes, I'm still here and ugh, stop calling me flower. You know I fucking hate it."

Ella turned in Morgan's arms. "I know that, and I also know you're not supposed to be here in my living room when I'm about to present my present."

"Present my present, cute," Lil teased. "And technically this is your kitchen. I know because I ran the gas line for that amazing cooktop."

"Not cute," Ella said, stretching her finger to point at the elevator. "Go home."

"Oh, honey, it's actually pretty adorable," Morgan quipped as she tightened her arms to keep Ella close.

"It's not adorable," Ella argued. "I had a plan and it did not include a third party."

Lil stepped into the loft, pulled the gate on the elevator door, and closed it behind her. "Phew," she said as the metal bits locked together. Morgan and Ella chuckled at the quirky sound effect Lil made every time she entered and exited through what she'd called the 'antiquated contraption,' as if she'd somehow escaped a treacherous ride. "Well, I have a plan, too," Lil added.

"Our plans better not be the same." Ella bristled.

Morgan squeezed Ella's hands. "They are not the same." She turned to look at Ella. "But you're going to like them."

Lil pushed the Briick set boxes aside, appreciating the thought that they both had building Briicks on the brain today. She made room for the tablet she'd pulled from her sling bag. "So I had an opportunity to get you something pretty cool." She activated the screen, opening the home page of the website.

"Briick Briick-tacular," Ella read the title. "What the hell is that?"

"Your dream come true." Lil smirked.

"Morgan's my dream come true. So you can take that and shove it—"

Morgan smothered Ella's mouth with a quick maneuver. "Let her tell you," she scolded as her hand fell away.

"I don't want—"

Morgan pointed. "Shh, let her tell you."

One of Lil's favorite parts of being with Morgan and Ella together was the way their love seeped into the room; even after eight years together, they acted like new lovers. "Wow, you two need to get a room," Lil teased.

"Lily Flower, if any of the next words that come out of your mouth include the word foreplay, I'm going to kick you out," Ella warned. "After I kick your ass."

"For the record you said foreplay first, not me." Lil opened the website on her phone.

"Why did you bring her over?" Ella harrumphed.

Morgan felt Ella's body tense. "She has a surprise for you, and I promise you're going to love it." She snaked her pinky around Ella's, tugging the firefighter in for a kiss.

Temporarily satisfied, Ella said, "Fine, what's the big surprise?"

"This." Lil tapped on a picture of *The Blasphemers* Briick set.

Ella steadied the page, not believing her eyes. "When did this happen?" She expanded the graphic and zoomed in on The Arsonist.

"It hasn't really happened yet." Morgan grinned. "The tickets went on sale this morning."

"I can't believe you didn't know about these sets," Lil said.

"I've been a little busy… ya know… fighting fires."

"More like signing your own boobs," Lil joked.

Ella reached to open her laptop and copied the link to the website. "My boobs, my crotch and sometimes strangers' boobs too."

"Ella!" Morgan scolded as she slid from the countertop. "You didn't."

"I did, and let me tell you it was a real show stopper." Ella used the touchpad on her laptop to expand the tiny Briick flamethrower on the page. "The flamethrower has a little glowy fire shaped Briick coming out of it."

Lil raised her hand. "Can we rewind to the boob-signing part of this conversation?"

"I second that." Morgan half-suppressed a laugh.

Ella continued exploring the images on her screen as she relayed the experience with more focus on the Briick sets than the story. "It wasn't that big of a deal. Marsh brought one of his dates and the dude had ridiculous pectorals." She cupped her hands in front of her chest. "Like, big," she chuckled.

"You signed man boobs?" Lil shook her head. This was not the detail she was hoping for.

"That sounds like something Marshy would do." Morgan pushed the barstool behind Ella, coaxing her to sit so she could occupy Ella's lap.

"Marsh set me up, and you should have heard Soot Boy and the rest of the team harassing me for the duration of that signing session." Ella grinned, thinking about her best friend and station captain, Lester Feller. The nickname Soot was complimentary to Ella's nickname Cinder. Family was built in the places you called home, and Ella had two homes: Station Eight-Eighteen and Morgan Hail's arms.

"I'm sure that boob signing was mamm-ry-able," Lil punned.

"Oh, that's horrible." Ella pinched her nose in disgust. "Marsh and Les mocked me as I made the largest scrolling E on the guy's chest. It was funny but it was also the last one, ever."

"Including women?" Lil bumped Ella's shoulder.

"Maybe." Ella's finger tapped the touch pad, opening the link to the convention tickets.

"Was that a statement or a question?" Morgan covered Ella's hand with her own.

"The only lady's boobs I'm interested in are yours." Ella tangled her strong fingers around Morgan's.

"Oh for crying out loud, I don't need to hear this," Lil said.

"You kinda started it with these." Ella pointed to the laptop screen. "Holy shit! The VIP tickets come with an exclusive pre-release building set." Ella's thumb and index finger danced across the touchpad. "Well, that sucks. Those tickets are sold out." Irritated, she leaned to look at her friend. "Why did you show me this?"

"So I could show you these," Lil emailed the ticket file from her phone to the computer. "Open the document, you goofball."

"I'm the goofball, Flower?" Ella accepted the download and the image of a VIP ticket popped up on the screen. "Did you do this?" She looked at Morgan.

"It was all Lil. She jumped on the website before the rest of the world."

Ella lifted Morgan, reversing position with her on the stool. "You got three VIP tickets for us?"

"I did, and before you try and wrap those muscles around me for a hug, remember I'm not a hugger." Lil made a cross with her fingers to ward off the display of affection.

"Fist-bump then?" Ella held out her knuckles and Lil tapped hers against them.

Morgan smiled at the exchange, leaning against her hand, elbow resting on the table. Her two favorite burly women avoiding affectionate contact was cuter than they'd ever want to own. "You two realize all that avoidance makes you cuddly and cute?"

"Cuddly and cute?" Lil guffawed as she stepped closer to Morgan.

"She means this." Ella flexed her bicep. "The left is cuddly."

"Don't say the right bicep is cute." Lil made a gagging sound. "I don't need to know you've named your body parts."

"You want to know the name of my—"

"Honey, be nice to Lil." Morgan interrupted. "She managed to put you in a VIP line for The Arsonist in tiny Briick form."

"Yeah, be nice to me." It was curious the way Lil didn't mind affection from Morgan. There was a bond between them that Ella didn't quite understand from the usually reserved friend.

"I can be nice." Ella scooted against Morgan, returning them to their snuggly position on the kitchen stool but also putting distance between the friends.

Morgan felt the possessiveness in Ella's actions but didn't say anything, waiting to address it when they were alone.

Ella scrolled through the details on the screen. "The dates are fairly close."

"Can you get the time off?" Lil asked.

"I'll get the time." Ella clicked on the event calendar in search of a costume opportunity. "There's a cosplay event too but I'm not sure I can put one together in time."

"I'll help," Morgan said. "It won't be our first collaboration."

"This is my cue to back out slowly. You do the cosplay thing and I'll be the protective best friend and beat the fans away," Lil joked.

"Sounds like a plan," Morgan said.

Ella downplayed how little time she had to make a costume. "I'm sure we'll all be fine."

"Great." Lil shrugged. "I'm gonna cut and run." She pushed the lever to open the elevator cage door. "I've got an early site visit in the morning." Ella's attempt to stand was met with a hand waved at her shoulder. "Stay and check out the event pages. I'll let myself out."

"Thanks, Lil," Morgan said.

"Yeah, thanks," Ella added.

"It's nothing," Lil replied as she stepped through the elevator door. "Let's just have a great time." The jaws of the elevator closed. "Phew," she said as it began to lower.

"Never gets old, how she thinks I don't know how to do a safety inspection on our elevator," Ella mumbled.

Morgan dismissed the comment as she tipped Ella's chin to her. "What was that all about?" she asked.

"What was what?" Ella misunderstood the question. "She always makes that sound when she gets in and out of it."

"Not the elevator." Morgan pushed Ella against the chair's back. "The look you gave her, and the extreme 'touch her and die' possessiveness you just displayed in our kitchen, and with Lil of all people?"

Ella frowned. Morgan's description of the exchange was confusing to her. "I don't even know what you mean by 'touch her and die'." She attempted to stand but Morgan held her in place with a glare.

"First, I am not a possession you get to drag around like a cave woman."

"Wait! Whoa... what are you talking about?" Ella was even more confused.

Morgan put a finger against Ella's lips. "Are you serious?"

Ella's lips puckered and she attempted to kiss the finger.

"Stop that. We need to discuss the little cave woman maneuver you just performed."

"Morgan," she said against the forceful finger before it moved away. "Cave woman?"

"You physically picked me up and moved me away from Lil."

"So?" Ella asked.

"So, what was that all about?"

Ella stood and with little effort reversed their positions so Morgan took her spot in the chair. "I don't know. I didn't even think about it."

"I'm with you and only you. You know that, don't you?"

Ella was shocked by the question. "Yes, why do you even ask?"

"Because that 'touch her and die' move was completely unnecessary."

"Morgan, honey." Ella leaned against the counter. "I don't have a clue what you're talking about."

Morgan didn't say a word as she spun away, leaving Ella staring at the vacant counter chair. A few seconds later, she returned with a tilted armful of books from her bedside pile.

"Sit," Morgan ordered.

Ella's brow peaked with curiosity as she lowered onto the barstool.

"This is *To Love Again*" Morgan raised the book. "It's a romance, and a really good one," she added.

"O…kay," Ella drew out the word, emphasizing her continued confusion. "And?"

"You frustrating woman." Morgan flipped the back cover around, scanning until she found the part she wanted to recite from the blurb. "When Autumn stands to defend her lover against the forces of evil, this touch her and die heroine rocks the damsel to her core…"

"Wait, it doesn't really say that." Ella tipped the book so she could scan the blurb. "Autumn and Juniper? What kind of names are those?"

"That's not the point," Morgan said. "When I said 'touch her and die', I was talking about a story trope."

"Honey, you're saying more words that I don't understand."

"Which?" Morgan asked.

Ella chuckled. "Story trope. I don't know what you mean."

Morgan sighed. "You should get comfortable, because I'm about to show you the ways of my book club world."

It didn't take long for Morgan to read the back cover blurbs from her small book stack and explain how certain predictable scenarios drove the plot of many of her favorite romance novels. She thumbed through social media posts of graphic depictions pointing literally to story trope words.

Ella was fascinated. "So if you and I were a romance story," she began.

Morgan blushed. "I think we are."

Ella nodded in agreement. "Well, for this example, let's say someone penned our love story, and if we go all the way back to the day we met we would fall into an enemies to lovers romance with a sprinkle of secret identity." She showed the squiggly-line graphic to Morgan.

"It was hardly a sprinkle, honey." Morgan argued. "You were in cosplay."

"Award winning cosplay," Ella corrected.

"Yes, but it was deceptive."

"Unintentionally," Ella corrected again. "Practically accidental."

"I suppose, but you could have told me," Morgan said.

"Yes, but I'm glad you forgave me that I didn't."

Morgan stepped between Ella's legs. "You made it very hard for me not to forgive, and it felt accidental when all was said and done."

"Ultimately it was the uniform, admit it."

Morgan smiled. It wasn't only the uniform; it was the tenderness, the attentive way Ella saw her, and also the way she changed little things so Morgan felt comfortable with the limitations her burn scars created. Truth be told, the uniform didn't hurt her cause either.

Ella tapped on another social media graphic, comparing it to a few books on the counter. "Oh, I'm another trope."

Morgan giggled. "Yes, you sure are."

"You got a sapphic in uniform." She pushed over the three-book series with flames and emergency service vehicles on their covers. "You seem to like that one."

"I like a predictable butch in a story or two by this author."

"Really, only by this author? What about in real life?"

"Truth?" Morgan kissed her.

"Mm-hmm."

She whispered across Ella's lips. "You, my love, are a walking, talking, romance reader's dream."

Ella smiled. "I kinda like the way you said that."

~~~~~~~~~~~

Two hours later, Ella lay in bed, Morgan's head resting across her abdomen. She scrutinized the stack of books on the floor, and couldn't chase the notion for a clever proposal from her mind. The blurbs were interesting and provoking a load of ideas. The current book she lay skimming through had a romantic, private proposal setting. Ella had a new florist she could use to create an atmosphere like it. She had a perfect rooftop patio for a private once-in-a-lifetime memory: rose petals, candles, their favorite song piped through the sound system, and a ring. The thought of a ring made her tense and she knew Morgan could tell.

"I like this," she said, wriggling to shake her sudden mood change.

Morgan adjusted to read the title. *"Like a Lamb for a Lion,"* she read. "Oh, out of all the books in here, that's the one you stopped on. The author is going to crush your soul."

"Really? It seems cute," Ella said.

"False sense of security, honey." Morgan faced her upside down. "The author is notorious for crushing souls."

Ella dropped the book to her hip. "But it's so romantic."

"What chapter did you skim to?" Morgan asked as she pushed to sit up.

Ella thumbed the pages. "Halfway through chapter seven."

"Yes, that's the very best part of their relationship," Morgan said, adding, "If you want them to live happily ever after, stop reading at chapter fourteen."
~~~~~~~~~~~

Ella closed the book. "Happily ever after ends two-thirds of the way through?"

Morgan caressed Ella's face. "Honey, this one is a love story. That's very different from a romance."

Ella set the book on the bed. "You finished this one?"

"It was a book club option." Morgan smiled. "I had to know what happened."

"But I don't?"

"Let's just say I know you, and you should work up to this one." Morgan took the book. After sorting through the untouched pile beside the bed, she gave Ella a new choice. "You should start with this one."

"Why?"

Morgan flipped to the inside flap. "It's a romance and they live happily ever after."

"Will it matter if I'm not actually going to read them?"

It was charming the way Ella 'read' books. She didn't have the patience for the slow-burn pace many were written in. "Maybe you should try the audio versions?"

"Is that considered reading?" The question was innocent and Ella had no idea the debate she'd stumbled into.

"You realize oral storytelling is older than written stories?" Morgan asked. "Didn't anyone read to you as a child?"

Ella shrugged. "My godmother did, of course."

"That's no different than plugging in a set of headphones and listening to a recorded narrator."

"I guess I never thought about it."

Morgan rolled to the side table for her phone. "I've got an account from the library. I can borrow a few books a month and we're lucky our library has a pretty diverse catalogue of romances about women who love women. You can also log into my book club account online. I've purchased hundreds of romances."

"Hundreds?" Ella asked.

"Yes, and I can set it up on your phone." Morgan switched her app to scroll through the book list.

"I can listen while I work out," Ella suggested.

Morgan snickered. "You can, but some of these get a little spicy." She was swiping through her audiobook list, searching for a great first listen. "This is my favorite narrator. She's done hundreds of books." Morgan adjusted the wireless headphone before pushing the second in Ella's ear.

The voice came on and Ella found it soothing. "She's nice."

"Yep," Morgan agreed. They settled against the headboard of the bed, Morgan's body relaxing against Ella's.

"Is this one of the spicy ones?" Ella asked.

"I guess you'll have to wait and see."

~~~~~~~~~~

The following day, Morgan visited Lil at a job site to look at a few dumpsters full of scrap she might use at the rage rooms. She left Ella sitting at the kitchen counter assembling a lighted Briick display case for their flowers and listening to her new romance.

"Honey, I'm home," Morgan said as the lift landed at their loft floor. Ella didn't answer but Morgan knew she was still there. She peeked around the corner, to see Ella adjusting the clamps on the wood and acrylic structure with corded headphones in her ears. She hated to interrupt.

"Hi, love." She raised her voice and waved to get Ella's attention.

Ella startled. "Oh, hi." She pulled the earbud from her ear and left it dangling.

"Good book?" Morgan asked as she slid an arm around to grab the earbud.

"It's a great book," Ella said.
~~~~~~~~~~

Morgan listened for a second before dropping the bud. "Are you listening at one-and-a-half speed?"

Ella nodded.

Morgan was horrified. "But it's a romance."

"I know, and I want to get to the good part." Ella tapped to pause the book.

"But how can you appreciate the narration if it sounds like squirrels fighting in a rock tumbler?"

Ella chuckled. "I'm impatient."

"But you're not getting the full flavor."

Ella disagreed. "Trust me, I got all the flavor in chapter seven."

Morgan checked the phone to see what book Ella was reading. "Oh. Oh yes, that's a flavorful book."

"I think you might have used a few of these spices on me?" Ella teased.

"Perhaps I have," Morgan said.

"I was wondering if you'd be interested in listening with me while I finish this build?"

Morgan pointed at herself. "You want me to listen while you work? Here? Right now? To his book?"

Ella placed the earbud back in Morgan's ear. "Yep." She tapped the file on her screen. "I'll even put it on regular speed."

"Baby, there is no way you're working through the next chapter."

Morgan was right. At two minutes and twenty-seven seconds, Ella was leading her lover across the loft and into their bedroom.

8.

The I Don't

The cellphone buzzed in Lester's pocket as he pushed through the door, juggling to keep the gym bag on his shoulder as he answered the call. The number on the display made him smile. "What's up, Cinder?"

"You on your way home yet?" Ella asked.

He could hear shuffling and the clunking of objects in the background. "Just finished at the gym, what's up?"

"I need an objective set of eyes on a project. Can you come to the loft and look at something?"

The tone of her voice lacked its usual playfulness. "Everything good, Cinder?"

"I think so, but I need a second opinion. I'll be on the rooftop."

"Be there in ten."

She disconnected without a sendoff and Lester worried as he hurried to his car. Eastman was definitely focused on something and she sounded a little off her game.

When he arrived at the loft's private entrance, he let himself in using the code to the door. It was quiet but he also knew Morgan was probably at the Sage Lounge taking a break from the chaos of the rage rooms.

"Hello, anyone home?" Lester peeked around the corner at the top of the staircase as he entered the loft apartment. Morgan was nowhere in sight so he made a quick dash to the steps leading to the rooftop patio. He could smell scented candles before he opened the door, and there were dozens of flower petals wedged beneath the threshold.

"Aw, Cinder, this cannot be your big idea," he said as he pushed through to the roof. The setup was stereotypical and not what he'd consider romantic, with scented candles so powerful he had to cover his nose. After a quick scan of the rooftop patio he counted more than two dozen flickering flames, and the mix of scents overwhelmed him.

"What do you think?" Ella asked.

"No, Cinder." He covered his mouth and nose.

"No?" Ella repeated the word. She was down on one knee, dressed in her perfectly pressed formal uniform, the tips of her polished boots reflecting the sun's light. She'd planned everything. The flowers, built from new Briick sets, not cut. The instrumental music playing through the speakers. The candles lit on the rooftop patio table flickering from the light breeze. The sparkling cider chilling in the ice bucket to celebrate with a toast.

It was not the answer she expected. It wasn't the dream come true. It was the implosion of a future she didn't know she wanted until she'd fallen for Morgan Hail.

Why was he saying no?

"Chees-y, Cinder." Lester shook his head. "This is the most predictable scenario I've ever seen. She deserves better."

"Cheesy? Better?" Ella's shoulders sagged. "Really?"

"With a double serving of crackers, seriously. And I think I need a breathing mask because the combination of these candles are strong. After reading so many of Morgan's books, this is all you've got?"

She dropped into the chair, blowing across the tabletop to extinguish the candles arranged around the Briick flowers she'd taken from the kitchen counter. "I thought it was clever and really romantic."

"For common folk," he said. "You and Morgan are not common folk."

Deflated, Ella tugged at the knot of her tie until it hung loose around her neck. "She deserves more than common."

"I agree. Any brighter ideas?" he asked.

"A river cruise, maybe."

Les shook his head.

"After dinner and a romantic comedy?" she suggested.

He wrinkled his nose, obviously unimpressed. "Think outside the box, Cinder."

"She really likes the uniform." Ella smiled.

"Obviously. Who doesn't?" he asked. "But that's not all she likes. What else?"

"Art. She lives for making art. And the rage room."

"A rage-room proposal seems completely off the rails," he joked.

"Not terribly romantic." Ella added.

He shook his head. "The champagne is nice." He flicked the glass.

"Sparkling cider," she corrected. "We're sober, remember."

"Right."

Feeling like the jacket was strangling her, she shoved it off her shoulders. "Am I being silly?"

"Nah, you're being you, but you're also forgetting that she loves you and whatever way you ask her, she's going to say yes."

"But not like this?" She sighed.

He shook his head.

"I only get to do this once," she persisted.

"What's in the ring box?" he asked, impressed that she had made a decision.

Ella popped the velvet-covered box open and flipped it around for him to see.

"It's empty."

Her forehead dropped to the tabletop. "I know it's empty." She groaned. "That's not perfect either."

"Hell, Eastman, don't you think you needed to get her a ring before you put all this together?"

Ella kicked her foot out from under the table. "That's why I called you instead of calling Morgan up here."

"Who polished the boots?" he asked, distracted by the ridiculous shine.

She peeked over the tabletop. "I did. Why?"

"I suppose you spent a lot of time with that."

She glared at him. "What's your point?" she snapped.

"My point is you should spend a little more time on the ring and less time on a spit shine."

He was right. She was putting on a show for Morgan without the key component for any proposal. "I know. I'm working on that too. I've found a jeweler, I just need to go."

"Do you need a wingman?" He touched her shoulder. "Cinder and Soot, we make a great team."

"Not this time." She patted his hand. "I think I need to be solo on this one."

"Okay, but the offer stands."

"Thanks, man," she said.

"Who knows, maybe getting a ring will inspire the perfect proposal scenario?"

"Maybe." She didn't sound hopeful as she stood, making her way to extinguish each candle on the rooftop, one by one. "It certainly can't make things more difficult."

"Don't get down, Cinder." He tossed his arm over her shoulder. "Just think of all the ways she loves you, and it'll come."

"I'll do that."

"You want some help cleaning the patio?" he asked.

Ella picked up a few flower petals. "Nah, I'd rather do it alone. It'll give me time to think."

"Okay." He backed toward the door. "Give me a call if you need an opinion."

She didn't look up as she scooped more petals into a bag. "I will."

It took half the time to clean the rooftop that it had to set it up. She collected everything into the garbage and took it to the dumpster behind the rage rooms. This was the only dumpster within five square blocks that Morgan wouldn't climb inside. Everything had already made its way through rage-induced pulverization. Ella could smell the blended scent from the candles and doubled down on scrapping every unoriginal idea in her proposal playbook.

"Begin at the beginning," she whispered as she closed the dumpster lid. "Start with Gems by Jem."

9.

The Stone

Ella stood outside the building with her hands jammed deep in her pockets, fiddling nervously with the gym-locker key she carried. She'd changed from her dress uniform back into jeans and her favorite and often lucky red flannel shirt. She called it lucky because somehow she managed to find it after Morgan's attempts to claim it for herself. Ella loved that Morgan's scent lingered in the soft fabric.

The store name, Gems by Jem, was written in dark block-style letters outlined with shimmering gold flecks. Ella stood frozen on the sidewalk, fighting the urge to turn around and go home, wishing she'd taken Lester up on his offer to accompany her. Why did this feel too big to do without Morgan's opinion? Was it right to do it alone?

She had no idea how long she'd been staring at the window display before a question interrupted her intrusive thoughts.

"Can I help you with something?" the store clerk asked through the partially-opened shop door. Dressed in a linen suit with a Windsor-knotted tie, she looked dressed for success, which was something Ella needed right now. "You've been standing out here for a while."

Ella must have made the store clerk nervous because she didn't come outside completely. "I suppose you can help, maybe," she said, but didn't take a step to enter.

"The shop is open, if you were waiting." The clerk pointed at the neon-styled sign hanging in the window.

Ella crossed the threshold, thinking again that she had no idea why she hadn't allowed Lester to come or asked Marsh or even Beatrice to help with this huge decision. The lighting inside the shop was brighter than Ella expected and the volume of cases and the assortment of rings were overwhelming. With every step deeper into the shop, it was clear she didn't know anything about jewelry and even less about what to buy for Morgan.

"What are you shopping for today?"

Ella stopped in front of the display case. She didn't need a watch, but nerves were taking over her usually no-nonsense decisiveness.

"A watch?"

Ella shook her head.

"Are you feeling okay?" the clerk asked, concerned about Ella's odd behavior.

"I, I'm..." Ella stammered.

"How about a glass of water, and maybe you'd like to sit down for a minute."

The offer with such kindness and care from a stranger was an unusual reversal of roles, snapping Ella from her stupor. "Oh, gosh. No." Ella said. "I'm sorry, it's nerves. I'm nervous and I probably shouldn't even have come here by myself." She jammed her hands back in her pockets.

"Nervous. So you're here for a big occasion?"

Ella grinned. "Very big."

"Proposing?" The woman asked.

Ella sighed as she said, "I am and I'm clueless about everything when it comes to anything related to what you're selling in here."

"Well, my name is Dru and I'll do my best to walk you through all of this."

Ella shook the offered hand. "Ella, and I appreciate the help."

Dru steered them to the center display, which must have been set up for indecisive shoppers like herself. "Do you have a style in mind?" Dru laid a card on the countertop with images of more than a dozen finger-band designs.

Ella shook her head.

Dru flipped the card over. "Perhaps you have a thought about the stone you're looking for? Diamonds are most common but there are also many other gemstone choices."

Ella scanned the displayed images, taking in the rainbow of colored stones. "I don't have a clue." It came out as a whisper more to herself than to the shopkeeper.

"Ring size?" Dru asked in a hopeful tone.

"I have no idea." Ella shook her head. "I probably should know all of these answers since we've been together for eight years."

"Does she wear a lot of rings?"

Ella fiddled with the chain of finger-sizing loops on the glass counter. "Depends if she's working."

"Great. Mission one will be to borrow the one she wears on her ring finger and bring it here for sizing."

"I can do that." Ella felt a hopeful turnaround.

"The rest we can figure out from there."

~~~~~~~~~~

Ella returned to their loft an hour later, armed with vital information but feeling disappointed by her experience in the jewelry shop. The radio hummed as she sat in Charlene's
~~~~~~~~~~

driver's seat. She and the car had been through some things, and she couldn't help but wish for a little of her godmother's wisdom as she stared through the windshield. How was she going to choose a ring for Morgan to wear forever without blowing the experience of a surprise proposal? Style, size, colors and cut were benign words, usually, but not now that the goal was designing the perfect engagement ring.

"Can't sit out here all day," she mumbled as she turned off the car.

The bell above the shop door announced her arrival. As she reached to silence it, Morgan spun around to greet her. "Hi, darlin'."

"Hi." She was disappointed Morgan was alone at the front reception. "You're working at the desk now?"

"Just for another half hour. I've got a group finishing up in room four."

Ella leaned against the check-in kiosk. "Can I smash something while you finish supervising?"

Curious, Morgan questioned, "Bad day?" She dropped her paint brush on the watercolor pad.

"Frustrating more than anything."

"What would you like to smash?" Morgan asked.

"Not sure, really. Maybe a toaster oven or two." Ella noticed the piece of artwork Morgan was working on. "What's today's project?"

It wasn't uncommon for Morgan to fill the studio time at the rage room with pencil sketches or commission work. Today it appeared she was experimenting with an unusual set of paints.

"I got these new colors." She rotated the book for Ella to see. It was a forest scene with a flowing river, detailed with multi-colored stones along the shore. It reminded Ella of a fantasy story she'd started listening to.

"Interesting," Ella said.

"That's what I thought when I saw the samples."

"The colors sort of shine." Ella tilted the page.

Morgan dipped her brush in the cup, swishing the paint from the bristles. "It makes everything shimmer."

Ella couldn't help but compare the artwork to some of the stones she'd admired in the jewelry store. "The way it dries really makes your rocks look like they came out of a river or a tumbler."

Morgan smiled. "I guess it could be like that, sure. This current project is for a children's petting zoo. The gift shop has an interactive mining station. You buy a bag of dirt and sift through it for gemstones."

"That sounds like fun."

"It does," Morgan agreed. "That's why I'm playing with the paints. It'll bring the little stones to life and make them look tumbled."

Ella asked, "Have you sifted through tumbled rocks to get a feel for what stones you'll use?

"I haven't. Rocks aren't really a medium I've ever worked with. I think I'll keep things neutral and use the promo card from the zookeeper's pamphlet. They have a list of most commonly found gemstones. And I went there yesterday to take a few pictures." Morgan opened her phone photo gallery to show Ella the snapshots.

"There probably aren't any emeralds or sapphires in that dirt?" Ella joked.

Morgan grinned. "Probably not. It looks like the most common treasures are agates and amethysts."

"Do you have a favorite?"

"Of those two?" Morgan studied Ella, thinking the conversation a little odd, and that perhaps her girlfriend was having a bigger off day than she'd thought. It was obvious that the firefighter was more than a little distracted.

Ella shook her head. "Not a favorite of those rocks specifically."

"Honey, are you alright?" Morgan asked.

Ella reached to rotate the chair, careful not to bump the project as she helped Morgan to her feet. "I'm fine." She shrugged and tried to use a casual tone. It was interesting that a pallet of paints could guide this conversation. Armed with the little knowledge she'd acquired at the jewelry store that morning, she might uncover an idea for the engagement ring stone. "I'm just curious if you have a favorite rock or gemstone."

"I do." Sensing some time in a rage room was definitely warranted, Morgan led Ella down the hallway toward room three.

"Are you going to tell me what your favorite stone is?"

Morgan paused in front of the storage room door, pushing it open with her backside. "Are you going to choose your target?"

Ella hesitated, surveying the room quickly but already sure what she'd want. "I'll take this." She picked up the cardboard box. The sticker on the side had an obvious graphic of a very outdated small appliance. Morgan held the doors as Ella maneuvered down the hallway and placed the target on a stand in rage room three.

"That's a good one," Morgan said.

Ella nodded her agreement. "These old toaster ovens are built different." She studied the tools on the cart, knowing she'd begin with the sledgehammer.

Morgan stood in the doorway with Ella's jumpsuit dangling from her fingertip.

"Are you going to answer my question?" Ella asked.

Morgan tugged the jumpsuit to her chest, teasing Ella in exchange for a kiss. "Kiss me first."

"Oh, the answer is that good, huh?" Ella leaned down, smothering her with a soul-searing lip lock.

The garment slipped through Morgan's fingers. "What was your question again?"

Ella chuckled as she bent to pick up the crumpled suit. "Rocks. You have a favorite and you haven't told me what it is."

Morgan fell against the doorframe, steadying herself. "I'm named after it."

Ella stepped into the jumpsuit. "Are you serious?"

"Yep, very," Morgan said. "It's a thoughtful thing my parents did for me."

Ella touched Morgan's chin, tipping it toward her. "I love you."

"I've noticed."

Ella shook her head. "Such a tease, Morgan Hail."

"And you love that about me too, Ella Eastman." Morgan spun away, leaving Ella to stare at the closing door.

Named after it, Ella thought. She gripped the handle of the fourteen-pound sledgehammer, completely distracted by the idea that there was a 'Morgan' stone. What color was it? Could it fit in a ring setting? What shape was it? How could she make a Morgan rock look beautiful on her girlfriend's delicate finger?

The frustrations from her morning jewelry disaster switched to excitement, energizing her with a new direction on the quest. Ella swung the hammer until there was nothing left of the outdated toaster oven.

~~~~~~~~~~~

A few days later Ella sat in the lounge at the station house scrolling through images on the computer.

"What the hell are you doing, Cinder?" Lester scooted the rolling office chair close enough to rest his chin and read over Ella's shoulder.

"Nothing." She tapped the X in the corner of her browser window.
~~~~~~~~~~~

"Porn on station time," he teased as he shoved her aside. With the click of a few keys he refreshed the browser display, opening her last page. "Alright." He hesitated. "Definitely wasn't expecting close ups of rocks. Are you a geologist now?" he asked.

"Knock it off." She pushed his chair, launching him a few feet away.

"Why the secrets?"

Ella turned the monitor screen so he could see. "Morganite," she said.

"Well that clears it right up." He pretended to stand up and walk away.

"Nosey asshole." She tossed her pen at him. "I'm trying to find the perfect stone for Morgan's ring."

"And you're picking that rock?"

Ella passed the pocket-sized notebook to him. "Long story short. She told me yesterday that her parents named her after this rock."

"Morganite." He read the perfect block print Ella had written.

"Read the rest." She flicked the pad. "It's like they knew who she was the day she was born."

"The stone of divine love," he read. "Damn, Cinder. That's pretty romantic, even for you."

"It's a gemstone, and if I read the information page correctly it can be cut a lot like a diamond for a ring."

"Why not a diamond?" he asked.

"Because this is her. Morganite is exactly what she needs."

"So you did it?" He smiled.

Ella nodded. "I did. Now all I have to do is figure out a band and fitting."

"How's that going?" he asked.

"Ask me next week."

"Aw, Cinder." He stood. "At the rate you're going—"

"Don't say it, Soot." Ella interrupted. "I've got it figured out. At the rate I'm going she'll be saying yes very soon."

10.

The Flame

Toni reached for the phone as the smoke detector blared in the flower shop. It wasn't a false alarm; she knew it when the scent of fire escaped through the forced air vents.

She was glad that Penny, her florist, had gone for the day, but that meant she was alone to find the fire. Flashing flames would be impossible to miss if they were coming from her shop, but she could not determine where the puffs of smoke originated. She couldn't see a fire, or feel the heat, but she could smell it. "911, what's your emergency?" As the 911 operator answered, Toni relayed what she could. She pressed the phone to her chest as the owner of the shop next to hers pushed halfway through the door.

"The north wall of my store is on fire," he yelled, holding tightly to the half-open glass panel door.

Toni knew his storage room was located there and that he used dozens of different chemicals in his salon. She answered the operator's question, thinking his north wall was her south wall. "We have a fire at thirteen-eleven Chestnut Avenue."

"Is there anyone in the building?" the operator asked at the same time the internal alarm system sounded over Toni's head.

The events happened faster than Toni could process and she couldn't answer as a loud explosion knocked the phone from her hand, launching it and her across the room. She rolled to the floor and covered her head to protect herself from the splintering slat wall of potted plants spattering the shop. Plant litter and clumps of potting soil rained down, and she struggled to stand.

She crawled through the debris, wincing as her forearm slid against shards of a shattered glazed pot. "Shit," she squeaked as she belly-crawled her way to the door.

"Are you okay, Toni?" the neighboring shopkeeper asked.

"It's only a cut. Nothing too big." She squeezed the wound with her hand, applying pressure that only made the gash ooze more. She was anything but okay and felt a wave of dizziness when she stood.

"It looks kinda big," he said as the call of sirens blared and fire trucks approached.

The experience seemed otherworldly; perhaps it was shock or a concussion from the explosion, but Toni was aware the whole time, even if it happened in slow motion. Toni only half registered the rough sleeve of a firefighter's coat coming around her shoulder. The garment was warm from the firefighter's body and the weight felt more like a hug than a burden. Disoriented from the blast and feeling faint from bleeding, she let the firefighter lead her across the street and help her into the back of the first aid vehicle.

"Sit down," the firefighter said.

Because there was nothing else she could do, Toni obeyed. The coat fell from her shoulders and the loss of the anchoring weight made her more lightheaded.

"Let me take a look at your arm." The firefighter removed their helmet. "This looks pretty bad."

"It's not real—" Toni's thoughts clouded, her eyes losing focus as the voice of the firefighter finally registered. She'd stopped trying to sit upright and instead used the sidewall of the emergency services vehicle to keep herself steady. She didn't want to lay down; it was only a cut on her arm, after all.

Ella chuckled. "What's not real?" she asked, fairly certain she knew what the woman meant.

"You were in my shop, and now you're preventing me from bleeding to death." Toni winced as Ella poured a cold saline wash across her wound.

Ella patted the gash with a gauze square. "I'm only a firefighter." She smiled.

Toni doubled down on her admiration, ignoring Ella's humble words. "You are aware that there is nothing *only* about you?"

Ella was trying to hide how much she hated the way a firefighter calendar occasionally got in the way of her job. Staying focused, keeping things strictly professional, she secured the bandage over the wound. "All set. You should go to the ER. Have that laceration looked at by a doctor."

Toni closed her eyes. This was the tough part of her decision to be independent and own her life. Hospitals and emergency health care were a luxury she couldn't afford. "I'll be okay." She raised her arm. "You did a pretty good job."

Ella didn't want to argue. "You should, at minimum, give your GP a call and follow up to get a tetanus shot. Even if there aren't immediate signs of infection, it is possible."

"Thank you," Toni said. "Not just for this but for the crew keeping the shop from burning to the ground."

"Eight-Eighteen is a team." Ella double-tapped the station logo on her shirt.

"Sure, but you are special." Toni paused, thinking twice before adding, "You know that, right?"

Ella folded the flap on the medical kit and pushed it inside the cabinet. "If you say so." She was embarrassed now, feeling more pressure to be a celebrity than perform the job she trained for and loved.

"If you didn't have a partner, we could have coffee and laugh about this," Toni suggested, with hope in her tone.

Ella raised a pausing hand. "Like I said, have the wound checked, and I'm sorry about the damage to your shop."

Toni's cheeks flushed. She'd taken a chance and fallen flat on her face. It wasn't the first time and it would probably continue to happen in the future, but without taking the risk she'd be single forever. "That was like a bad pick-up line moment. Wasn't it?""

Ella collected the empty bandage packets from the bench. "It wasn't bad, just not appropriate in this situation." She held the red contaminate bag open so Toni could drop her blood-soaked tissues inside.

"You never know. Things happen for a reason, and you've now been to my flower shop twice." Toni shrugged. "I had to shoot my shot."

Ella thought back to the day she'd met Morgan, remembering the moment she knew she had to take a chance of her own. They'd spent the last eight years together after the reward of a very similar shoot-your-shot risk. She couldn't hold that against this woman. She did own a flower shop; maybe she could break the tension by changing the subject. "Have you ever watched *The Blasphemers*?" She smiled.

"Not you, too." Toni's attempts to smack her forehead led to a squeal as she raised her forearm, absentmindedly flexing her wound. "Please don't make a joke about my secret lair."

"I suppose you get that a lot?" Ella asked.

"More than you can imagine, and what's funnier is I'm not a florist." Toni scooted along the cot, wishing she could fade from the rapidly declining and embarrassing situation. "I own a flower shop. That's it. Penny does everything else."

Ella hopped from the back of the first aid vehicle and assisted the smaller woman to the city street. "But on the show it's mostly a front," Ella joked. "And the character's a badass."

"He knows his stuff." Toni forced a smile.

"So... you're saying we aren't going to find a secret computer lab in your basement?" Ella chuckled.

"It's fiction." Toni cradled her arm against her chest.

Ella shrugged. "Until it's not." She winked.

"No, there's not a super secret computer lab in my basement," Toni answered. "Well, not unless it belongs to the shopkeeper next door, and the explosion blew it through the wall." She stopped, realizing for the first time how much potential damage there was. The fire was out, but so was a section of the wall separating her flower shop from the salon next door. She raised her elbow to point at the pool of water collecting on the sidewalk. "I kinda wish this was fiction."

"Do you have someone to call?" Ella asked.

"For?"

Ella sidestepped the stream of water making its way to the drain near her boots. "Someone who can pick you up and take you home?"

Toni slumped against a lamp post in the parking lot. "My car is over there. I can manage the short trip."

"If you don't want to go to the ER, I have to insist someone takes you home," Ella said. "I can ask an officer to drive you."

"I'm fine." Toni forced a straight posture and tapped her fingers to her nose a few times. "See, totally good and sober."

"That'd be great if I was here for drunk driving, but I'm not." Ella wasn't going to continue to argue or even ask again. She whistled loudly and an officer raised their head.

"Sup, Eastman?" they asked.

"The shop owner needs a ride," Ella called. "Can you arrange for one?"

The discussion was over, and before Toni could further argue her position the officer was opening the door and Toni was resting in the front passenger seat. Her head fell against the cool glass. She didn't remember telling the cop where she lived or even how long it took for them to arrive at her apartment, but she was glad when her front door came into view.

"Would you like help inside?" the officer asked.

Toni stumbled getting out of the vehicle. "Maybe to the door. I seem to be slightly more tired than I thought I would be," she said. Fortunately she lived on the first floor and although she was slow, she didn't need physical assistance.

"It's most likely the adrenaline wearing off," he said. "Are you certain you don't want to go to the ER?"

Toni nudged his arm away. "I'll be fine." She fumbled to release the keys from her belt loop. "I appreciate the ride." She unlocked the door, relieved to be in her space.

"Have a nice night," the officer said. Toni closed out reality as she shut the door.

She was exhausted and her arm was beginning to throb. She knew she should call someone to help her or listen to the suggestion that she have a doctor look at the wound. "I'll rest, just for a minute," she said as she slid into the high-back recliner. The next thing she knew, it was morning and someone was pounding on her apartment door.

"Open the fucking door, T!" It was Cove and they were obviously aware of the fire.

"Hold on, I'm coming," Toni yelled. "Stop pounding." Her head hurt and she was sleepy as she shuffled the short distance before opening the door to a very disheveled best friend.

"Where the hell have you been?" They made a quick survey of the wounded woman, noticing first the dirt on her face and then the blood crusted on her pant leg. "You're hurt. Shit, T. Did you see a doctor?" Cove's questions came faster than Toni could answer.

"It's only a little cut." She held the door to steady herself and show off the bandage. "They cleaned it before I got home." She dragged herself away, her body aching everywhere as she collapsed into the chair.

"Let me look." Cove peeled the tape from the gauze and unrolled the wrap. There was a light stain of dried blood that seeped through the pad. "Why didn't you go to the ER?"

"And pay a zillion dollars?" Toni asked. "I'm already trying to figure out how I'll fix the building damage. " She rotated her forearm, getting her first real look at the gash. "It's not so bad. This will heal."

"You're a freaking wing nut," Cove said, obviously concerned about their best friend. "What did you cut it on?"

"A flower pot, of all things."

They rotated Toni's arm. "Nothing metal?"

"Ow," Toni pulled away. "That's attached, ya know!"

"Sorry," Cove said. "When was your last—?"

"Stop." Toni covered their mouth with her free hand. "I was examined at the shop and they suggested I see my GP." Her chuckle was bitter. "Like I have one of those."

"Well whoever examined you should have taken you right to an ER."

"Co, you do realize who you're talking to. An ambulance ride?"

"But you're hurt," they argued.

"Tomorrow, it'll be a scratch," Toni said. "I have to focus on getting back to work." She combed her fingers through her hair. "Obviously you've been by to see it?"

"The shop?" Cove began.

Toni waved a hand, fighting back her tears. "It's bad, isn't it?"

They knelt in front of their friend. "Hell, when I saw it and you didn't answer your phone… I went a little mad."

"That sounds very very bad," Toni whispered.

"There's a lot of water all over, and the wall has a hole as big as me, but any contractor can fix that." Cove stood, taking both of Toni's hands and guiding them to the bedroom. "You should take a shower. I'll make you breakfast and then we can head over to check out the shop."

Toni let her friend guide them both. "You're the bestest bestie anyone could ask for."

Cove chuckled. "And don't you forget it."

~~~~~~~~~~

"It's not that bad," Cove said for the tenth time in the thirty minutes they'd been inside the flower shop.

Toni lifted the water-soaked pile of paper she used to fold her origami creatures. "This entire box of paper is a loss." She turned her laptop computer sideways and water poured from every key on the keyboard. "Computer's toast."

"When was your last backup?" Cove set the monitor and laptop in a plastic tote.

"Can't remember." Toni raised the portable drive and water dripped from it onto her desk.

"More than moist."

"I'd say so." Toni laughed because the alternative was to break down in tears.

"You have your files stored in the cloud?" Cove asked hopefully.

"As per your suggestion." Toni sighed. "See, I listen sometimes."
~~~~~~~~~~

"So we can get the place up and running without a ton of elbow grease." Cove stepped in a pool of water as they tugged the trash bin behind them.

"I've made a few calls to commercial contractors." Toni shrugged. "I'm not excited to see those estimates." She blew a loose strand of hair away from her cheek.

"Get more than one," Cove suggested.

"Yep." Toni passed a waterlogged box of ribbon to her friend. "See if any of that is salvageable."

They picked through the spools one by one, dropping every roll into the trash bin. "Sorry, bestie, these are not good."

Toni dropped into the chair, leaping up quickly when water from the saturated cushion soaked through her jeans. "This feels impossible."

"It'll be okay."

"Dunno, Co. This is a real mess." Toni wasn't convinced she'd ever get through the catastrophe that was her life as she watched it drip, literally, into her livelihood.

"Maybe we need to take a break," Cove suggested.

"We've only just started."

Cove took her hand and led her around the service counter toward the door. "I've got an idea. Give me two hours and then we can come back."

Toni forced a smile as she raised her index and middle fingers. "Two hours."

"Maybe three, but trust me, it'll be worth it."

"I guess I have to trust you."

They nodded. "That's what besties do."

11.

The Rage Room

The bell jingled over the door when Toni and Cove entered. There were plenty of emotions as awareness hit the three people standing in the room. Toni looked at Cove, and Cove looked at Beatrice. Exes weren't always able to be in the same room but Cove's reaction was not ex material. There was still affection, still an attraction bigger than the mile of disappointment between them. Toni had glaring eye-daggers loaded with more daggers, directed at the cold heartbreaker also known as Beatrice.

Toni had never met Beatrice in person, had never wanted to, and was unprepared when the woman was standing in front of her. She was cute with her straight black and white streaked hair and dark eyeliner. Toni couldn't tell much more about her but she understood Cove's attraction.

The silent, circular stare-down ended when Morgan entered the room.

Morgan could feel the tension but also had a lot of love for Cove that they needed to know. "Well, hi there." Morgan smiled with outstretched arms open to hug them. "How have you been, my beautiful friend?"

"I've been good," they said, and although hugging wasn't their thing, Morgan's gentle demeanor was the mother of all embraces their heart needed.

Morgan whispered, "That's wonderful. It's been a while." She was trying to be sensitive to Beatrice but also welcoming as she noticed the other person standing behind them. "You brought a new *friend*," She was uncertain if this was a partner or only a pal.

"Sort of," Cove elbowed Toni. "Ella invited her, actually."

Toni wasn't starstruck, but she was nervous and a little intimidated to be around Ella's partner. She noticed the little Briick potted plant on the counter. "I helped her with that." She pointed to the fake plant.

"Oh, you're the florist." Morgan smiled. It wasn't a secret that the constructed plants had rekindled her and Ella's fondness for the building sets.

Toni shook her head. "I own the shop. I hired the sweetest florist to do all the dirty work for me. Pun intended."

Beatrice groaned almost as loud as Cove.

"How you doing, B?" Cove asked but Beatrice didn't stay long enough to respond. "I guess that's an answer."

Morgan waited for the rage room door to close before saying, "Moving on takes time." She paused to adjust her thoughts and not deadname them. "Cove. The name suits you."

"Thanks," they said. "I—"

Toni interrupted. "She's the one who chose to move on," she said, defending her best friend and a little edgy from Beatrice's abrupt exit.

"T, it's cool. Morgan is cool," Cove said. "You don't have to defend me here. Not with her and—"

Toni interrupted. "Well Beatrice had a chance to make it right and she didn't." Her voice rose. "Who abandons someone, and then wraps it with the word love?"

"She didn't abandon me," Cove argued. "We've been over this."

Morgan placed a hand on Cove's. "You're still hurting?"

They nodded.

"And so is she," Morgan said with a tone so soothing Cove couldn't avoid the tenderness.

Toni was quick to add, "They don't date and they don't do anything but work."

Cove elbowed her. "I take care of your sorry ass, don't I?"

"As a friend, Cove," Toni emphasized. "A friend. She was more than a friend, and some people need more than friends. Even big, tough, stubborn mules like you."

"Can we stop discussing my past?" they barked. "That's not why we're here."

"Sure," Morgan said as she sidestepped to the check-in podium. "I'm guessing you're here to rage?"

"Like an inferno," Cove joked.

"Would you be C. T. at three?" Morgan chuckled.

Cove shrugged. "I didn't want to piss Beatrice off by using my name."

"You could have used mine," Toni said.

"You're being dramatic," Beatrice said as she returned. "I set up the Exes Wreck room for them. I assume you're raging together."

Toni pulled the card from her back pocket. "I have this."

Morgan recognized it. "Oh, that's one of the promo cards I made for Ella."

"She gave it to me when she was buying plants for you at my shop a few weeks ago."

Beatrice couldn't hide her smile. "Ella Eastman is very good for business."

"I wasn't planning to use it, but I'm having a shitty week." She raised her bandaged arm.

Cove coughed. "Nah, T. You're having a monumentally shitty week. Also, I'm not here to rage. I'm just her emotional support person."

Beatrice chuckled. She'd once had Cove as her emotional support person and the memory of it sparked pleasure.

"Why don't you follow me and I'll run you through the rules of the room," Morgan said as she pushed the door open. "B, can you do the audio setup?"

Beatrice didn't want to be out there with Cove. She wanted to be in the room full of hammers and baseball bats, and was careful not to touch her former partner as she walked behind them to the computer.

"You can go in with her, ya know?" she asked.

Cove leaned over the countertop, interested in the bank of monitors showing live video feeds. "That's quite an upgrade from four years ago."

"Once Ella moved in, she and a contractor friend of hers went crazy converting the wasted storage space to usable rage rooms." Beatrice keyed the mic. "Morgan, you good?" she asked and Morgan moved into frame to deliver a thumbs up in the video feed. She watched Toni step into the jumpsuit, fighting with herself not to comment but losing the battle. "She's pretty."

Cove chuckled. "I'm surrounded by pretty people," they said.

Beatrice looked over her shoulder, finding them staring directly at her. "Really, Cove?"

"My name sounds nice coming from you."

Beatrice shook her head. "You don't get to say things like that."

"She's only a friend," they said.

"Aren't they always?"

Cove rounded the counter. "You still believe I could have done that to you?"

"You did do that," Beatrice said. "Who takes their top off with just their friends?"

"It was a binder," they argued. "I was trying to figure out a damn binder. That's all. And so what, I didn't tell you right away. I was figuring out a lot of things." Cove turned into the gift shop area, slapping at the rack of shirts to avoid the disappointment in Beatrice's eyes. "I know I should have told you first, but I didn't want you to leave."

"So instead you pushed me away."

The bell over the door jingled, and then was silenced from a hand grab. Beatrice let out a sigh knowing it was Ella. It seemed fitting that the firefighter's quirk would interrupt a conversation that was fast-tumbling toward a full-on argument. "Hi, Ella." Under the circumstances her greeting bordered on pleasant.

Ella frowned. "What?" She adjusted the paper bag of groceries from one arm to the other to avoid the closing door.

"Hi?" Beatrice said, but it sounded more like a question.

"That's all you've got?" Ella wondered what was going on. This was never the way Beatrice greeted her. "What's wrong?"

"Why would something be wrong?" she asked.

"You never only say hi. It's always hot stuff or hot firefighter or some other weird thing you come up with to irritate the hell out of me." She set the bag on the check-in podium.

"Hey there, Fire Mama," Beatrice teased, but the sentiment fell flat. "Is that better?"

Ella crossed her arms. "That's worse. What the hell is wrong?"

Without saying a word, Cove stepped from behind the rack of shirts.

"Oh," Ella said.

Beatrice turned away. "Yeah." She didn't need to watch the monitors yet but it was easier than continuing the conversation with her ex.

"Hey Ella." Cove gave a brief wave.

"Cove, buddy. How the hell have you been?"

Beatrice sighed. Of course she was Miss Congeniality. Of course the perfect woman for Morgan was also perfectly neutral in an emotional storm.

"I'm good. Great, I guess."

"The new style suits you," Ella rubbed the top of her own head, making note of the shorter buzzed cut Cove was sporting.

"Yeah? I was worried when the barber took out the number two, but since then it's made the rest of… all of me easier."

"How's that going?" Ella asked. "And tell me to shut up if that's too personal."

"You were there, Ella," they said. "It got personal a long time ago."

Beatrice hadn't moved. She stared blankly at Morgan helping Toni fill out her waver form, but all the time more focused on the conversation between the people behind her.

"We love you, ya know." Ella said.

"Yeah," Cove said. "But it was loving myself that was the real issue that needed sorting."

"I'm glad you're still here, buddy. No matter what."

"Thanks," they said. "It means a lot because I know you're not a bullshitter."

"She might give you shit, but she's not full of it," Beatrice inserted.

"There she is." Ella chuckled. "That's the sweet little bean counter I know and love."

Beatrice raised her middle finger. "Bite me, hot stuff."

"Hey! Hey." Morgan tossed the clipboard on the counter. "Why is it I'm always coming out to find the two of you verbally sparring? And with this." She tapped Beatrice's middle finger.

"Ask her," Ella and Beatrice said at the same time, pointing at the other.

Cove stepped away from the dueling duo. "I'm not a part of it."

Morgan tipped onto her toes to kiss Ella. "Hi, love."

"Hi," she said. "I finished my errands. I thought I'd make an early dinner." She crumpled the paper bag to carry it in one hand.

"How about a half hour, give or take?" Morgan suggested.

"Sounds perfect," Ella said. "I'll take this up and get cooking." She turned to Cove. "Don't be a stranger."

"I won't," they said.

Ella bumped their shoulder. "I mean it. You need anything, you call and we'll show up."

"We both mean it," Morgan reiterated. "Family means something around here and together with B or not, you belong with us too."

"I know," they said, and they did know. This reunion brought on by Toni's fire was a reconnecting they'd worried about since the separation.

"B, I'll be right back," Morgan said as she followed Ella to the loft elevator. They watched the couple disappear to the second floor.

"Ella's right," Beatrice said without turning to look at Cove.

"About what?" they asked.

"That buzz cut suits you."

Cove fought the urge to run their hand across it. "Yeah?"

"I wouldn't say it if I didn't mean it."

"Oh, I know that about you." Cove shrugged. "If I know anything, I know you'll come at me with the truth."

Beatrice turned away, whispering, "Too bad it doesn't work both ways."

Cove didn't respond. They wouldn't defend who they were or how they'd decided to live their truth. It wasn't a choice, it was just the way it had to be.

Beatrice spun in her chair when the bell over the door jingled. She hadn't meant to chase them away. "Shit!" she mumbled. "One step forward and ten bitchy steps back."

Cove leaned against the cinderblock wall, just past the Rage Room window. They'd run away again, something they'd been determined not to do. They turned back, pushing through the door and into Beatrice's space. "I didn't betray us."

Beatrice tried to speak.

"No, let me say this." Cove held up a pausing finger. "I kept one secret. Which, for me, in that situation, is how I stayed alive."

Beatrice didn't say another word. What could she say when Cove was right? She'd ended their relationship based on her perception, and sometimes that was miles from the truth.

"I am sorry…" Cove forced out the words, "that you weren't the first person I told."

"Me too," Beatrice said.

"You didn't know what I was going through."

Beatrice wanted to say she didn't know because they didn't tell her, but she waited. Cove needed understanding not anger. "Maybe you'll tell me one day?" she asked.

Cove shrugged, not sure Beatrice meant it.

"You know where to find me if you ever want to share." Beatrice turned back to the monitors.

"Yeah, I do."

12.

The Challenge

Cove was sitting on a chair in their apartment, watching their friend read through the document in her hand.

"Thousands," Toni said. "This one is for thousands and thousands of dollars I don't have." She'd arrived in a frenzied state.

As hard as Cove tried, they could not settle their friend with food or a beverage. "That's only one estimate. Get a couple more and then see what your insurance agent has to say."

"They'll say tough luck, loser." She flopped onto the couch. "This doesn't even include the inventory I lost."

"Slow down. I have an idea; let me make a call." Cove dialed a number, one they had called so often they would never forget it.

"Why are you calling?" There wasn't a friendly greeting, but Cove hadn't expected one.

"Hi, B."

"Hi." She paused before asking again, "Why did you call my personal line?"

Cove expected the emotional wall. "You mentioned Ella had a friend who's a contractor. I wondered if you'd give me their number."

Beatrice was concerned, asking, "You alright?"

Cove grinned, recognizing the milestone moment Beatrice's concern meant. "I'm fine. It's for my friend Toni. She needs someone who can do commercial construction who won't take her to the cleaners."

Beatrice felt relieved. "Her name's Lil and she'll give an honest estimate or Ella will kick her ass."

"That's great," Cove said. "Thanks, B."

"You're welcome." Beatrice ended the call.

"You must really love me." Toni threw an arm over Cove's shoulder, and the level of affection took them by surprise.

"Mush, yuk," they pushed away. "You know I love you but what does that have to do with anything?"

"You called her, for me."

"So," they said. "I'll text the number to you."

Toni knew she had to let it go. Making Cove uncomfortable was the last thing she wanted to do. "Thank you."

~~~~~~~~~~

The flower shop door was wedged open and Lil could hear the sound of a vacuum but didn't see a person operating it. She could also smell the remnants of fire and something she couldn't yet identify. She had expected to see more initial damage after receiving the voice message from her assistant.

"Hello," Lil said. When no one answered, she spoke closer to a yell. "Hello, Stacey Construction. Anyone here?" She knocked against the glass on the shop door before walking further inside. The front section of the floor was dry, which was a great sign after a fire. Most of the shop looked ready for business until she noticed the person sucking up
~~~~~~~~~~

pools of water from the floor behind the service counter. The damage was impossible to miss, as was the person with their back to Lil. She waited for them to turn around and when they did, Lil was startled by how much the frightened person jumped.

Toni ripped the headphones from her ears. "Holy shit, you scared the hell out of me."

"It wasn't my intention. I knocked and called out a few times." Lil held a hand to her. "Lil Stacey, Stacey Construction."

Toni looked at her watch, realizing the last hour had passed in what had felt like minutes. She wiped her hands on her smock. "Toni Peters." She kicked the vacuum canister aside. "This is the shop and there's the catastrophe." Her tone lacked humor as she presented the damaged wall.

"I see. It looks like you're managing the water cleanup," Lil observed as she stepped closer. "Mind if I assess your catastrophe for myself?"

Toni chuckled as she slid aside. "Please." She pushed the shop vac toward the utility sink. "I'll get rid of this and give you time to..." she paused, lost for a descriptor. "Do whatever it is you do."

"I'll be fine," Lil said. She began the assessment, noting the permit for construction and additional paperwork tacked beside a singed calendar image of her friend. She snickered. This was Station Eight-Eighteen's service zone, and someone from the arson investigation team, possibly Ella herself, would have caught the obvious picture modification to feature only Ella Eastman.

This shopkeeper was so far ahead of the game. Although Lil had been told there was an explosion, the structural framing was mostly intact. She tore a section of gypsum board away, confirming the wall wasn't weight-bearing and that most of the repairs would be cosmetic. She jotted a few notes on her clipboard, filling in the estimate for repairs as she went along.

"What's the bad news?" Toni asked as she locked the lid onto the vacuum canister.

Lil swiped her hand on her thigh. "You've already done a lot of the work for me."

"It's not much, but this place is my livelihood. I can't open until they check the right boxes on that." Toni pointed to the paperwork tacked to the cork board. "Plus my best friend helped a lot."

"Best friends are—" Lil smiled.

"—the best," Toni finished.

"Exactly." Lil tucked her pen into the clipboard. "Before I got here, I'd given my best guess for repairs, and from the information you left with my service I expected a bigger job." She released the form from her clipboard and handed it to Toni.

"I was lucky Station Eight-Eighteen responded to the fire so quickly, and their inspection team came almost the next day." Toni read through Lil's notes, and her first reaction was disbelief. "You can really do all the repairs for this amount?" She was surprised and also had feelings about the two estimates she'd already received.

"I reviewed the building plans last night, and now that I've seen the damage," Lil shrugged, "it'll probably fall under that number since I can do most of the work alone."

Toni turned away, reaching for the file folder under the counter. "I got this estimate yesterday morning, and this one yesterday afternoon." She spread the papers out side by side, adding Lil's to them. "These guys are almost ten times what you're estimating."

Lil knew what she was about to read; she saw it all the time. "This one is mostly legit if you wrote the estimate based on the incident report." She wasn't defending the contractor, only explaining why they might be different. "This one." She laughed. "He's telling you the job is too small to be profitable for him and his crew. The labor estimates are ridiculous; there's no way he'd need four people for these repairs."

"His was the first and I almost broke down." Toni stacked the paperwork, keeping Lil's on top. "No, I did break down, and then my friend found you."

"I like your friend already," Lil joked.

"Me too, now that I see your estimate. When can you start?" Toni asked.

"How's tomorrow?"

"Are you serious?" she asked.

Lil nodded. "Yep, I can be here at seven."

"In the morning?" Toni asked with more doubt in her tone than intended.

"I'm not your average contractor." Lil grinned.

Toni picked up a pen. "Where do I sign?"

Lil tapped the line at the bottom of the estimate and didn't waste time putting together a plan for supply deliveries. "I'll have a dumpster dropped off later today. Is there a location you'd prefer?"

"You can put it in the parking spots behind the service door out back." Toni moved toward the exit. "I'll show you."

"Great." Lil followed. "It'll be small, and feel free to dump any damaged materials in if you need."

"My desk is trashed." Toni opened the door to show a metal office desk and two waterlogged chairs.

"This is yours?" Lil asked.

Toni nodded. "I was trying to figure out if I could hose it down, but the little chunks of pot embedded in the side put me off the entire idea."

Lil picked up the corner of the desk, and water dripped from the riveted seam. "I can help you turn these over and we can see what might be salvageable."

"If your estimate holds true, I can afford to replace it. I do feel a little guilty about just dumping it though."

"Can I tell you a secret?" Lil opened the top drawer, releasing more water from the empty tray.

Toni forced a smile. "Sure."

"Your desk will go out with a bang."

Curious, Toni asked, "What does that mean?"

Lil squatted to pull out the bottom drawer. It was empty but the scent from the smoke fumes was intense. "Have you ever heard of RATS Rage Rooms?"

The smile on Toni's face was an answer. "Yes, I've been there. That's where I got your number."

Lil released the locking latches on the drawer, pulled it from the desk and flipped it upside down. "This little baby is going straight to RATS, and in a day or two someone will take all their rage out on one or all of these drawers."

"That almost makes me feel good," Toni said.

"Almost?" Lil asked, as she flipped the rest of the drawers.

Toni was curious to know why the contractor was taking out the drawers but didn't ask. "Almost, because I'd really like to give that sucker a sendoff myself." She kicked at the leg of the desk.

"I can probably arrange that," Lil said. "If you don't mind, I'll pull my truck around and throw all this in. There's no sense putting it in a dumpster just to take it out."

Toni fell back against the side of her building. "Are you for real?" she asked.

Lil shuffle-stepped closer and tipped her elbow toward the woman. "You can touch my arm to be sure," she joked, and was surprised when the shop owner did.

"This feels too good to be true."

Flattered, Lil didn't know what to say. "Uh, thanks."

"That sounded weird didn't it?" Coming off of a breakup, feeling like she should hold back before jumping at something new, she couldn't help but move toward the extraordinary thoughtfulness.

Lil shook her head, pausing long enough to regain the woman's attention. "It looks and sounds like you're going through something big and you needed a little kindness."

"And here you are giving it to me."

"Don't worry," Lil said, hoping to break the intensity. "There's no charge for it and it's what I do best."

Toni pretended to wipe her brow. "Whew, I'm glad for that because I'm not sure I could afford your skills."

13.

The Gym

Ella was done waiting for the right moment, holding on in hopes he would bring up the subject. After months of wondering, she had to ask. "How's your breast man?" she teased as she positioned the anchoring pin on the weight stack. They were meeting early in the morning, hours before the building was fully staffed, and with no one else in the gym, she was very interested in the status of the man he'd brought to the calendar meet and greet.

"Ew, don't say breast like that." Marsh was walking on the treadmill, very near the end of his fifteen minute warm up before they started their arm day routine. "He's delicious, if you really want to know."

"Delicious, nah," Ella raised her hand to stop his next words. "Please, that's enough detail for my little sapphic heart."

"You asked, I offered." He giggled, not from the humor of their exchange but more like a person in love. Suddenly very serious, he said, "I could see myself with him?"

She stopped, her weight stack hovering mid-lift as she tried to unscramble the sentence he'd blurted out so casually. "What?" She stared. "Like… with him, with him?"

Marsh nodded and the motion threw his balance sideways so he grabbed the safety bar on the treadmill. Putting their hands on the treadmill railing was a no-no between them, but it was Marsh's moon-eyes that were throwing Ella off. "Yeah, I like him, like him."

"Really?" Ella released the handle on the stack of weights and dropped to sit on the bench. She fussed with the support around her wrist; it wasn't loose but the fidgeting deflected her sudden curiosity. "How long have you been seeing this breast man?"

"That's not…" He didn't want to make light of his feelings. It had been years since he'd found anyone who wanted more than a night. "You're going to be mad when I tell you." He reduced the incline on the treadmill and halved its speed.

"I'm only going to be mad if you tell me that my embarrassing pectoral signing was your first date."

He raised five fingers and hid behind them, afraid to see Ella's reaction.

"It was your fifth?"

Marsha shook his head. "Kinda, but no. It was our five-month anniversary and I wanted him to meet you."

Ella threw a lifting glove at him. "Five months?"

Marshall kicked his legs to the side of the treadmill so he could straddle the rotating belt. "You can't be mad at me."

"Yes I can." She wasn't mad, not in her heart. How could she be when Marsh looked so happy? She was hurt. They'd been friends for years, longer than she and Morgan had been together and almost as long as she'd been a firefighter. Until this moment, she'd thought they told each other everything. "Five months, man. Why didn't you tell me?"

He shrugged. "There wasn't much to tell."

She absolutely knew there was so much more. "Bullshit," Ella said through a cough.

"Shut up." He ended his treadmill session and sat on the edge of the machine. "It was just coffee."

"Five months of coffee?" Ella scoffed, circle-wave motioning repeatedly to coax more detail out of the usually loose-lipped storyteller.

"Okay, there was hand holding."

"Marshall Marshy-plum Rexton there is no way *you* are the hand-holding guy in this weight room right now!"

He smirked as he tossed the lifting glove back to Ella. "Obviously there's great fucking sex but I know you don't want to hear about that."

"Dude, you're one of my best friends," she said. "I want to hear about your happiness."

Marsh chuckled. "I'm kinda really happy, Ella."

"That's wonderful."

"It is," he said, about to go into more detail about their relationship.

"Don't do it." Ella pointed, knowing exactly where his story was going next. "If you say one word about your bedroom, I'm going to say twenty about mine."

"Ew, vaginas," he teased. "It's four-thirty in the morning. I can't handle those this early."

"You can't handle those at all, bud-dy." She pulled down on the handle, feeling energized as the resistance of the weight stack flexed her muscles. The half shirt barely covered her chest, leaving her abdominals visible. She stared at the contour of her body in the wall covered mirror, trying to build the rip of her physique and liking the escalation of definition reflecting back.

"Don't be such an ass, Ella." He waited for her to finish her set. "I know you'd never kiss and tell."

It was the way he called her out that made Ella turn serious. She didn't kiss and tell. "She's my everything," Ella admitted as she sidestepped so Marsh could set up his weight stack.

"So when are you gonna put a ring on her finger?" He grunted as he started his set.

Ella fiddled with the wrist strap on her glove again. The scar on her forearm made her think of Morgan. Her girlfriend was so many individual positives rolled inside a compact yet feisty woman. Morgan's heart was kind; so kind that she managed to soften Ella's hard edges. And compassionate in a way that had their no-touch friends always lean in for a perfect Morgan Hail hug. And patient… so very patient that not once had she ever put pressure on Ella to be someone she was not. But there was something else, something Ella had longed for but could never define. The woman was exciting even with every stitch of clothing on and Ella was drawn to that part of her. "I'm trying to figure out how to do more than put a ring on her finger."

"It's a good thing she's so patient." Marsh sidestepped for Ella's next set.

Ella looked up, catching his smirk-filled expression beside her nervous reflection in the mirror. "What do you mean?" She adjusted the weights. "Has she said something?"

"Nah, she hasn't and probably wouldn't say anything to me," he said.

"I can count on one hand the times she's spoken about marriage—"

He interrupted. "Maybe she doesn't want to—"

Ella cut him off. "She wants to be married. I've listened to everything she's ever said about forever and I'm hers as much as she is mine. I know it in my bones."

He shook his head. "It's been eight years, my friend. If you know all of this, what are you waiting for?"

Ella pulled the weights. "I want it to be perfect."

"The proposal?"

"No." She paused. "Well yes, that, and our lives. All the things in it that aren't settled."

Marshall watched their reflections in the mirror. As Ella stared at the weight stack's rise and fall, he knew she was avoiding saying the words he waited to hear.

She glanced up. "What?"

"You're scared."

Ella lowered the weights but what she wanted to do was slam them to the stack. "No."

"Ella Eastman, girl, you are all talk and no walk," he accused.

"No, I'm not." Ella knelt to find her phone in her gym bag. "I've got this." She thumbed through the pictures, looking for a very specific one.

Marshall leaned in. "A bookcase?"

"Not the bookcase." She thumbed through a few more pictures until she landed on the one she was looking for. "This."

"It's a ring." He took the phone. "You got her a ring?" It was his turn to be disappointed. "You bought her a ring and you didn't take me along?"

"Come on, man." She wiped down the machine so they could move to the free-weight room. "It's a picture. I didn't buy anything."

"But this is the one you're thinking about?" he asked.

Ella followed. Even if he wasn't holding her phone, she would have moved with him. "I like this one."

"You know, she should like it too." Marshall tucked his gym bag beneath the bench before Ella helped raise his weights into position.

"Seriously, I was pretty sure I knew what I was doing before today."

"You were *doing* nervous and indecisive from where I'm sitting," he teased.

Ella tapped his elbow. "Shut up and lift."

Marshall grunted. "Yes, ma'am."

Ella was silent as he finished his set. They'd managed this routine for years, each counting on the other to keep them on track. Although Marshall's body had developed in mass, Ella's had developed with more definition. Her goal had always been about fitness for the job, until Morgan. She loved the way Morgan looked at her. The way her ink-stained fingers tickled the ridges of her muscular definition. The sensation was beyond words, and all Ella wanted now was to give her lover the best possible playground for those fingertips.

"Ella," Marshall called to her.

"Oh, sorry." She took the weights from him.

He shook out his arms, feeling the fatigue of his set. "Maybe we should cut this workout."

"What are you talking about?" she asked as she sat.

Marshall set her weights. "Your head is all over the place this morning."

"I'm only ever going to do this once," Ella said as she pressed the sixty-pound weights.

"That's what I mean." He was spotting her, paying close attention to how disconnected she was. "You're going to hurt yourself or me."

Ella felt the heaviness on the last rep and Marshall tapped his fingertips to her elbows, coaching her through it before taking them from her hands.

She was fighting back her tears, overwhelmed by the idea of the perfect proposal, and anxious about disappointing Morgan with a proposal flop like her rooftop catastrophe. "Will you help me?" She didn't look at him directly, knowing if their eyes met she would lose any sense of control and cry.

"Propose to Crumbly?" He set the weights on the floor, suddenly aware of the flush on Ella's cheeks. Her eyes were focused on her reflection in the mirror, and Marshall was prepared to tease her until he saw her face. "Hey." He put a hand on her shoulder.

Her big brown eyes turned to him. "Yeah."

"Whatever you need," he said.

Ella cleared her throat. "Thanks, Marsh. I'm…"

"I know, Ella, and I'll make sure whatever you decide, wherever you decide and however you decide, that when you're ready to pop that question you're not on your own."

14.

The Repair

Toni stood in the doorway of the store room. She'd given Penny, her florist, the afternoon off once their orders were fulfilled and safely stowed in the refrigerating units. Lil had arrived at seven a.m. with tools, trash bins and a delivery of materials planned for nine a.m.

She watched the contractor work, solo and more efficient than any team she'd hired before, and was impressed by this one-woman show. "Do you always work alone?"

Lil didn't stop as she stretched a tape measure across the bare wall studs. "I hardly ever work alone."

"So this *is* a really small job?" Toni asked.

Lil repeated the dimensions of her cuts in her head as she measured the gypsum board. "Nah, I'm in the middle of a few projects that I delegated so I could manage this one alone." She ran a blade edge using a square to make a perfect score line and Toni was fascinated by the technique.

"You've done this before?"

"More times than I can count. I grew up with a hammer in my hand." Lil carried her cut piece to the wall. The balancing act was quite the maneuver as she held the gypsum board in place with her knee while sinking three screws to quickly anchor it in place. It was almost a dance as she repeated the process four more times to cover the damaged wall.

"Wow, you're impressive."

Lil triggered to rev the drill twice. "Thanks."

The room fell silent again as the contractor remained laser focused on the job. When she'd estimated a day to do the repairs, she wasn't kidding.

"Do you mind if I work around you?" Toni asked. "I have a few customers coming in."

"I'll have the trash out of your way and then I'll tape and mud this. I'll be done for the day in a few hours," Lil said as she collected her not-very-messy mess. "Tomorrow morning I'll be back to sand and put on a finish coat, and you can paint the day after."

"Just like the estimate estimated," Toni said.

"Yep."

Toni couldn't determine if the woman was disinterested in conversation in general or only with her. She decided to give up on chit chat and return to the temporary table she was using as a service counter. Mandy came to mind as she shuffled forms around. She couldn't help but question every decision she'd made about the relationship until coming to the conclusion that she'd left Mandy long before the breakup. Days apart outnumbered their days together, and that was a sure sign things were going nowhere. More than anything, she wanted to be seen and cherished for the person she was.

"Will this bother you?" Lil asked again.

The question drew her from her thoughts. "I wasn't listening. What did you ask?"

"I asked if my troweling would bother you." Lil scraped and scooped the white mud-like compound in her metal trough.

"I hadn't even noticed." Toni spun around to see that most of the horizontal lines were already covered. "You're fast."

"I wasn't kidding," Lil chuckled as she turned back to the wall. "This is an incredibly small job." Her tape knife floated across the line where the seams came together.

"Thank you," Toni said.

"It's what I do."

The sound continued, a strange, soothing rhythm—scrape, swipe, swipe… scrape, swipe, swipe—until it faded into the background of the next half hour.

"I'm going to use this to help dry things out and I'll come back later tonight to check it," Lil explained as she adjusted the small industrial fan to its lowest setting. "I'm about to take a lunch break." She rolled her wrist to check the time. "You interested?"

Toni was surprised—not only for the offered meal but for how quickly her day was progressing. "Wow, the morning flew by."

"Yep, so would you like to break bread with me?"

"Sure. With that thing blowing, I'd probably leave for a while anyway."

Lil took her tools to the back of the store. "I'll wash these up and then we can go?" She pushed through the door with her backside.

"I'll meet you out there in a minute." Toni hadn't unlocked the shop that morning in anticipation of Lil's work. Having scheduled all of her deliveries and pickups for later in the afternoon, she was free to enjoy a longer break for lunch.

Lil was kneeling over a five-gallon bucket, plunging her tools in the water for a final rinse. "I usually go to the Sage Lounge for lunch. It's my favorite place. You ever been?" She didn't stop working as she waited for an answer.

"I went once with my ex but only for drinks after dinner service." Toni shrugged. "I've never had their food."

Lil was more enthusiastic about taking her there. "So you haven't experienced Marshal."

Toni laughed nervously. "What's a Marshal?"

"He's a who, not a what, and he's my favorite reason to go after noon." She wiped the tools dry and tossed them into the side cabinet of her work truck. "I can drive, if that's alright?"

It was alright, more alright than she could know. Toni drove everywhere when she and Mandy were together. The attorney was never at rest, always working on something, and had become a bit of a demanding yet princess-y passenger. "It would be great, actually."

"You mind?" Lil asked as she reached to open the passenger door.

Toni shrugged. "Mind? Why would I mind if you open a door for me?"

"Some people, well, they might not like it."

Toni, a few inches shorter than Lil, needed the running board to climb into the truck. The cab was spotless, which wasn't a surprise after experiencing the way Lil worked. She watched the contractor circle the front to get in the driver's seat. She was nervous, but didn't know why. Lil made it obvious she was interested in spending their lunch break together.

"Was this weird?" Lil asked, sensing the nervous fidgeting beside her.

"It's not weird. It's kinda nice."

"Oh," Lil said. "Then I guess it's good that I asked."

"Very good."

When they arrived at the restaurant, Marshal was at the door to greet them. "Hey girl, hey." He popped a fist for a bump and Lil tapped it with hers. "Who you bringing today? No—" he held out a hand to shush her. "Let me guess." He eyed Toni up and down. "Hmm, not in construction with those pants."

Lil winked at Toni and the shopkeeper blushed. "She's definitely not," Lil agreed.

"Oh, you're a designer. Are you looking at swatches?" he guessed again.

Toni shook her head.

Marshal held a finger, guiding Toni to give a little twirl. "Business or pleasure?" he asked Lil.

Lil cleared her throat. This location might have been a mistake as she rarely came to the Sage Lounge in the afternoon for anything other than a business lunch.

"It's a little of both," Toni answered as the door behind them opened.

Marshal smiled. Lil chuckled and Toni gasped when she recognized the new arrival.

"Well, well, well," Ella said as she paused in the doorway. "Look at this little family reunion."

"What are you doing here?" Lil asked.

Ella waggled her eyebrows. "Lily Flower, are you here on a hot afternoon date?"

"Lunch with a client," Lil corrected but Ella was skeptical.

"Business and pleasure, according to... sorry, I didn't catch your name," Marshal said.

"It's Toni, right?" Ella asked as she held her hand out. "The florist."

"She owns a flower shop," Lil corrected. "We're taking a break. I've been repairing some damage to her flower shop after a fire."

"Oh, yeah," Ella remembered the shopkeeper's previous correction. "How's the arm?"

Toni tugged her sleeve to show the oversized bandage covering the wound. "No infection. No lockjaw," she joked. "Didn't need that tetanus booster after all."

"Excellent. I guess my first aid did the trick." Ella slid past her to give Marshal a hug. "You got a few minutes?" she whispered in his ear.

"Give me two seconds to seat them and I'll be right back."

Marshal led them to a table. "How's this?"

"It's perfect," Toni and Lil said at the same time.

"Keith will be your server," Marshal said as he walked back to talk with Ella.

Toni opened the menu, trying to be as inconspicuous as possible, but also incredibly curious how Lil was such good friends with her secret firefighter crush.

"How do you know her?" Toni didn't look up from the menu, afraid the flush of her cheeks was obvious to the contractor.

"Ella?"

"Yep," Toni squeaked out.

Lil didn't need to look at the menu. "Her partner and I go way back."

"Oh? How?" Toni tried to keep her voice casual.

"We've already established you've been to RATS rage rooms," Lil said, and when Toni nodded she continued the story. "I met Morgan when she was diving into one of my job site dumpsters."

Toni was shocked. "Really? Diving into it?"

"Yes, she's a wild one. She even convinces Ella to jump in on occasion."

Toni considered the trash they'd thrown into the dumpster behind her shop this morning. "That seems dangerous."

"It can be," Lil agreed.

"Hello, I'm Keith," the waiter interrupted as he placed two glasses of water on the table. "What can I get you today?" he asked.

They ordered sandwiches and the waiter tucked the menus beneath his arm and walked away.

"So Morgan introduced you to Ella?" Toni asked.

Lil nodded as she sipped her drink. "About eight years ago. You obviously know she's a firefighter."

Toni's eyebrows raised.

"I saw the calendar hanging on the cork board wall." Lil shrugged. "I figured you either like firefighters in general, or just Ella Eastman."

"Both, I guess," Toni said.

"Ella's a great friend, and the hardest working person I know. Well, aside from me." She chuckled at her own joke.

Toni didn't know what to say. She was very curious about Ella, but more curious about Lil. "So Lily Flower… what's the nickname all about?"

"You caught that?"

Toni nodded. "I did. How'd you get it?"

"Ugh, I don't know." Lil hated the nickname in private and hated it twice as much in public. "I made some kind of joke when Ella and I were working out once, and she called me a wilting flower. With a name like Lilith, it was inevitable."

"That's your full name?" Toni asked.

"Lilith Vilda Stacey."

"Vilda?"

Lil explained, "According to my mother I was very active in utero." She paused, waiting for a reaction but Toni was waiting for more. She sighed. "My parents are a bit eccentric and Vilda means wild and I guess the Lilith Vilda combo was setting me up for the extreme rebelliousness."

Toni whispered, "Queen of all, mother of night, I whisper your name to guide me to light."

"What does that mean?" Lil asked.

Toni smiled. "Lilith is the mother of all. She's bigger than anything. The first of the first. It's a lovely name."

"You make it sound kinda beautiful."

The waiter returned with a tray of food, but Lil was less interested in the plates as he set them on the table.

"Anything else?" he asked.

"I'm fine," Toni said.

"Me too."

Toni draped the napkin across her lap and looked up into Lil's questioning stare.

"What?" Toni asked.

"No one has ever said anything as beautiful as what you just said."

"Well, Lilith Vilda, you wild Goddess, I guess that streak has come to an end."

Lil sipped her water. "I guess it has."

"Can I assume your coming out was part of this rebelliousness?" Toni chuckled as she asked.

Lil shook her head. "Hell no. My parents knew before I did and when I sat them down they practically told me."

Toni laughed. "It feels good to be accepted for who you are."

"Yes, it does," Lil said, adding, "I'm guessing you had a similar experience?"

"My dad is a bit of a character." Toni smiled. "I was so girly playing with dolls and wanting to wear dresses even when I was climbing trees."

"A real wild child," Lil teased.

"So very," Toni said. "But he was always there cheering me on even when I chose to open a business instead of going to school."

"From the looks of the shop, I'd say it was a great decision."

Toni cut her sandwich in half. "It was great up until a few days ago."

"The shop'll be ready to go before you know it." Lil's reuben sandwich was twice as thick as Toni's BLT, but she didn't bother to cut it. She took a bite and let out a sigh.

"That good?" Toni asked.

"Even better," Lil said after washing down the food with a sip of water. She dipped a fry in the dressing. "You never mentioned a second parent."

"I don't have one."

"Oh," Lil said.

"It's not tragic. My dad wanted to be a dad so he used a surrogate."

"Really?"

"Yep," Toni smiled. "Just the two of us for much of my life."

"Even now?" she asked.

"He's got a boyfriend. Had a girlfriend before that, but I don't usually meet them until he's serious."

Lil raised her eyebrow, expecting more.

"What?" Toni asked.

"So is he serious?"

Toni chuckled. "Hardly ever."

15.

The Tome

Ella raised her hand to catch the bell above the rage room's entrance. The morning wasn't going as planned, and she was hoping to surprise Morgan with an impromptu session in one of the rage rooms. The muffled clang in her hand captured Beatrice's attention instead.

"She's not in the shop, hot thing," Beatrice said as a greeting.

"Or you could call me Ella," she shot back. She was having a day, she knew, and it wasn't fair to bring it into this conversation, but she didn't have it in her to play this never-ending game of banter.

"Calling you Ella would hardly be as much fun as calling out the hot stuff you are."

"What if you gave it a try?" Ella argued. "Just for today."

"Nah," Beatrice shrugged off the suggestion. "Plus, you walk in here all pumped up from the gym. What's my happy little pansexual heart supposed to do?"

Ella ignored the shameless flirtation, and asked again with less patience, "Can you just tell me if she's in the building?"

"Yep." Beatrice grinned.

"Upstairs or down?"

"She had a bit of a wrangle with a few door panels."

"Wrangle?" Ella paused to lean over the check-in desk to look at the monitors. "Did she hurt herself?" she asked.

"No, Ella. Jeez, she's more than capable."

"That's not what I meant. You said wrangle and—"

Beatrice interrupted. "Yes, the stand fell over and so did the door, so we need to rebuild the stands. That's all."

"Where is she?"

Beatrice's eyebrow raised, teasing. "Now?"

Ella tugged the shoulder-strap on her gym bag. "Yes, now. For crying out loud. Does it always have to be such a game to talk to you?"

"Gotta keep you on your toes," Beatrice teased.

Ella shook her head. "Just tell me if she's home."

"She is."

Ella turned to leave. "Thanks, and for the record I live my life on my toes. It would be nice if you'd give me a break when I'm in my home."

"I'll see what I can do."

Ella turned down the corridor, yelling back, "Yep, I've heard that before too." She peeked through the rage room windows as she passed each studio looking for the panels Beatrice mentioned. Room five, their recent remodel, had two newly acquired 'Axel's Towing' truck door panels anchored to wood and cinder block pedestals. *I can rebuild those*, she mused as she took the stairs two at a time to the loft.

"Morgan," she spoke into the echoing apartment. The open-air space was as quiet as it had ever been at three in the afternoon. Ella dropped her gear bag on the floor beside the table and kicked out of her boots. She was coming off the four-day shift at the station house, and although she was professionally satisfied as a firefighter, the last day of her shift was often welcomed. It wasn't excitement from leaving the station house, but a void filled from missing her life partner and finally crawling alongside her for a cuddle.

The loft smelled of incense and something else. Ella peeked inside the half-open oven door, finding three misshapen loaves of bread. She could deduce from the cool surface that the loaves had finished baking a while ago, and she smiled knowing they were part of Morgan's kitchen experimentation inspired by book club research. It was adorable and unpredictable, and she didn't mind being the victim of Morgan's culinary curiosities. She checked the powder-smeared clipboard stand on the countertop where Morgan's hand-scribbled recipe lay. "Pea protein flour, yum," Ella said with a chuckle.

"Morg?" She whispered this time, knowing exactly where the woman would be. She unbuttoned her pants and tossed her belt on the duffle. In nothing more than a Blacktree Fire Department t-shirt and a pair of *Blasphemers*-logo printed boxers, a sentimental season four convention gift from Morgan, she rolled the bedroom door open.

Ella paused in the doorway, the full weight of her body leaning against the rustic trim as she admired her partner. Morgan's hair was bundled up, the tips freshly dyed bright green. It was always a guess as to what her girlfriend might get up to during Ella's extended length shifts. She wanted to touch her, to reconnect after their days apart, but Morgan looked so content with the book resting against her chest.

Another romance, Ella chuckled to herself. Her lover was obviously reading something sapphic; whatever genre, there was always romance. Ella couldn't remember this cover, but the artwork looked like a period piece. Historical fiction was not Morgan's usual go-to. Ella stepped closer, tilting so she could skim through the blurb on the back of the book. Sword fights and rescued damsels now that sounded like a book Ella could get into.

She didn't say a word or make any adjustments to her girlfriend's position, keeping quiet as she moved around their bedroom. She changed out of her shirt and into a sleeveless sleep t-shirt before slipping beneath the blanket and snuggling against Morgan's side. This was what she wanted, what felt solid and normal. Morgan felt like home and there was no place else Ella wanted to be.

"I love you," she whispered as she removed the book from the sleeping woman's hands, careful to check the page number before laying it on the side-table stack of books. Morgan didn't make a sound as she curled against her lover's chest. Ella held tightly to her and to the moment. It felt like a dream written in one of the hundreds of books stacked on the floor of their bedroom. She'd build those shelves for Morgan. *Maybe I can hide the ring in a book and put it on the shelf. We could be a great romance*, Ella thought, and then smiled and amended, *maybe we already are.*

Morgan stirred. "Missed you," she whispered, half asleep, as her sock-covered foot hooked over Ella's ankle.

Ella didn't fight the smile. "I missed you, too."

"Are you home?"

It was a silly, sleep-induced question that had an obvious answer. Ella remained in the moment. "Yes, baby. I'm home."

"Good," Morgan whispered against Ella's shoulder.

It was late afternoon and the two lay together like it was the dark of night. Ella closed her eyes. She was definitely home.

~~~~~~~~~~~

"You should have woken me." Morgan said as she climbed to cross over her partner.

Ella held her in place, keeping her Morgan straddled across her hips. "You looked so cute all snuggled in with your book."
~~~~~~~~~~~

Morgan stared at the novel, cover closed on the bedside. "What page? I think I was on—"

"Page one-seventeen. You were a few pages before chapter thirteen."

Morgan leaned closer, kissing Ella as she tried again to cross over. "Of course you'd memorize it."

Ella held her. "Don't go yet."

"I have to go now, baby." She tipped her head toward the bathroom. "Give me a second."

Ella's hands fell away. "I guess peeing is a necessity." She pushed upright to rest against the headboard.

"It is." She hurried to the bathroom, aware Ella was unhappy about her quick hop from their bed.

Ella kicked the blanket off her legs and waited for the always predictable questions to come. The toilet flushed and Morgan hummed a little song as she washed her hands.

A hushed moment was shared as Morgan leaned against the frame of the bathroom door, eyeing Ella, and Ella stretched a hand to lure Morgan back to their bed.

"How was the shift?" Morgan waited, watching, reading every little change in Ella's body language.

Ella shrugged. "Nothing super big. Little of this and a little of that."

Morgan wasn't pleased. This response was avoidance and protectiveness, and she wasn't letting Ella carry it into the loft. "Let's go to the rooftop."

Ella knew what it meant and she loved Morgan for it. Over time, as their lives grew together, the rooftop patio had become an important conversation place. Gone were the elements from the botched surprise proposal but Ella couldn't help the emotions that came with the thoughts of failing Morgan.

Maybe she was sensing how much Ella was holding back because of the proposal, but Ella couldn't share that. It would spoil the dream, and Morgan deserved perfect memories.

"Are you angry with me?" Ella asked as she pushed the rooftop service door open. She spun around, offering a hand to help Morgan across the threshold.

"I'm only angry if the little bit of this and that involves big this-es and bigger thats."

Ella sighed. "We lost a kid last night."

Morgan kept her distance, preparing for the answer, asking, "Did you go through the after-event protocols?"

Ella dropped into the chaise chair, kicking her bare feet up on the cushion and Morgan sat on the edge beside her. The after-event protocols were part of a research project from a local PhD candidate. His former role as a firefighter was the driving force behind these guided mental health small-group sessions. They were off-the-record conversations focused on the painful realities emergency services team members faced after traumatic incidents. What happened in the sessions stayed in them unless there were conversations about self-harm or an escalation in decline of mental health.

"Yes," she paused before adding, "Roger and I ran the protocols together."

"And?"

Ella wasn't trying to be evasive, but she wanted to protect Morgan by keeping the darkness of her job from invading their lives. Child loss was always tough for the team, but particularly difficult on Ella. "Died on the scene. We were mostly there out of obligation."

"Accidental?" Morgan asked. This was the hardest loss for Ella to reconcile and a struggle to hide how it made her feel. Their relationship began soon after a child was lost in a fatal collision more than eight years prior. It was never easy to discuss but always necessary and something she couldn't tough her way through.

"Overdose," Ella choked out.

"That's terrible," Morgan said. "I'm glad you talked with Roger."

Ella shook her head, lost in the fog of the scene. The girl was barely old enough to experience life. "He's got a niece that age."

Morgan smiled. "Yes, we met at a signing once. She loves her uncle."

"Yeah." Ella blew out a slow breath.

"I don't know how you do it," Morgan whispered.

"We just do." Ella forced a smile.

"How's the rest of the team?"

"Shook, like me. We hate when it's kids."

"I know, sweetheart." Morgan nodded. "And there's more? I can read it all over your face."

"It's Seb," Ella said.

Morgan clutched Ella's hand with a sharp grip. "Is he okay?"

"Mostly." Ella gave her a calming kiss before explaining the events of the previous morning. "Seb had left a message to call him, and I did. Right away." She was still anxious about their conversation. "He said he was scared, and I said that was not the way to start a conversation."

"He wouldn't call you at the station unless it was important." Morgan understood Ella's fear. Over the last eight years, Seb had undergone multiple surgeries, rehabilitation and long-term care for the double amputation. Ella was there with him for every one, even after he married Sally, his high school sweetheart. Morgan hesitated before asking, "And what did he call about?"

"He had some news about the implant surgery," Ella explained. "They said there was no sign of infection."

Morgan smiled. "That's such amazing news."

"It gets better though." Ella had tears in her eyes as she added, "Sally is expecting."

"She is?"

"I'm going to be an auntie."

"You're not that great with babies." Morgan chuckled. "He knows that, right?"

"I reminded him, trust me." Ella hugged her. "We both agreed that you get to be the lead aunt when little baby Wilson arrives."

"I'd be proud to have that title." Morgan relaxed in Ella's arms.

Ella stared at the setting sun, quiet for a long moment until Morgan squeezed her hand.

Morgan turned to face her. "You can see the good in all of this, can't you?"

Ella nodded. "He's going to get through and build the family he almost gave up on having."

"A lot can happen in eight years." Morgan hesitated. "You don't have to protect me, you know." She drew her fingertip along the length of Ella's forehead to brush away the loose hair.

"You?" Ella chuckled. "Protect you... we both know you're the badass in this relationship and I need that. You."

Yes, Morgan did know. To the world, her lover was the big, strong, brilliant, least-femme person anyone could be, but on the inside she was the fragile girl, frightened by loss, who didn't mind being the little spoon once in a while. Knowing what might help Ella enjoy the next few days peacefully, Morgan suggested, "Baseball bats or sledgehammers?" She smiled.

Ella pulled the petite woman onto her lap and without pause stood with Morgan in her arms. "Why choose only one?" It was a statement punctuated with a smoldering kiss.

~~~~~~~~~~

Ella had pulled the protective coveralls on over her t-shirt and boxers without any additional clothes. The only person who'd witnessed them enter the rage room was Beatrice, and
~~~~~~~~~~

after an approving whistle she'd left the couple alone. "Falling in love with you was such a smart move," Ella huffed through excited breaths after she smashed the final blow to the window frame.

"A smart move because of that outfit," Morgan joked. "It's definitely so… right."

Ella fanned the length of her torso. "Definitely because of this fashionable jumpsuit. It has nothing to do with the shrapnel surrounding us."

"So you're saying you love me for my rage rooms." Morgan took the sledge hammer from her girlfriend. "And not the wardrobe selections I've added to your life."

Ella lifted her lover. "You know me so well, Morgan Hail. You get me and I see it." Her stare went from playful to hungry.

Morgan's back met the wall. "No, Ella Eastman, we are not doing anything in this room that you are thinking about." She tipped Ella's chin, locking eyes.

"I could do one thing." Holding Morgan with one arm she slid the other between them to tug at the zipper pull.

Morgan looked down as her jumpsuit opened. "Beatrice is sitting in reception—"

"Yes, I am!" The intercom interrupted. "And the last thing I want to see are my best friends' personal assets."

"Party pooper." Ella tugged the zipper back in place.

The intercom crackled again. "Big sister is watching you, hot stuff."

"Not fair," Ella said.

Morgan draped her arms over Ella's shoulders "Let's go take a shower and wash away the rest of the rage."

"What if I want to do something else," Ella waggled her eyebrows.

Morgan giggled, playful as she attempted to stop the eyebrow action. "That's not as sexy as you think it is."

Ella turned her head, burying her lips to her lover's neck. "Better?" she whispered against goose pebbling skin.

"Maybe," Morgan hissed.

"Your body is saying more than maybe," Ella said seconds before the rage room lights began flickering.

"Go get a room," Beatrice screamed through the sound system but left the lights dimmed and gave it a second before realizing she'd created mood lighting. The women were pressed against the door so Beatrice adjusted the dimmer to full brightness. "I meant, get a room upstairs!"

16.

The Artist

Inspired by a social media post pairing the perfect food to eat while reading, Morgan had chosen a very unforgiving recipe. "This isn't right." She had the book weighted to keep it open as she followed the detailed directions on the page. "There are so many don'ts listed." She was talking to the empty loft, trying to reassure herself that this would work. Her butter was cold and the dough was a little tacky—everything the recipe called for, but the first batch was a dense dry mess.

"Good thing failures are as tasty as success." She chuckled as she popped a chewy piece in her mouth. She tried not to handle the dough too much as she pressed lopsided wedges from the pile.

The oven dinged, preheated, ready to bake the next batch, and with as little jostling as possible she transferred wedges to the parchment-lined tray, shoved them into the oven and set a fifteen-minute timer.

"I think the bread was easier," Morgan said as she swiped the flour off the pages of the open book. She turned to address the image of Ella pinned to the refrigerator door. "It's a good thing you're not a bad sport when it comes to my baking trials."

~~~~~~~~~~

Ella followed the aroma up the stairs. Morgan's culinary experiment paired with her romance novel of the day was becoming a delightful and often delicious game.

"Hi darlin', I'm home." Ella dropped her gear on the floor beside the kitchen counter and snuck a quick peek beneath the tea towel. It wasn't bread this time but inconsistently shaped attempts at something resembling a biscuit. She couldn't wait to try whatever they were.

Morgan was working at her drawing table and spun around in her chair to greet her partner. "Hi." She waved Ella to come closer. "Good workout?" she asked.

"Great one. You've been busy." Ella nodded toward the kitchen. "They smell wonderful."

"My floppy scones?" Morgan chuckled as she turned back toward her current project.

"But how do they taste?" Ella teased, avoiding the obvious observation that they looked nothing like scones.

With the pen tight in her fingers, Morgan gave a noncommittal wave. "They're so-so."

"Sounds delicious." Ella leaned close, sweeping Morgan's hair aside to kiss her neck. "Hi."

Morgan closed her eyes, enjoying the brush of lips against sensitive skin. "Hi."

"You taste delicious, too. Better than so-so scones."

"Have I ever told you how adorable you are?" Morgan reached to hold Ella in a lopsided hug.

"Yep," Ella said.

"Modest, too."

Ella supported the sideways compliment. "When a woman, my woman, calls me adorable, who am I to disagree?"

"Exactly."
~~~~~~~~~~

Ella eyed the projects on the table. "What are you working on?" She tapped the drawing.

"Lil emailed earlier and sent me a sketch of the bookcase."

It was a professionally drafted diagram, measuring the height of their ceiling and spanning the wall behind the couch. It was a massive undertaking Ella would never have attempted. "Is that what you had in mind?" Ella asked.

"Not by a mile." Morgan opened her notebook to show the small side-table sized shelves she'd hoped Ella and Lil could assemble in an afternoon. "You know Lil. She doesn't do anything on a small level."

"This is pretty cool, though." Ella skimmed through the side note. "I like the little display cubbies."

"She added lighting so I can put my Briick flowers inside."

"And the *Blasphemers* Briick sets."

"Sets?" Morgan questioned.

"There are five," Ella said. "If we get one, we have to get them all."

"Lil had no idea what she was doing with those convention tickets."

"She was doing us a favor." Ella opened the bookmarked page on her phone's browser. "I might have missed all of these."

"Have you been coveting *The Blasphemers*?"

"Maybe." Ella tucked her phone to her heart playfully.

"It's a good thing Lil planned to use the whole wall." Morgan flipped the page. "She wants to add a little rolling ladder, too. What do you think?"

"Sounds very Lil." Ella ran her finger along the image. It looked like a mini stairway used to retrieve products from the top shelves in a hardware store.

"It'll collapse and fold into the wall so you won't see the ladder or even know it's there, but it'll be accessible any time you bring me not-flower flowers."

"I like it," Ella said and she did like it even if it was ten times the project she'd anticipated. "Did she give you a schedule for this monster bookcase building plan?"

Morgan spun her chair around. "After that's gone." She motioned toward the stack of crates piled in front of the wall where the proposed book case would be.

"Your art for the Briick show," Ella said. She was excited about the convention not only for the release of the *Blasphemers* building sets, but also for the merchandise table Morgan was able to secure in the vendor space. "So next week?"

"Lil said she'd be here the next time you have four days off."

"After the convention."

Morgan chuckled. "Yes, after the convention."

Ella was trying not to be obvious as she read through the listed materials to estimate expenses. "How much is this project going to cost?" she asked.

"There're no numbers listed." Morgan noticed a few loose prints and tucked them into protective sleeves for the show. "Lil insists the lumber is less than we think."

Ella wasn't convinced. "Did she at least give you an itemized materials list?"

"She knew you were going to ask." Morgan handed her the note card. "She said you have rescued her enough to cover ten projects like this and more."

"That's ridiculous," Ella scoffed. In anticipation of Ella's reaction to the plan, Lil had included meticulous notes comparing rates of service with the supplies they'd use.

Morgan nodded. "I said that, too."

"It's very generous." Ella was at a loss. It was futile to argue the arrangement with Morgan when her girlfriend agreed it was too generous. She'd save that argument for the long drive to the convention and let it go for now.

"Lil reminded me that we're family and that's what families do." Morgan stacked the art prints into a container and handed it to Ella. "You get to do something you're very good at and muscle up." She patted Ella's abdomen as she passed by.

"A floor to ceiling bookcase will be a huge project." Ella was like a kid, bouncing on her feet as she adjusted the stack of prints for Morgan's art event. "I'm excited to help."

"I'm excited for this show." Morgan checked the list of things to prepare for the Briick Briicktacular maker's market. "I haven't done a show like this, or this size anyway, since before we met."

"I'm ready to muscle-up for setup and tear down."

Morgan tipped onto her toes to kiss her girlfriend. "That's exactly what I'll need from you before you and Lil go off on your Briick adventure." She tugged the shoulder strap of Ella's sleeveless shirt.

"You're not going to have FOMO?" Ella asked, not for the first time.

"I promise there will be no fear of missing out. I'm more excited to be a vendor than a patron."

"It is how our worlds collided," Elle teased.

"Best event ever."

Ella kissed her. "I couldn't agree more."

Parting, Morgan whispered, "You ready to taste my scones?"

"Oh, honey. Am I ever."

They sat together at the table. Morgan watched every bite as her girlfriend devoured the scone without discrimination. Ella had fantastic cooking skills of her own, and was the perfect subject to test kitchen experiments on.

As Morgan washed the dishes, Ella went through what was remaining on the list Morgan needed to finish for the event. A delivery vehicle was at the top and Ella chuckled. It would be hilarious and quirky and even a little romantic to rent a U-haul and propose from the back.

Her idea was a ridiculous trope, but an excellent one. The timing would work. The Briick event could be a romantic lead-in, as they were spending the weekend in a beautiful suite Lil booked with the VIP tickets. Ella was distracted as she tried to devise a plan she could execute in the next few days.

"Do you mind if I take a quick shower?" she asked as she set her dish in the sink.

"Not at all," Morgan said. "I kinda stole you away."

"You can steal me any time." She kissed Morgan, shouldered her gear and left the room. With the same practiced routine, Ella hung up her equipment bag but paused to make a call. The phone rang five times before Marsh answered.

"Hey, Ella." The noise in the background was loud.

Ella checked her watch, realizing he was probably just starting the evening shift. "Sorry, I wasn't watching the time, Marsh. I was wondering if you'd like to help me with a little project?"

He was quiet for a moment and Ella wondered if the phone cut out. She checked the screen and the call time continued to increase.

"Did you hear me?" she asked.

"Is this about Operation PP?"

She could imagine him cupping the phone to whisper the question. "What the hell are you talking about, PP?" Ella asked.

"Operation Perfect Proposal," he teased. "It needs a codename if you want to keep Morgan from finding out."

Ella pulled her shirt and sports bra off and kicked out of her running pants. "Ugh, we are not calling it that, and yes it's about my new idea for a proposal."

"I'm in. Tell me where and when, and what you need."

"I'll be in touch," Ella said as she turned the shower on. The water temperature felt cool as she stepped beneath the spray. This would work. All she needed now was a twinkly fairy light show and the perfect ring.

After the shower she walked into Morgan's studio with a towel around her neck, swiping the remnants of water from her hair. Her girlfriend was back at her desk focused on another project. "What are you working on now?"

"The art heist," Morgan said without explanation, but Ella knew exactly what she meant. It was the penultimate episode of season five from *The Blasphemers*, the make-or-break moment that changed the Florist forever.

Ella had an idea. "You should do a freeze-frame from the proposal," she suggested.

"Really?" Morgan's hand stilled on the page. "I guess that was a cute scene."

Ella smiled, leading Morgan to the perfect proposal conversation. She woke the computer and queued an episode to the thirty-second scene. "This is beautiful." She paused the frame and although it was a little fuzzy, it captured the chase across the pier and through the beachfront crowd. "With the way the sun sets, this would be amazing if you use the new paints you got."

Morgan often used visual cues for inspiration, freezing the frame on a movie or TV show to sketch the image. Ella's suggested scene made her curious and she tapped the keyboard to advance the video a few frames at a time. "I see what you're saying about the scene, but the *Blasphemer* team isn't a big part of the shot for very long; they only run through it."

"But don't you think it adds a little romance?"

Morgan turned the page on her sketchbook and drew a quick image based on the fuzzy, frozen screen. It was a rough line drawing but Ella appreciated how easily Morgan could draw what her eyes could see. After eight years, she was still mesmerized by Morgan's view of the world and how it translated to something she could hold.

"It's kinda corny," Morgan said without looking up from her work.

"The sketch?" Ella was confused.

Morgan shook her head. "No, the proposal scene."

Deflated, Ella huffed. "Oh." This was not the reaction she had anticipated. "You don't like the down on one knee, open the ring box proposal?"

"It's on a beach," Morgan explained. "All that sand in my socks. I couldn't handle it."

"I know how much you hate sand on your feet, but this isn't your proposal. It's a made-for-TV proposal. People like to watch that kind of thing."

"They knock the ring in the sand and have to search for it." Morgan snickered. "It's so cliché'."

"Maybe, but any and everyone would crawl around looking for a rock like the one they dropped on that beach."

"Another cliche," she added. "I'd never wear a ring like that."

This was the conversation Ella needed. "Too fancy?"

Morgan shrugged. "It's a big clunky thing, not exactly for practical people."

"So you're saying size matters?"

Morgan chuckled as she closed the laptop and turned to face Ella. "It most certainly does." She wriggled her fingers displaying the lack of jewelry. "Do you realize how many times a day I wash my hands?"

"I never thought about it," Ella said as she noted Morgan's ink-stained fingers.

Morgan stood, holding Ella's hips as she reversed their positions and walked the taller woman to the chair. "I love wearing rings, don't get me wrong, but they spend most of the day in that bowl by the sink."

"I don't think I've ever paid attention," Ella said. This conversation was answering questions she hadn't considered asking. "Everything you wear is small, kinda delicate, like you."

Morgan walked away and returned with the little cup from the cabinet above the utility sink. "Hold out your hand." Ella did and one-by-one, Morgan slid her rings onto Ella's fingers.

Ella wriggled them. "These are not made for fingers like mine." She flexed her hands, displaying that not one fit over her mid-finger knuckles. "I couldn't wear a single one of these."

"Right, that's why the ring has to suit the wearer and this wearer would choose something small, like this." Morgan picked the last ring from the dish. The oval stone had a light pink tone with facets that dazzled from the light of her drawing-table lamp.

"I don't recognize this one," Ella said.

"I don't wear it." Morgan slipped it on her ring finger. "It was my grammy's. It's one of the few things I've kept through the years and I'm so afraid to lose it that I never wear it."

"It's beautiful," Ella said. "What's the stone?"

Morgan's smile was brilliant as she teased a question. "Guess?"

It was not clear like a diamond or colorful like a ruby or sapphire. Ella had some experience looking at stones very much like this one, but she played innocent.

"Was it named after you?" Ella asked. She had to be careful not to reveal what she'd learned from the jeweler, but if her girlfriend was teasing, it made sense to guess. "Morganite?"

"Very smart." Morgan touched the stone. "I was the only grandchild and she got it when I was born. I played with it," she continued. "She never took it off but when I sat in her lap

I would try to spin it on her finger. Her hands were so worn and arthritic that it was difficult to remove, but even now I can still feel her hand and how she let me hold it and play."

"You should wear it."

"I've thought about it, but some things can't be replaced." She set it back in the ring dish.

"Yeah," Ella whispered.

"So that's the history of my rings." Morgan said. "Probably more than you wanted to hear,"

"It's the story of you," Ella said. "I want all of it, every detail."

"Even the less important ones?"

Ella took the cup from Morgan's hand. "Especially the less important ones."

~~~~~~~~~~

Ella waited outside the jewelry store, arriving ten minutes before their opening time. She had a picture of the Morganite ring her girlfriend treasured and knew exactly what she wanted made.

"Daydreaming again?" Dru asked, skipping a formal greeting.

With excited energy, Ella stumbled to get out her words. "The stone is perfect, and I know what I want."

Dru held the shop door open as Ella stepped through. "I think I'm going to need a little bit more detail."

"Right." Ella shared the photo on her phone. "This is what I need."

Dru knew the stone. "Morganite, interesting choice. Quite romantic."

Ella couldn't suppress her smile. "This ring has quite the history," she began and proceeded to share the details behind Morgan's treasured ring. In less than an hour, the sketch was
~~~~~~~~~~

made and they were narrowing choices until Ella settled on the exact design. "It's perfect."

"When are you planning to propose?"Dru asked.

"As soon as you've got the ring made." Ella smiled.

Dru stepped behind the counter and began detailing the ring order in writing. "I'll call you in a few days."

~~~~~~~~~~~

Ella sat on the living room floor, half-propped against the couch with Morgan leaning against her. "Hold my hand."

Morgan dropped the book to her lap. "What?"

Ella plucked the earbud out and paused her audiobook. She'd given in to Morgan's request to listen to her favorite stories on regular speed when they were together. "Hold my hand. I'm trying to visualize something."

Morgan wriggled her fingers against her girlfriend's. "Okay, what are you trying to see?"

"No, tell me what you see?" Ella flipped the question around.

"Our hands." It seemed like the most obvious answer.

"Yes, okay," Ella agreed, encouraging the conversation with a more direct question. "Are they entangled, entwined, laced or tangled?"

"Oh, um." Morgan thought. "I think they are laced. We sort of zig-zagged them together."

Ella rewound the audiobook back thirty seconds, popped an earbud in Morgan's ear and pushed play. "Listen to the sentence."

The narrator spoke, "...their embrace was passionate as the lovers tumbled, their bodies entwined like pieces..."

Ella pushed stop. "Entwined?"

Morgan smiled. "Your curiosity is cute."
~~~~~~~~~~~

Ella wasn't looking for adoration, she was having a serious crisis of visualizing the act that paired with the word. "I don't understand how bodies entwine."

"Really, love?" Morgan wondered if Ella was setting her up for a little romance-novel-inspired role play.

"I'm not kidding."

Morgan marked the page in her book and stood. The earbud tugged free as she held a hand to her girlfriend. "Come with me."

Always ready to follow her lover, Ella let Morgan guide her to the bedroom.

"Sit."

Ella grinned. "Am I about to get some action?"

Morgan knelt to straddle Ella. "Maybe." She tugged the bottom of Ella's shirt guiding her lover forward so she could remove it, but she stopped halfway.

"Uh." Ella struggled. "Love. It's kinda stuck."

Morgan adjusted the fabric to uncover Ella's face. "Not stuck, tangled."

"More like strangled," she quipped.

"Think about it, El." Morgan pushed the shirt to get it around her lover's broad shoulders. "You asked for one so I'm giving you the answer."

"Oh, so I *am* about to get some action." She wriggled her torso until the shirt was over her hands.

"Maybe." Morgan pushed their bodies against the mattress, catching Ella off-guard. "I have always appreciated your kinesthetic style of learning." She captured the fabric around Ella's wrists, locking them over her head.

"It appears you're about to teach me some more."

Morgan smiled. "I am."

"And what hands-on approach is this?" Ella gasped.

"Do you have a guess?" She tugged Ella's boxers down.

"Uh." Ella's breath hitched. "No guess."

Morgan leaned close, a breath away from Ella's lips. "I would call this entangled," she whispered. "Lover."

Unable and unwilling to alter their positions, Ella moaned as Morgan ground their hips together.

"I like entangled," Ella said.

"I like it too," Morgan agreed. Ella didn't change her position as Morgan removed the shirt binding her hands. She tickled the back of her taut biceps, trailing slowly along her muscled forearms until her palms slid perfectly into Ella's. Her knuckles whitened as their hands clasped together. Morgan thrust again. "Do you know what this is?"

"I have no fucking idea." Ella's body clenched as pleasure obliterated her senses.

"Lacing." Morgan squeezed her hands. "We are laced together, honey." The strap of her sundress fell, revealing a brief glimpse of her breast.

"Yes," Ella hissed. "I like lacing. I like lacing a lot."

"I thought you would." Morgan chuckled as she kissed her way down Ella's neck, nipped her shoulder and paused to whisper, "Do you remember what comes after lacing?" Her hands moved to cover Ella's breasts.

It was too much to lay still as Morgan topped her. Ella rolled, her body reversing them so quickly that Morgan gasped. "I know what I want to come next." She thrust her thigh against Morgan's center, never breaking their laced-finger connection.

"Yes." Morgan kept pace with Ella as she rolled them back to their original positions.

"You're so…"

Morgan wanted to be closer, needed the contact, as Ella rolled them again. "Don't stop," she begged.

Ella raised her lover's skirt, freeing the final barrier between them as she tugged her panties aside. The moment was frenzied as their time apart drew out the craving for pleasure.

"Yes," Ella whispered as their bodies met, fulfilling hunger, satisfying need. "More," she begged, and Morgan delivered for hours.

~~~~~~~~~~~

"Holy fucking." Chests heaving, Ella's forehead touched Morgan's. "Who… was teaching… who?" She forced the breathy question.

"Mm-hmm," Morgan struggled to form words.

Ella tried to work the bedsheet over her naked torso and Morgan giggled as her lover struggled.

"Not funny." Ella strained to raise Morgan enough to tug the fabric free.

"Entangled." Morgan arched as Ella propped with one arm to wrestle their bodies loose.

"You're so incredible."

"I hope I cleared up your confusion." Morgan pushed the sheet from beneath her until they were both lying under it.

"Crystal clear from this angle."

Morgan squeezed Ella's hip. "I love this angle."

"So do I, love." Ella took a deep breath. "So do I."
~~~~~~~~~~~

17.

The Rental

Marsh steadied himself as he lifted the bench up onto the truck. "Is this truly what you want to do?" he questioned as he pushed the bench over the rental truck's chipping metal bumper. "Because Operation PP in a hired moving truck seems a little unromantic."

Ella was arranging the string of fairy lights around the interior of the short box truck. "When we're finished decorating the inside, it'll be very romantic, and for the millionth time we are not calling the proposal to my girlfriend Operation PP."

From the minute Ella had picked Marsh up that morning, he'd insisted on using the ridiculous title. "Are we really going to keep arguing over the name?" Marsh opened the base of the bench and began fluffing the vacuum compressed seat pads.

"When the name sounds like a child's pit stop, yes, we are going to argue," Ella barked.

He stuck the pillows to the velcro strips, securing them in place. "You're the one planning to propose to their partner inside the back of a rented moving truck."

"She'll never expect a U-Haul proposal. It'll be cute and unforgettable."

Marsh slid the box beneath the 'marry me' banner Ella had already stapled to the slats bungeed in place for the big question.

"I kinda get the humor." He plopped on the box.

"It's more than that, man," she explained. "You roll up and she's standing on the sidewalk waiting to load everything for the convention. I'll be back here, and when you walk around to open the overhead slider, I'll be down on one knee. It's the perfect proposal trope."

It was obvious by the way his eyebrows raised toward his sweat-shiny forehead that he didn't understand the perfection of her plan. "You must explain," he said as he swiped the moisture with the towel tucked in his back pocket. "I don't understand what you mean."

Ella continued decorating as she repeated Morgan's definitions of predictable situations in the romance novels her girlfriend read.

"So a trope is a story plot?" he asked.

"Something like that," she agreed.

"U-Hauling is a very lesbian story plot." He punched her shoulder. "You and Morgan are a prime example."

"We didn't even U-Haul," she protested. "It was years before I sold the cottage and moved into the loft with her."

"Officially." His fingers hovered, making tiny quotation marks. "But you were at her place more than anywhere besides the station house."

"That's called dating, asshole," she punched back, nearly tumbling over the roll of carpet in the process.

"I hate to tell you this, Ella, but dates end at the door."

She shook her head, laughing. "Marshal, Marshy-plum Rexton," she punctuated each name slowly, "when was the last time your date ended at the door?"

"My dates, and where they begin or end, are not the point of this conversation, Ella Lane Eastman," he teased back.

"You're right, they're not." She cut the plastic zipper ties around the rolled up rug and kicked it open across the floor of the moving truck. "Today it's finally about showing Morgan how much she means to me and that I want to be partnered with her and no-one else."

Marsh could see the frustration in Ella's expression. "Okay, okay… I'll stop teasing you."

"Good, now stand over there and tell me if the setup works." She knelt and was pleased to find the cushioning of the rug would create a comfortable spot to kneel.

"I'd say Operation PP's mobile proposal lair is a go." Marsh gestured two thumbs up. "And a ring?"

Ella patted her pocket. "To the exact specifications as described by my future fiancée."

"Very sneaky move."

"You have no idea," Ella said.

"Now that we've got the decor finished, how long until we can cruise over to the loft and set this plan into action?"

Ella smiled, a grin so big Marsh grinned too. "I'll call her as you pull up. She has no idea what I'm really doing today but when I thumbed through her convention itinerary she didn't have a rental confirmation number for a truck on her list.We talked and I suggested using Charlene. I'll tell her I'm out front and she can come meet me, you open the door and I'll propose. We can load her artwork tomorrow morning for the convention's artist's market event. Easy!"

"Don't you think you should have told her about the rental?" He asked.

"No way. I'm pretty sure I convinced her we could make everything fit in Charlene."

Marsh was skeptical. "There is no way you can get those crates in that car. It's big, but I saw the totes full of product Morgan had stacked in the loft."

"Trust me buddy, I've got it all under control."

"Operation PP is a go." He clenched his hand for a fist bump.

"Nah, man." She waved him away. "I'm not encouraging that codename."

Fifteen minutes later Marsh drove up the street, approaching the back entrance to the rage rooms, but slowed when he saw the activity in front of the overhead door. "Uh, Ella. We're gonna have to redirect Operation PP," he said through the wall of the truck.

"What?" Ella asked. She was nervous. Her hands were sweaty and she could feel a collision of emotions tearing at her perfect moment.

Instead of pulling over, Marsh drove on to circle the block, and stop far from the shop. He parked and raced around to explain the activity he saw at the rage room.

"What the hell," Ella said as the door rolled up to reveal her.

"Operation aborted." Marsh's pout was adorable.

"Explain," she said.

"Morgan, as always, was one step ahead of you."

Ella jumped to the ground. "What does that mean exactly?"

"Your bestie Lil was out back with a Stacey Construction company box truck and Morgan was helping her load a cart full of totes inside of it. This stage of Operation PP is a bust."

"Well shit." She slumped down on the bumper of the truck.

"Do you have an alternate plan?" He asked.

Ella rubbed her palms across her thighs. "This was the alternate plan, remember. Soot pulled the plug on my rooftop proposal, so now I'm back to square one."

"Got any other tropes up your sleeve?" he asked. "Wait, is having a trick up your sleeve a trope?"

She punched his shoulder. "Nah, man. It's not."

"Maybe it could be." He teased as he tugged her to her feet. "Let's get your truck back to the rental place and maybe go work off a bit of this disappointment at the gym?"

"Can't do the gym right now, man." Ella secured the rear door of the truck and ran around to climb in the passenger seat.

"Sorry this wasn't the proposal you wanted." He said, almost as disappointed as Ella looked.

"Not to worry, Morgan's got about a thousand romance books and I've got time to do more research."

"A thousand?" He asked. They drove a few blocks to where Charlene was parked.

"Okay, maybe not a thousand, but it feels that way sometimes."

"I can return the truck," Marsh said. "You head back to your place and I'll call you when I'm done."

"Are you sure?" She asked. "I'm not dumping it on you?"

"I am the driver and technically I rented it so Morgan wouldn't see the deposit charge, so It's on me." He hitched his thumb toward the passenger door. "Get out. Go see Morgan and try not to focus on Operation P P for the afternoon."

She unclipped her seatbelt. "That's a tall order, man."

"Maybe, but the way you love that lady, you'll get it right."

"Thanks Marsh," She said as she stepped to the curb. "I appreciate you."

"I love you too, Ella."

She sat in her car, sorting through the disappointment of her second failed attempt. This one should have been it. She felt for the box in her pocket and pulled it out. The hinge clicked as she opened it. The ring was beautiful, delicate with a morganite stone faceted with cuts that sparkled in the sunlight. She set it on the dashboard, staring, dreaming.

"Time to move on," she whispered as she tucked the ring box beneath the registration paperwork in Charlene's glove box. Ella arrived at the rage room's back entrance as Lil was loading the final tote of artwork.

"Look at you," Lil teased. "Getting here just in time to pat me on the back for a job well done."

"Lily Flower, you are so onto my plan." Ella swatted her friend's shoulder. "I was parked down the street, watching and waiting until you loaded the last one. It took you long enough."

"Bitch," Lil said and punched back.

"She was not." Morgan stepped between them. "She was helping Marsh. He just messaged me to apologize."

Ella's eyebrow peaked, anxious about this little redirect Marsh had shared. She leaned down to meet Morgan's lips. "Hi,"

"Hi, yourself." Morgan's voice was hushed, lingering over the pleasure of Ella's nearness. It didn't matter they'd been together for years, the woman's greeting still made her body tremble.

"I thought we were using Charlene for the convention?" Ella asked, trying to keep the tone of the question neutral. Neither of them had a clue about Operation PP. She groaned internally knowing Marsh's title was fused in her thoughts. Ella needed to move on from her second failed plan.

"Although I believe Charlene is up to the task of hauling all of this," Morgan patted the closest storage tote. "It'll be easier in the long run and Lil is attending anyway." Her shoulder shrug was so casual, it annoyed Ella. "We can all drive to the conference together."

"We should have discussed this plan." She said, suppressing her disappointment.

Lil slapped her friend's shoulder before draping an arm around her neck. "Don't worry, Cinder-Ella, there's plenty of heavy lifting in your future tomorrow."

Ella shoved the hand away. "That's not the point."

The rage room phone rang in Morgan's pocket and she returned to the desk inside leaving the two standing next to the loaded truck.

"What gives?" Lil asked.

"Damn, Lil. I had a whole proposal planned today and your stupid box truck got in the way." Ella kicked at the tire.

Lil froze. "You did what?"

"It doesn't matter now, but yeah I was going to propose today."

"What the hell. Why didn't you tell me?"

Ella shrugged. "The less people who know, the easier it is to pull off the perfect surprise."

"But you didn't pull it off."

"It's not the first time it's happened, either," Ella shared as she stepped up to pull the box truck door down.

"Explain," Lil said, and Ella proceeded to share every detail of her two disastrous attempts at proposing to Morgan.

"So you'll come up with another plan," Lil said.

"It's not that easy."

Ella's disappointment was obvious so Lil decided to share the surprise she'd made. "I was going to wait until tomorrow to give you this, but since you're so down in the dumps..." She ran around to the driver's seat and returned with a cardboard box. "I 3D-printed these for you."

Ella opened the flaps to find two bright yellow, oversized Briick figure costume hands.

"I know you worked hard making some out of foam, but I thought these would have a more authentic feel," Lil explained.

"Wow." Still emotional from the blundered proposal plan, and feeling touched by Lil's thoughtfulness, Ella was caught off guard. "They're amazing."

Lil helped hold the box. "Take them out, there's something underneath."

Ella dug around until she found the rest of the 3D printed pieces.

"It's a flamethrower," she explained. "It's not exactly like the Briick set piece because I couldn't find a print file, but this one is from the series."

"You made a neon flame."

Lil smiled. "I did. But you'll have to glue it all together."

"If this was part of a real Briick set I'd never use glue."

"It's blasphemous," Lil teased back. "Every Briickhead knows that."

"This is so cool. I don't know how to thank you."

"Win the cosplay contest," Lil cheered.

Ella shrugged. "I'll do my best and these will definitely help."

18.

The Check-in

It was the third time circling around the parking lot of the hotel and conference center. They'd decided not to split the three-hour drive after witnessing Lil's territorial horn-honking when she picked them up that morning. Ella was comfortable, stretched out against the passenger side door with Morgan leaning beside her on the bench seat. The totes of artwork were secure in the back of the company truck along with Ella's Briick figure cosplay costume.

"There's one." Morgan pointed to a space wide enough for the truck.

"Finally," Ella chuckled. "I didn't know this convention was going to be so big."

"There has to be another event here," Morgan said. "This conference center has three separate venue spaces."

The plan for the afternoon was to check in and then help Morgan set up her merchandise table in the designated seller's hall. Morgan recognized a few business names on the trucks as they walked through the parking lot.

"Oh, that guy is the builder from social media." Ella pointed. "I wonder if he's setting up his Galaxy Explorer theme or ancient Greece?"

Lil scrolled through the last few social media posts from the builder's hall. "Looks like Galaxy Explorer and oh, he's got the first run Lunar colony."

Ella stopped to look over her shoulder. "They haven't made those brick colors since I was a kid."

Lil was practically salivating. "This is going to be so good."

Ella settled her arm around Morgan's waist. "Are you sure you're not going to have FOMO as an artist instead of walking around with us?" she asked.

"I'll be fine," Morgan confirmed for the tenth time in as many days. "Plus, I have access as a vendor so maybe Lil can sell the VIP ticket to someone."

"I'll probably just find a day pass holder to give it to. I don't like the idea of selling it now." The entry doors slid open, revealing a giant glass table in the lobby. "Are those folded paper cranes?" Lil asked before picking one up.

"They are," Morgan said. "What a cool way to greet guests."

"Definitely different," Lil said as they approached the check-in desk.

Ella attempted to pass some cash to Lil as they waited for the hotel clerk. "This should cover our half."

Lil pushed Ella's hand away. "Nah, seriously. I've got this."

"How can I help you?" the clerk interrupted. His forehead was sweaty and his shirt was moist with perspiration under his arms, and he looked like he was ready for the day to end.

"Reservation for Stacey," Lil said, noticing the name 'Randy' pinned to his shirt.

He typed on the computer. "I don't see anything. Can you spell the last name?"

"S-t-a-c-e-y." She said the letters slowly.

"First name?" he asked.

Her response was sharp. "You've got more than one Stacey registered?" Lil knew what was coming as the snark in her tone caught Ella's attention. She didn't want to say her full name because until this day she was able to defend the 'Lily Flower' teasing, but she wasn't sure she could manage whatever was coming next. She spoke softly. "Lilith."

Ella chuckled.

"Not a word." She pointed at Ella. "I didn't pick the name, my parents did."

Ella made a zipping motion across her lips but it was obvious she had something to say.

"Yes, I see you right here." Randy printed a page and fiddled with the stack of room cards. "Two keys?" He gestured toward Ella.

"Can we have three, please?" Lil asked.

Ella leaned in, adding, "And extra towels."

"Absolutely. Sign here and initial the three boxes."

Lil read over the document. "We should have a suite?" She tapped the circled description on their room reservation.

The clerk looked at his screen. "I have you down for four nights in a double, double."

"That's not what I reserved." She opened the app on her phone and showed the email confirmation. "I made this reservation months ago."

He tapped the keyboard. "I'm sorry, Ms. Stacey, but this is the only room I have available for you."

Lil took a deep breath, forcing calm as she insisted. "Check again."

He tapped the keyboard, all the while increasing the shadow of sweat on his shirt. "The number on your reservation clearly shows a double, double."

Lil looked at Ella who'd taken a step closer. "Do you have another suite available?" they asked at the same time.

"With the Briick event and the Origami convention, I'm afraid we are completely full."

"Origami convention?" Lil said.

"Completely full?" Ella said.

Morgan chuckled. "The double, double will be fine."

Lil scribbled a signature across the bottom of the registration paperwork. "There's a gym?

"Down the hall and across from the pool." He pressed the keycards into the programming device and passed them to Lil. "Hot tub is on the fifth floor. Right down the hall from you. No children allowed."

Lil looked around them. "Cool, we didn't bring any of those."

He chuckled, disinterested. "Room five-twenty." He stepped behind the office wall and returned with two towels. "Enjoy your stay," he said as he disappeared behind the office wall again.

"Enjoy our stay," Lil grumbled. "The reservation was for a suite."

"Not today." Ella tapped the button to call the elevator. When the elevator door opened, they found a row of origami folded cranes taped to the handle on the back wall, beside a poster reminding attendees of tonight's paper-folding mixer.

"These are so cute," Morgan said, her tone more cheerful than Ella or Lil's. "I hope we see more of this. They're fun."

"He said there was an origami convention here." Ella pushed the button for the fifth floor. "So we probably will, but I'd rather see more Briick builds than folded paper animals."

"Both sound like a great way to spend the weekend." Morgan pecked Ella's cheek.

"Yeah," Ella agreed as they rode the elevator up. "I guess you're right. We could be terrorized by a clown convention instead."

"Not all clowns are creepy," Lil defended a little too quickly.

"Name one?" Ella asked.

"Clowny-O," Lil said.

Ella gasped.

Morgan laughed. "Isn't Clowny-O from a horror movie?"

Lil shrugged. "Really, horror? I've always thought it was ironic humor." She played with a paper crane, unfolding it to see if she could figure out the technique.

"There was a scythe, and the eyebrows had a hugely exaggerated villainous arch," Ella argued. She wasn't ready to admit that clowns terrified her, and there was no way Clowny-O was the character in a comedy. "Remind me to never let her pick the movie," Ella whispered loud enough for Lil to hear.

"Noted." Morgan imitated ticking a box on an imaginary checklist.

"I hope the room is nice," Lil said as she handed the towels to Morgan. "Sorry we were downsized."

"The lobby seemed modern," Morgan said with enthusiasm. "At least we have a room."

Lil distributed the key cards as they stopped on the fifth floor. "We're only in here to sleep. In the big picture, clean sheets and clean towels are all I need." She followed Ella down the hall.

"And a bed," Ella added. "At the very least we should expect that. " She tapped the card against the door lock, and found it odd that the television was on. As she entered, she could see an open suitcase on the floor and could hear the shower running. She stepped backward, leaving the room to double-check the number on the wall outside. It was the same as the little envelope Randy had given them, but the room was already occupied.

The front desk clerk came bursting out the stairway door. "Please stop," he huffed, realizing they'd already entered the room.

"There's someone in the room already," Ella said, with more calm than she felt on the inside.

"I'm so sorry, I entered the wrong number." He was huffing from his obvious sprint up the five flights of stairs.

Ella was not amused. "Man, that's dangerous. There's someone in the shower and I just walked right in."

He began a slow walk, leading them down the hallway to the elevator. "The room I have for you is four-twenty. I'm so sorry."

Lil and Morgan followed Ella and the front desk clerk into the elevator and they rode one floor down. He handed the keys to Ella but didn't follow them when they stopped on the fourth floor. "Please let me know if I can help with anything else," he said as the doors closed.

"What the hell just happened?" Lil questioned, thrown by the mixup.

"I can't believe he made a mistake like that." Morgan held Ella's hand, tugging her to stop. "You okay?" she asked.

"I'm pissed." Ella turned to her. "What if that was you in the shower and some stranger walked in without you knowing?"

"Shit, I hadn't thought about it like that," Lil said. "We should probably file a complaint or call his supervisor."

"I'll make a call." Ella handed the new room keys to the pair before tapping hers against the door lock. "Hello," she said to the silent room. "Wait here a second." She entered, passing a large accessible bathroom before rounding the corner. "Oh hell no!" she yelled.

Morgan stepped behind her. "This is not a double, double room."

"That's a king-size bed," Lil spat, pointing out the obvious. "Maybe it's his first day on the job?"

Ella picked up the phone and dialed the front desk. "Randy, we have a problem with this double, double." Ella said. She could hear the keyboard clicking in the background

"What seems to be the prob-lem?" he paused, saying. "Accessible king."

Ella was losing her patience. "Do you see how our suite that you reduced to a double, double has now morphed into a single accessible king?"

"I see that." He continued clicking at the keyboard. "I don't have anything else for the night."

Ella almost felt bad for Randy, but the emotion faded quickly. "There are three of us, Randy. You do realize this?"

"Yes, I'm aware of that, ma'am." More keyboard clicking. "I'm very sorry. This is the only room I have available this evening and unfortunately I don't have a rollaway."

Ella's fingers clenched around the telephone receiver. "Thank you." She wanted to slam the phone but that wouldn't change their situation. When she turned to look at Morgan, Lil was laughing behind her.

"It'll be fine." Morgan tapped Ella's chin. "It's a big bed."

"I'm a cuddler," Lil teased as she wrapped her arms around herself. "Can I have the middle?"

Ella slumped into the corner chair. "You and your smart ass can have this seat, Lilith."

"I'll sleep in the middle," Morgan interrupted Ella. "You'll behave and you," she pointed at Lil, "you'll stop antagonizing my girlfriend."

"Only for the night, though. Right?" Lil teased.

Morgan kicked her suitcase over. "For as long as we are cozying up in this bed."

Ella took a long shower, hoping to wash away the disappointment of the last twenty-four hours. She was feeling the pressure of a perfect proposal, and hating that the title of

Operation PP was sticking when she strategized her next steps. She swiped the fog from the bathroom mirror, cursing the lack of a vent in the space. This was supposed to be a five star convention center and they should be celebrating their engagement this evening.

She heard laughter from the room and opened the door to see Morgan and Lil sitting together on the bed. Ella didn't consider herself a jealous person, but she couldn't get the concept of the 'touch her and die' trope out of her head. This wasn't a good way to start the weekend. She pulled the shirt on and struggled into her shorts, her body still damp from the steam of the room.

"What's so funny?" Ella asked as she toweled her hair.

Morgan patted the bed beside her. "Come look at this with us."

Ella hooked her towel on the bar in the hall before sitting on the bed. It was softer than she expected. "The mattress is nice," she commented.

Lil bounced. "We've thoroughly exhausted this sucker."

Ella glared.

"Stop it." Morgan swatted her friend. "You said you'd be mature about all of this." She whirled her hand, gesturing to everything happening in the room.

Lil stood and bounced a few times. "We jumped on the bed, Ella. Calm down."

"Come here." Morgan held a hand to Ella. "Sit with me and let's figure out how we are going to share close quarters for the next few days." She addressed Lil. "You need to be serious for a minute."

"Fine." Lil flopped in the chair. "Obviously you two need time together to be couple-y, and I need to find someone to couple-up with."

"Sex free!" Ella blurted. "Let's agree that there will be no walking in on any under-the-clothing action while the three of us are sleeping in this bed."

Lil nodded. "Agreed."

"Perfect," Ella said. "Stick to this rule and I'll do my best to lighten up."

"That sounds like a plan." Lil tucked a room key in her wallet. "I'm going out so you two can enjoy some quiet time." She winked.

"Thanks, Lil," Morgan said and bumped Ella to do the same.

"Ow." Ella rubbed her side and noticed Morgan's glare. "Yeah, thanks, Lilith."

"See you later." Lil groaned as she opened the photo she'd taken of the meet and greet info from the elevator. "I'm not sure what's worse. Lily Flower or using Lilith?" she mumbled as she pushed the elevator call button.

~~~~~~~~~~

"Did you hear the door?" Ella whispered as she squeezed her eyes shut, averting the sunlight breaking through the curtains that didn't close completely.

Morgan was tucked against her chest, barely awake. "Lil went for breakfast."

Ella rolled her wrist to look at her watch. "It's five-thirty."

"She said she's meeting someone." Morgan nuzzled closer. "Apparently they're an early riser."

Ella relaxed on her back, keeping the two of them together as she did. "I am, too, but we don't have anywhere to be until nine-thirty."

Morgan made tiny circles on Ella's abdomen. "Shh, I'm sleeping."

Ella chuckled. "Your hand isn't."

A pinky finger wriggled beneath the wide elastic of Ella's boxer briefs. "My hand behaved all night."
~~~~~~~~~~

Ella was slow to move, not eager to stop the sensation but eventually pausing Morgan's hand. "No under-the-clothing action, remember."

"If you were paying attention last night, I never agreed to your silly restrictions."

Ella craned her neck to look at her lover. "We are not."

"You're right, *we* aren't." Morgan's hand dipped lower as her lips moved close enough to rub Ella's breast through her t-shirt. "We know you never break the rules." Although it was meant as a tease, it was also true. She was honorable, often to the extreme.

"Morg…" Ella hissed.

"Yes, love."

Ella did the opposite of relax as fingers slipped beneath her shorts and the t-shirt bunched up beneath her arms. She wasn't thinking about anything but the way her lover was commanding her body.

"There's something very exciting about touching you this way." Morgan meant every word as she teased a nipple with her teeth. She knew Ella, understood every subtle flex and moan in response to her attention. Ella's shoulders tightened as she arched into Morgan. "That's right, love."

"Fuck, baby." Fingers dipped and lips moved but all Ella could do was let go and feel the love Morgan held in the moment. It was glorious, void of proposal anxiety, doubt of perfection or fear of failure. "Don't stop."

Morgan grinned. "I don't intend to." She kissed her way down Ella's chest, across each ripple of her abdomen. "Too much clothing. It needs to go." Ella attempted to move but Morgan pushed her down. "Uh-uh, this is my job, you can't break the rules."

"You—" Ella could hardly form words. "Yes."

With a finger hooked over Ella's waistband, Morgan slid her boxer shorts down one leg, leaving them half on. She was focused, licking then sucking hard on the jutting bone of Ella's hip, tearing Ella farther from Lil's restrictive rules.

"Yes," Ella groaned.

Morgan stilled, a second or two of hesitation, driving Ella wild with need before she took her with her mouth.

Ella reached for the sheet, grabbed Morgan's tangled hair, grasping and arching to anchor herself to something as the orgasm strung her body tight. The release was intense as her pulse throbbed everywhere Morgan's mouth had touched. Morgan slowed and her fingers dipped as a featherlight touch of lips danced across the heightened awareness. It was erotic but Morgan was hardly finished as she retraced the path she'd followed to Ella's sex.

"Love," Ella gasped, nearly incapable of forming words.

Morgan nipped Ella's rib. "Mm-hmm."

The hum vibrated, and Ella felt the sensation between her legs. "You undo me."

"I know." Morgan smiled as she pulled Ella's t-shirt back into place.

The pleasure continued as the fabric moved across her nipple. "You're going to wreck me for the rest of the morning if you don't stop."

"We can't have that." Morgan made a feeble attempt to cover Ella with one leg in and the other out of her boxers.

"Morgan Hail, you're the best decision I ever made."

"Am I?" She chuckled, knowing exactly what the orgasm-induced proclamation meant.

"One hundred percent," Ella affirmed.

"You're the best decision I ever made, too." Morgan kissed Ella's throat before snuggling against Ella's exhausted body.

~~~~~~~~~~
~~~~~~~~~~

Ella's smile wasn't fading, and it wasn't only from their love-making that morning. She was fascinated by the Briick architecture displayed in the creator center. The venue was near the size of a football field and hundreds of Briick builders were there to share the creations they'd assembled.

They'd started their adventure in the secondary sales room where Ella's wallet fell victim to the used and retired vendor salespeople.

"This was a great deal," Ella said as she twirled the bag holding a twenty-five-year-old retired Briick World set that she'd longed for as a child.

"If it's possible, I think your smile is larger than the one you left the room with," Morgan teased.

Ella chuckled. "Maybe it is. We couldn't afford this fire station when I was a kid. I had the smaller set, which was okay." She leaned over the barricade to get a closer look at a tiny retractable ladder on the Briick World fire engine set on display.

"Did you know you wanted to be a firefighter at that age?" Morgan asked, feeling like she was seeing a side of Ella she'd never met.

Ella grasped Morgan's hand. "Not at all. I only wanted to play and build, and Lou encouraged it."

"They were so good to you." Morgan wanted Ella to know that she understood those memories were special. "They'd be very proud of the person you've become."

"Yeah?" Ella squeezed her hand.

"Never doubt you're a good person."

They continued up and down the row of displays, pausing again when the Briick flower garden came into view.

"Wow, that looks so real from back here," Morgan said.

It was like a fantasy-world botanical garden with Briick flowers and plants in every color. "I had no idea you could do so much with Briick building sets."

"We're gonna need another loft," Ella teased.

"We just might." Morgan checked the time on her watch. "I need to head over to my table."

Ella didn't want to let her go. "Already?"

"Come with." Morgan tugged her toward the exit. "You can wait for Lil and people-watch with me."

"People watching is almost as fun as Morgan watching," Ella said.

"Silly." Morgan flashed her vendor badge to the security person.

"Maybe, but definitely not the silliest here."

19.

The Recon

Day two was off to a smashing start as Ella sat through the first of five panel discussions similar to those the day before. Each one focused on a variety of topics in the Briick collecting world. Today, the history of Briicks was the most interesting, as the company's hundred-year existence survived many highs and lows of the ever-changing toy industry. The last topic of the day was related to STEM focused on empowering young people and Ella was excited to see dozens of girls in the crowd.

She could relate to the staggering gender bias and imbalance, as one of a few at Station Eight-Eighteen not identifying as a cis-gendered male. She listened to corporate execs break down the demographics and wanted to know more about the company's push to get building sets into the hands of the next generation of scientists and engineers.

She'd wandered through the vendor hall a few times, making sure to pass by Morgan's space to see how sales were going. Morgan's art design style was very different from the other fan art sellers and Ella was excited to see some of the poster-sized pieces were no longer hanging in her booth. She stopped to take a few pictures.

"Looking for something special?" a vendor said, interrupting Ella from what must have looked a little stalker-ish.

"Uh, not really." She turned to them.

"Saw something you like but don't want to buy it?"

The question seemed snarky and Ella wondered why. "No, that's my girlfriend and I wanted to capture the moment."

"You're her partner?"

"Ella." She raised a hand to shake theirs.

They pointed to their name tag. "Allison, but everyone calls me Alli." She waved off the name tag spelling. "Next time I'll know to shorten my name on the registration form."

Ella understood that mistake, having had her name mispronounced during a cosplay event many years before. "Nice to meet you." Ella took a moment to scan Alli's booth, enjoying the diverse items for sale. "You've got a lot of goodies here."

"I guess." Alli picked up a crocheted replica of a Briick styled figure. "I made all of these. Had to create many of the patterns myself."

"That's impressive. Anything from *The Blasphemers*?" Ella asked, seeing a few superhero-themed creations alongside cartoon and anime figures.

"You're not the first person to ask." Alli turned to the container on the table beside her chair. "I'm working on—"

"The Arsonist." Ella could identify the little figure anywhere and specifically from the colorful scarf it had on. "Season two."

"You're a fan?" Alli asked.

"A ridiculous fan." Ella was excited. "I had a meet and greet with Dracea Barnes once."

"No way!"

"She was the nicest person." Ella opened her phone to skim through photos looking for the picture of herself with the actress who portrayed the Arsonist on TV.

"You're a cosplayer, too?"

Ella chuckled. "Yes, and it's how I met my partner. Are you planning to sell that little Arsonist when it's done?"

"Sorry, it's a commissioned piece, but I can make another one just for you."

Disappointed, Ella considered a special order. "Would you ship it?"

"Sure, I can even customize it for you if you wanted me to add elements," Alli explained, going into detail about how she could make it even more special for a mutually enthusiastic fan.

"I like one-of-a-kind." Ella accentuated the descriptor. "I'm sold. Let's do it."

While Alli wrote down Ella's details and filled out the order form, Ella scanned the social media code for Alli's work.

"Oh, please follow me. Thanks," Alli said. "It's fun to do events and meet people who follow my page. I have a little over a thousand followers now, and that boosts internet sales from my website."

Ella chuckled internally; she was about to shock this seller. "Well, now you have," she checked the number on Alli's page, noting the she/her pronouns listed with a tiny blue, pink and white striped flag beside it, "one thousand and fifty-seven." Ella waved her phone screen.

Alli accepted the follow request, and her reaction to Ella's page happened like a slow motion scene from her favorite television show. "Holy crap."

Ella got that a lot.

"You're @Cinder_EllaE? I've been following you for years." She showed her screen to Ella. "Your cosplay is ridiculously amazing. I can't believe I didn't recognize you from the picture."

"Dracea Barnes is very distracting," Ella teased.

"Wow! Just Wow!"

"Thanks." Ella recognized the currency of her online presence, and wasn't shy about its value in the independent creator world. Yes, her posts included the firefighter calendar events and her costume creations even before the award-winning Arsonist outfit, but it was her reach with the charitable fundraising communities that she cherished most with Seb's Project Lifeline calendar.

"Over five-hundred-thousand followers," Alli said. "That would be a dream come true for me."

"Yeah, it can also be a lot of work," Ella said. "How about we give a boost to Alli's creations?" She pointed at the hand-painted sign.

"You'll post with me?"

"Heck yeah." Ella waved her around the table. "Stand here so we can get your stuff in the background."

Ella knew how to set up the picture, framing them perfectly to capture the most colorful crocheted pieces. "Hold this one." She picked up the nearly perfect replica of the Briick figure made with blue yarn.

"Thanks for the picture, Ella. I can't believe…"

"Alli, my partner is an artist before anything else, and I understand how hard it is to be a creator." Ella typed out a quick description of her interaction with Alli and posted it on her page.

"That's really cool."

"I tagged you in it, and when you finish making my special order, I'll post that, too."

Alli had a crooked grin, almost a grimace. "To a million followers? I hope my hands can keep up." She tapped the page of her order-form booklet.

"What's the damage?" Ella asked.

"I can't charge you." Alli heard the tone on her phone, alerting her to the reactions from Ella's single post.

"You should charge me double," Ella teased. "But I insist. Charge me whatever you charged the person you're making that one for."

Alli finished filling out the fees. "Shipping is extra."

"Add it in," Ella encouraged.

"Total at the bottom and also fill in your address." She handed the clipboard to Ella. "It feels weird to ask you for it."

"It's okay. I've had a public mailing address for a long time. Please don't feel anything but excited for a sale." She printed her post office box address in precise, block-style letters.

"Thank you, Ella."

"You're welcome. I'm so excited to see what comes." She tucked the receipt in her pocket and walked away. She had a few minutes before she would meet up with Lil so she finished wandering, taking a moment to watch Morgan work.

Ella was unaware that Morgan had enjoyed the entire interaction. She had taken two photos and couldn't help but relive the moment she and Ella had clashed during a very similar fandom exchange. Their first encounter did not end in a selfie, but it did ultimately end in a happy relationship.

Lucky didn't describe how it felt to be loved by Ella.

~~~~~~~~~~~

"Did you hear Cinder_EllaE is in the house?" Lil teased as they sat down for dinner.

"Really?" Morgan smiled. "I hadn't heard." She waved her phone.

"I heard about a zillion times." Lil opened her menu.

"Huh, that's kinda cool." Ella was tucked behind her menu trying not to giggle.
~~~~~~~~~~~

"I browsed that woman's webpage. She makes some great crochet pieces."

Morgan closed her menu. "Cinder_EllaE is very good for business." She kissed her girlfriend.

20.

The Con

"How was day three?" Ella asked through her oversized headpiece as she slipped behind Morgan's table of art. The venue hall was the largest she'd ever been in and that didn't include the Briick displays in the exhibition hall. She was glad it was a three day event.

"I only have two prints of the Bruiser left," Morgan began. "I sold most of the Briick-style character art I had, and that case of holiday ornaments is empty." Morgan kicked the plastic tote. "Empty." She kicked two more. "Empty."

"Holy shit, Morg," Lil said. "You're killing it."

"One of my best shows yet." Morgan sat. "How was the Briick set release event?"

Lil shook the poly-bag. "It was amazing." She opened the video app on her phone. "I recorded it for you."

"You didn't have to do that," Morgan said.

Ella dangled two poly-bags in front of her. "I got mine and I got yours. Since we didn't sell the ticket, they let me scan your voucher."

"Don't let this Briick nerd over here fool you." Lil flicked her thumb at Ella. "They loved her cosplay, and when they heard Cinder_EllaE was in the house they probably would have let her take the whole case."

Ella squatted so Morgan could help take the headpiece off. "It kinda killed." Her smile was wide. "I know the original Arsonist costume was the best, but the modifications I made to it for this convention fit seamlessly with the Briick figure."

"The 3D-printed hands were the absolute win, though," Lil interrupted. "People kept stopping her to see them and play with the flamethrower."

Ella set the bags in Morgan's lap and dug out the plastic molded Briick hands. "They were a great idea." She had to give Lil credit for producing them.

"I'm happy they were so cool," Lil said, adding, "I should have printed more. I could have sold at least a dozen pairs, and you haven't done their cosplay contest yet."

Morgan propped her head against her hand, leaning on the table to watch the pair retell their adventures. "The two of you are adorable."

Lil guffawed. "What?"

Ella grinned. "Are we?"

"After everything that happened when we checked into the hotel." Morgan tugged at the costume hand grenade draped across Ella's shoulder, pulling her in for a kiss. "Ridiculously cute."

"She's cute for sure." Ella pointed at Lil. "I'm not even sure I was cute when I was a baby."

Always the peacekeeper between them, Morgan teased, "Don't fight it." She smiled. "When the two of you aren't acting like enemies, you make great friends."

"We do okay," Ella said.

"Okay?" Lil huffed. "Your lady just complimented us, me. I think we do better than okay." The argument died as a pair of teenagers approached the table.

"Time to get back to work." Morgan kissed her girlfriend. "You two go out there and play."

As Morgan patted her cheek, Ella had a sense of déjà vu, reliving their first meet, which hadn't been cute for either of them: Morgan hating on the Arsonist character from their favorite show as Ella defended the character's story arc. There was no miscommunication, only Morgan realizing she'd stopped watching at the wrong time.

Ella smiled, all too aware that she'd won Morgan's heart and they'd made a home together because of that initial dislike. Conventions would always feel special. How had she not recognized an opportunity for the perfect proposal would have been here and right now?

She followed Lil down the aisle toward the ballroom, heading to the costume contest stage.

"Hey, you okay?" Lil asked.

"Just thinking about a missed opportunity."

Lil nudged her, whispering, "Operation PP?"

Ella spun around. "Fucking Marshal."

Lil chuckled. "He warned me you'd say something like that."

She glared. "He's been calling it Operation PP and now I can't stop and…"

Lil fought the belly laugh. "He also said you're putting too much pressure on yourself. Anyway, why don't you just propose? You're both here and it is kinda romantic."

"I left the ring in Charlene's glove box."

Lil shook her head. "Rookie mistake."

Ella pulled her headpiece on, frustrated and in a hurry to disappear from her reality. "Don't remind me."

~~~~~~~~~~
~~~~~~~~~~

"Your pants have to be full by now," Ella teased.

Lil was sticking the origami cat face into her front pocket while balancing Ella's giant, plastic Briick figure hands. "These work pants have very deep pockets, my friend."

"How many have you got in there?"

"Cat faces or folded paper art in general?" Lil asked.

Ella had her cosplay headpiece tucked beneath her arm, flipped upside down so she could carry the 'best dressed' trophy as they walked to the box truck. "What are you going to do with them?"

"I don't know but I might have a new hobby." She held up a pocket-sized 'Art of Origami' pamphlet.

Putting two and two together, Ella figured out why Lil kept disappearing. "Is that where you went for breakfast on the first morning?"

Lil untangled the lanyard around her neck to show off the second convention name tag. "And day two and three."

"You're two-timing on us," Ella accused with an edge of playfulness. "Unacceptable, and with paper folding."

"I am not." Lil laughed, loud enough to attract attention. "You're not the boss of me and anyway, there are some very queer women at that paper-folding convention and it's so much more than folding paper." She made little quotation marks.

"So you bought three one-day tickets?"

Lil unfolded the pamphlet. "I went to their meet and greet mixer the first night and introduced myself to the woman checking people in. She was a little gruff initially, thinking I was mocking the art form, but after I explained my curiosity spurred by the elevator cranes she sat me down and we folded paper together for almost an hour."

"You folded paper," Ella repeated. "Together?"

Lil nodded. "She had great hands. It was kinda erotic."

"Paper folding is a turn-on for you?"

"Maybe, maybe not."

"Play-er." Ella tapped the lock on the truck's rollup door.

"Nah, it was more than that. I've folded about a hundred different paper animals and listened to the life history of more than a dozen strangers." Lil keyed the lock and opened the back of the truck. "It was very social."

"Are you going to ditch us again tonight?" Ella dropped her costume head into the storage tote and began the adventure of disrobing.

"I am," Lil admitted. "You two can enjoy the vendor dinner and I don't have to be the single third wheel."

"You know that doesn't add up?" Ella teased.

"So?" Lil smiled. "I'll have fun and so can you."

"We'll enjoy the couple-time."

Lil sat on the truck's step-up bumper. "You realize if you had that ring, a proposal would have—"

"Don't remind me." Ella folded the jumpsuit and bundled it with the grenade-covered shoulder bandolier.

"Have you figured out a new idea for Operation PP?"

Ella waved for Lil to get out of the path of the overhead door. "Not yet."

"What if you just walked right up to her and asked?"

Ella scoffed. "You're kidding." She flipped the handle of the truck's latch.

Lil secured the lock. "No, your inability to execute a plan is stressing me out."

"Stressing you out?" Ella rested against the truck. "It needs to be—"

"Perfect, yeah. I got that."

~~~~~~~~~~

Lil was juggling the two cans of non-alcoholic beer with the paperwork she'd downloaded using the concierge printer. The dew from the ice cold cans dripped along the featured
~~~~~~~~~~

guest list on the origami event packet's first page. She'd read through the information a half dozen times, close to memorizing the last day of the event.

"Hey, you made it back." The man greeted Lil.

"I did." Lil set her cans down so she could add the bundle of paper squares to her pile. She tipped the corner, flipping the multi-colored stack, wondering what exciting creations she was going to fold at the evening event.

"You're aware tonight's panel is alcohol free?" he asked, nodding toward her sweating cans of beer.

"Oh, these." Lil spun the can around so he could see the cute long-necked bird on the label. "They're a non-alcoholic malt beverage. It's from a local brewer I met. She's on a mission to create safe sober spaces."

"That was our mission for tonight, too." he said.

"Sobriety has enough judgement attached," Lil said. "Thanks for recognizing it."

"Our conference coordinator is on that same mission," he said as he leaned across to check the number on her pile of paper. "You're at table ten. She'll be at eleven. I'll make sure to introduce you to her. I'll show you where to go."

She followed him through the maze of round tables to a mostly occupied one near the front of the room. Lil appreciated the signs on each as they landed at table ten. She was glad the empty chair was facing the long banquet-style head table with a single microphone on it and a huge projection screen wall behind. They meant serious business when it came to the art of folded paper, and Lil wondered who was presenting.

"We are so lucky to have Mara this year," he said, answering her thought. "Mathematical paper architecture. She's a genius."

Lil had no idea when she'd stepped into the event that such an enthusiastic convention crowd could exist around the ancient art. "I'm an absolute novice," she confessed.

"I know." He tapped the list in front of him, pointing at the line of information from her registration form. "That's why we ask these questions when you sign up, and also why you're at table ten." He grinned. "Some of our best guests are next to you. Antoinette is leveling up this year. You two will have a great time." He tapped at the little rainbow sticker on her name badge.

Lil greeted the table full of people with a hand wave before pulling out her chair, and noticed that a not-so-strange stranger was sitting beside her. "Hello, funny bumping into you here."

"Well, hi." Toni didn't try to hide her surprise. "Funny meeting you here, for sure."

"Funny." Lil juggled the items in her hands, unsuccessfully, dropping a can on the carpet. Her pile of paper slipped, fanning a rainbow of pre-cut squares to the floor. She felt the heat in her cheeks as she ducked beneath the table to escape embarrassment. *Dork*, she thought.

Adorable, Toni thought as she flipped the length of tablecloth covering her lap and knelt beside Lil, asking, "Can I help?"

Lil groaned. "Ugh, how embarrassing." Adding to her awkwardness, the badges around her neck fell forward, swinging to bump her face. "I think I'm beyond help."

Toni stopped the swing before it could hit Lil again and was very curious to see the Briick Briicktacular VIP badge. "Are you here as a Briick-head too?"

Lil paused, her body physically freezing from the use of the term. Only a Brick-head would know that a Briick-head existed. "I am, sort of."

"Sort of?" Toni questioned.

"Knock knock," someone said as they banged on the tabletop.

"I guess we've been discovered," Toni whispered.

Lil froze, the pounding startling her. "Could this be more embarrassing?" She blew a slow breath, shaking off the momentary sense of panic.

Toni noticed the emotional shift but instead of drawing attention she winked, "Yes, I'm certain it could be a lot more embarrassing."

Lil's lips formed a tight O of surprise as Toni returned to her upright position. *What just happened?* she thought as she grabbed the pieces of paper and returned to her chair.

~~~~~~~~~~

"Mara's work is so inspiring," Toni said with such enthusiasm that the shoulder strap on her bag slipped to the bend of her arm.

"Yes," Lil agreed. "She put on a great talk, and the demonstration was so good even I could follow along."

"She travels all over the world," Toni said as she tried to lock the bag strap on her shoulder while maintaining the enthusiastic hand gestures she made as they walked.

"Can I carry that for you?" Lil asked.

"I guess I should have brought a backpack like you did."

Lil shouldered the additional bag. "Maybe next time."

Toni was enjoying the company and didn't want the night to end so she slowed her pace. "What are you doing for the rest of the evening?" Lil was about to answer when Toni added, "Whatever you had planned, maybe we could do it together?"

"Not shy, are you?" Lil chuckled.

"I guess not," Toni said.

"I like that about you. No pretense."

"Yeah?" Toni slowed her pace to a rambling zig zag down the carpeted hallway.

"Yeah."
~~~~~~~~~~

Toni stopped in front of the glass table to arrange the pocket full of paper cranes she'd folded during the evening's presentation."Would you like to take a walk with me?" she asked. "There's a path along the river."

The lobby doors slid open and they passed through. "I'm going to toss the bags in my truck."

"Great idea." Toni smiled.

"We could put yours in your car if you'd prefer."

Toni gave a quick head shake. "We could if you wanted to drive back to Blacktree since I took the train here."

"You took the train?"

She nodded enthusiastically. "It's my favorite way to travel and the station is four blocks from the hotel so I can walk everywhere I need to go."

Lil unlocked her truck and tossed their bags on the floor of the passenger side. "I took a train with my parents when I was a kid."

"You make it sound un-fun," Toni teased.

"It was a four-day trip across the country," Lil shared. "I was nine and I'm pretty sure my parents didn't enjoy it as much as I did."

"So that's the only time you've ever ridden the train?"

"Yep." Lil added, "I like the freedom of driving."

Toni leaned against the side of the truck. "Sure, but I haven't left the hotel all week so the train made sense."

"Smart lady." Lil locked the door. "How 'bout we take that walk?"

They set a slow pace, winding through the park across from the hotel. The night was cool and a refreshing change from the stagnant, recirculated air in the conference center. The sidewalks were designed for wandering and Lil felt an unexpected sense of calm after a very busy day.

"The river water is so high," Toni observed.

"It rained yesterday." Lil smacked her forehead internally as she realized she was talking about the weather.

"I didn't know that," Toni said, adding, "I had a pretty full schedule yesterday." She sidestepped around a park bench. "Should we sit?"

Lil nodded as they sat with the setting sun behind them. "How did the painters do?" Lil asked, curious about the final outcome of her repairs to the flower shop.

"They were wonderful and it looks nice, but I had a great contractor who gave them a perfect canvas."

"Just doing my job, ma'am." Lil pretended to tip a hat.

Toni should have found it corny but she believed the gesture was authentic to Lil's character. "I've had a great time tonight," she admitted.

"Yes, I have too. I was expecting to cram into a very crowded hotel room, but instead I'm walking the river park with you."

"Why is the room cramped?" Toni asked.

"Mix-up with the reservation. There are three of us sleeping in a king-sized bed."

Toni leaned closer. "Three of you?"

"Oh, right. I forgot." Lil explained, "Originally, I bought the tickets for my friend Ella and her partner Morgan. They are *Blasphemer* fanatics."

"Ella, from the rage rooms?" Toni asked to clarify but she knew the answer.

"The very same." Lil gave a crooked half grin. "Morgan has a fan-art table in the merch area so I've mostly been hanging out with Ella."

Toni nodded. She was fan-girling again and listening through a haze of adoration.

"There was an insane problem with our reservation." She retold the story of check in and the mix-up with their rooms, all while Toni nodded in the appropriate places.

"I should see what they're up to. Maybe we can hang out for our last night."

"That sounds fun, but won't they have plans of their own?"

"Let's find out." Lil scooted closer so Toni could read the screen as she sent a message to Ella.

> Lil: What are you and Morg up to?
> Ella: Just got back to the room from the vendor hall. Gonna grab dinner. Join us?
> Lil: Can I bring a friend?
> Ella: You have one?

Lil held the phone to her chest. "She likes to tease."
Toni found the playfulness endearing. "Seems like it."
The phone vibrated with a new message.

> Ella: She cute?

Lil shook her head. "I'm so sorry. Ella really isn't objectifying. She's just…"

"Playful," Toni interrupted.

"Exactly."

"Let me see your phone," Toni requested, and Lil handed it over.

Toni typed a message.

> Lil: She's hideous

There was a long pause, obvious typing and editing and typing again.

"Morgan is probably censoring her," Lil chuckled.

> Ella: Bring her and your ugly ass to the Italian place across the street from the hotel.

"You hungry for Italian?" Lil asked.

Toni typed a response.

Lil: See you in ten minutes.

"Can we walk there in ten minutes?" Lil asked, turned around by their pathway wandering.

Toni held the phone to her. "We can make it if you can keep up with me."

"Oh, I can keep up." Lil's grin was visible even in the low light. "Let's go."

21.

The Inquisition

Ella wheeled the cart across the plastic film covering the carpet in the merchant hall. Many of the vendors had packed up the night before while Ella, Morgan, Lil and Toni had enjoyed a not very delicious Italian dinner.

With mostly empty plastic totes, Ella didn't struggle following the pathway to the loading doors where Lil was waiting with the truck door open.

"Come on, slow poke, we have places to be."

It didn't take long to shuttle everything into the truck and by the time Ella returned the cart, Morgan was there with the paperwork from checking out.

"You'll be happy to see that Randy reduced our nightly rate." Morgan held the receipt to Lil.

"It should have been free after his fuck up." Ella opened the passenger door and helped Morgan climb in.

"This is crazy." Lil passed it to Ella. "That's half the original rate."

"He probably lost half his ass after talking with the manager." Ella had taken the time to report the incident, worried more about personal safety than reducing the cost of their stay, even if Lil was paying. With Ella and Lil in a heated state about the entire incident, Morgan volunteered to take over the hotel check-out process.

"It was a big mistake," Lil said.

"Dangerous. Imagine if I had nefarious intentions," Ella said. "All I could think was what if it was Morgan in that shower."

"Maybe Randy will be more careful." Lil started the truck. "We set?"

"Let's do this." Morgan fastened her seatbelt and settled in against Ella's side.

Lil grinned as she circled the hotel to detour through the park. The bench she'd shared with Toni was empty, but the memory of the talk made her want more. She tapped her thumb against the steering wheel as she waited at the stoplight in front of the train station.

"She's grinning," Ella whispered loud enough for Lil to hear.

"Yep," Morgan said.

"It's weird," Ella whispered again a little louder.

"I can hear you." Lil turned to enter the highway.

"What's up with you?" Ella asked.

"We passed the park and the train station."

Ella turned to look back. "We passed it coming in, too, but it wasn't out of the way then."

"Toni came to the conference on the train," Lil explained. "She left early this morning."

"Of course," Ella teased. "Hot for the florist."

"Toni was very sweet." Morgan elbowed Ella lightly.

"Way too sweet for Lily Flower," Ella teased again.

"Bite me," Lil huffed. "And she's not a florist. She's a shop owner who loves making people happy with botanicals."

"Ella, stop giving her a hard time. Their interaction was charming."

Lil tossed her arm over the back of the bench seat. "Yeah, listen to your girlfriend."

Ella didn't listen, doubling down on her inquiry. "How did you manage to lure such a sweet person into your clutches?"

"With paper boxes." Lil grinned.

"Paper boxes?" Ella repeated, skeptical about the answer as she took a sip from her water bottle.

"We were learning about three-dimensional folding with interlocking techniques, and Toni is very talented at demonstrating precision fingering." The explanation sounded innocent in her head.

Ella choked on her drink.

"You okay?" Morgan asked as she patted Ella's back.

"Fine." Ella coughed. "I need to look up the definition of origami because she just made it sound like foreplay."

"Maybe it was."

Morgan squeezed Ella's thigh, easily able to predict what was about to come out of her girlfriend's mouth.

"Lily Flower, I slept next to you last night and I know you didn't get any action."

"Not from Toni." Lil waggled her eyebrows.

"Stop it." Morgan swiped at Lil.

Ella leaned forward. "You did not just say that!"

"Your girl is very cuddly." Lil slowed the truck as she attempted to merge into traffic.

"I know I'm not driving, but if we have to pull this truck over, the two of you are riding in the back." Morgan scolded.

"This is a lot of truck," Ella said.

"Can you even reach the pedals?" Lil paddled her hands, imitating dangling feet.

"Hands on the wheel, Lily Flower." Ella reached for the handle above the door as the truck came to a stop.

"Damn traffic." Lil honked the horn to wave the car in front of her to move in.

Morgan repositioned herself against Ella. "The only person I cuddle is you." She turned to Lil. "And we both know that you had one foot on the floor every night we spent at that hotel."

"Really?" Ella leaned forward again. "You really did that?"

Lil slid into faster moving traffic. "I did." She propped her elbow on the door's armrest. "I tend to wrap around whatever is beside me when I sleep and as much as we joke…" She shrugged. "I respect Morgan and you too."

"Thanks." Ella was sincere. "That's… that means a lot."

"It does," Morgan agreed.

"The whole situation was weird and I didn't want to make it worse," Lil explained about the awkward last couple of nights. When she spent time with the couple, she almost always felt like a lost puppy trying to keep up.

"We love you," Morgan said in a gentle tone. "Never worry that we don't want you to join us."

"She's right," Ella added. "You are one of our favorite people."

"Thanks, guys. I—"

Ella interrupted to add, "When you're not being a complete dork."

"I'm the dork?" Lil hitched her thumb to point toward the back of the truck where Ella's cosplay was neatly folded in a crate beside a huge bag of retired Briick sets.

"Yep, I said it."

"Who in this truck cab has more than one replica of an imaginary flame thrower?"

Morgan poked Ella. "That would be you."

"And who in this cab had an entire room in their house dedicated to making cosplay costumes?"

"Award-winning cosplay," Ella corrected.

"You make my point for me, dork."

"You have a room too, it's just full of Briick sets, and who in this truck cab waited on the phone for hours to get VIP convention tickets?" Ella shot back.

"For you!" Lil smashed the horn hard as a sports car cut her off. "Asshole!" She quick-peeked at her passengers to clarify. "Not you, that car."

"We saw."

"So I guess we're both dorks," Ella said.

"I'm happy to be one."

Ella was itching to ask more questions about Toni and her talented fingers. "Since we are in the land of oddity, and not to make a weird conversation weirder, can we talk about dinner last night."

"Can we not?" Lil reached to turn the radio on. "80s rock, anyone?"

Ella smacked her hand away. "Nuhh," she scolded. "I want to know why she blushed half the time we were in the restaurant."

"Maybe they were playing footsie under the table," Morgan suggested.

"Ooh, that's so high school freshman."

"Are you serious?" Lil said. "I could hardly talk to a girl in high school, let alone play footsie." She imitated an idea flying over her head. "Oblivious."

"That matches the Lil of this decade," Ella teased.

"I could say the same about you."

Ella was offended. "What do you mean?"

"I think she means that Toni was blushing last night because she's got a little crush on you." Morgan patted Ella's thigh.

"Who's oblivious now?" Lil teased. She set the cruise control and waited for Ella's reaction.

The firefighter was often clueless about flirting when it was happening to her, inside and out of the calendar signing events. The idea that Toni would still act nervous around her was hard to believe.

"We've met so many times. I don't get it."

"You're a celebrity," Lil said. "As much as you like to deny it, that news thing they did after the fire and the calendar publicity are bigger than you realize. You've got over a half million followers, nerd!"

Ella shrugged the idea away. "That's silly."

"It's not, baby." Morgan snuck a quick kiss. "Lil makes a good point."

"I do," Lil explained. "If we used your toaster oven haul as an example, you've got what… ten, eleven?" she asked.

"Twenty-seven," Morgan corrected.

Lil gasped. "No way."

"Way." Morgan chuckled. "I've got the full shelves in the storage room to prove it."

Ella's head dropped back against the seat as she blew out an exasperated breath. "That's not including the first few I left at the station house, one for the kitchen and one for the thrift store."

"You've been doing this for almost ten years. That's, like, three a year if you break it down." Lil was shocked, believing that was a lot.

Ella shook her head.

"Oh, no. The toaster oven thing started with the last calendar," Morgan said proudly. "October. It was the vampire theme that left half of the population on the floor."

"Ella Eastman." Lil whistled. "Converting the masses with plastic fangs. Girl, no wonder you make Toni swoon. I should pay more attention."

"It's so awkward and embarrassing."

"You represent a different time," Lil said. "Embrace it."

"With a sledge hammer," Ella snarked.

"If it helps, do it."

Ella returned to the conversation Lil was obviously trying to avoid. "Speaking of doing it—"

"She's nice and I like her, but she's coming off a breakup and I'm not interested in being the rebound screw."

"Maybe she's not looking for that?" Morgan suggested, always the optimist.

"Maybe." Lil adjusted the cruise control. "It's nice to talk with someone who isn't a contractor, and we have a lot in common."

"Romance is budding for our little flower," Ella joked.

"It appears so," Morgan said. "You let us know if you want another dinner together."

"I will," Lil said. "But only if I get to pick the restaurant."

22.

The Bookcase

"Hey Crumbly," Marsh greeted Morgan at the Sage Lounge reception table. "What are you doing here? Slow day?"

It wasn't uncommon for her to come in before they opened officially, and Morgan sidestepped the kiosk for a hug.

"Ella is working on a project with Lil, and I have work that requires a bit of quiet." She waved the book in her hand.

"Is it spicy?" he asked.

Morgan chuckled. "Has Ella been talking about romance novels again?"

His nod was enthusiastic. "She has, and I feel educated, although I lean more toward men who love men in my fiction."

"Are you reading romances, too?"

He put a finger to his lips. "I am, and I'm not ashamed to talk about them."

"Good for you," Morgan cheered. "So can I sneak in the corner upstairs for some quiet time?"

"I got you, girl." He removed the velvet rope blocking the stairs. "You okay on steps today?"

"Lead the way."

~~~~~~~~~~~

Ella raised the lengths of lumber to shift them off the painter's tarp. "Did you call her?" she asked.

Lil ignored the question.

"You didn't, did you?"

Lil tipped the board, continuing to fit the framework of the bookcase together as the sun went behind the clouds. The rooftop patio was the perfect place to stage their project, and now that a day had passed since the parts were stained and sealed, they could proceed with the installation of the massive bookcase.

"This is the last one," Ella said as she double-checked the positions that Lil had staged the labeled pieces in. "You're just going to ignore the question?"

"Yep." Lil began loading her tool pouch and Ella watched every move. "I don't want to talk about it."

"We're going to eventually."

"Can we focus on the bookcase?"

"Those are really small nails," Ella observed, letting her curiosity go for the moment. When the time was right, she'd dig deeper into why Lil was avoiding Toni's obvious attraction. "Will that hold the weight of all this?" She kicked the top board.

"Nah, the nailer is for finishing." Lil torqued a bit into her drill. "The frame is anchored to the studs with these babies." She scooped a few long bolts from her tool belt.

"Impressive." Ella was intrigued. This project had grown from a cute little prefabricated side-table case into a full floor-to-ceiling work of art.
~~~~~~~~~~~

"Thanks, Ella. I wanted to make it nice for the two of you."

"Your idea of nice is…"

Lil interrupted. "Let's build the wall, and when it's up you can shower me with accolades."

"There's the humility I was waiting for."

"Less talking, more holding. Put those muscles to use and square this up."

~~~~~~~~~~

For the next few hours, Lil ordered Ella and her physical strength around. The layout was more than satisfying as they stood shoulder to shoulder to admire the nearly completed wall of shelves.

Lil tapped the brad nailer against the baseboard trim pieces and paused, the hose of her compressed air nailer hissing as she disconnected it.

"You want to use the nailer?" Lil asked as she loaded another clip of finishing nails into the tool.

Ella licked her lips. "You know I do."

"Quick safety lesson," Lil said. "It doesn't shoot. It's more like a single blow hammer. You touch it to the trim and then pull the trigger. If it isn't depressing the latch, it won't fire." She picked up the hose. "It also requires this." She reconnected the nailer to the air compressor nozzle. "I never make changes to this tool with the hose attached."

"I was paying attention," Ella said as she climbed the ladder. "Better safe than sorry, and for the record, I have responded to job sites for nail gun accidents."

"They can do a lot of damage, especially with larger nails." Lil handed the tool to Ella. "You ready?"

Ella was ready, and handled the finishing job like a pro as she tapped the first few pieces of trim into place.
~~~~~~~~~~

Lil held the next one upright and Ella secured it to finish the edges along the wall. "You're having a little too much fun."

"I'm pretty sure it's because we're doing it for Morgan," Ella said. "She deserves this and so much more."

"I'm also here for you, and you know it." Lil climbed the second ladder to stabilize the longest and last piece of decorative trim at the ceiling. Ella passed the nailer to Lil so she could drive in the final brads.

"This might be the hottest scene I've ever come across." Morgan gave a slow intentional whistle.

"She got a carpenter's crack?" Lil teased.

Ella adjusted the tool belt around her waist and checked the tuck of her shirt. "I do not have, and never could have, a carpenter's crack. I've got too much ass for my pants to fall down."

Morgan patted Ella's behind. "Not too much ass, sweetie. I'd say just the right amount."

"Stop it," Lil groaned. "I'm already jealous enough of the two of you."

Morgan held the ladder as Ella stepped off. "Aside from my ass, do you like what you see?"

"Like?" Morgan shook her head. "Love is more like it. Lil, the bookcase is amazing and I can't believe you did this in one day."

Lil tipped her wrist to check her watch. "Not completely in a day. I'm pretty sure it was your girlfriend and her intense work style that pushed this project through in two days instead of two weeks."

"Nah." Ella wasn't going to take all the credit. "It was teamwork and excellent project management. Plus staging everything on the roof made the assembly part a dream."

"Yay, we get the rooftop patio back." Morgan ran her finger along the edge of the shoulder-high shelf.

"I'll tidy it up now." Lil disconnected the nailer and placed it in the case beside the elevator door.

"No way," Ella intercepted. "I'll take care of all the cleanup. You get to sit in the chair, sip something cold, and relax."

"You think I'm going to watch you clean up after me? No way, Eastman."

Morgan side-stepped, interrupting her construction crew. "Maybe the two of you should enjoy the last bits of sunshine on the rooftop while I clean up. I think it's the least I can do to thank you for this."

Ella held Morgan from behind, walking them slowly toward the patio. "How about no way are you cleaning up after us," Ella said as they climbed the steps leading outside.

Lil managed to roll the fifty-gallon trash bin toward the short staircase while carrying the folded tarp. "This is nothing."

Morgan was skeptical until she saw the staging area. It didn't look like a construction site, it looked more like an exercise in tool organization.

Ella was quick to return with drinks. "You are supposed to be relaxing up here." She carried three glasses along with a bottle of chilled water.

Lil was wiping down every tool before returning them to their proper kits. "We're done. There wasn't much to do because you hardly let me make a mess before you and your broomstick came along to sweep it all away."

"Genius plan, if you ask me," Ella teased as she filled their glasses. "And broomstick?"

Lil stacked her tool boxes by the door. "I'm not calling you a witch, although I've enjoyed the company of a few. I'm only saying you're too tidy for a job site."

"Maybe." Ella shrugged. "But we built a very impressive bookcase and that's all that matters. And speaking of enjoying company…"

"She hasn't responded to any of my messages," Lil said, finally answering her questions about Toni.

Morgan shook her head. "What are we talking about?"

"Toni the florist," Ella said as she wriggled into the lounge chair so Morgan could sit in her lap.

Lil spilled a little water when she picked up the glass. "She's not a florist."

"Right," Ella said. "She owns the shop, and maybe you should get in that truck parked downstairs and go see her at said shop?"

Lil shrugged the suggestion off. "I think maybe she just isn't interested and I should let it go."

"She's interested," Morgan interrupted. "I saw her at the restaurant and she was definitely having a great time."

"You think?"

"Now I know why you're still single," Ella snarked.

The contractor slumped into the chair. "I'm not good at this. I've never been good at this."

"Would you like a suggestion?" Morgan asked with kindness in her voice that was so achingly sweet no one would say no.

Lil nodded.

"Don't call or text anymore. If you're interested, go and see her."

"Just like that," Lil said. "Go to her place of business and ask?"

"You're her contractor." Ella winked. "Swing by, check and see if she's satisfied with your work."

Lil began to feel empowered by the couple's encouraging words. "Maybe I'll go there now."

"That's a great idea," Morgan said.

"Do it!" Ella chanted as she joined Lil to carry the tool kits to the loft elevator. "Quick tip," she whispered.

"What's that?" Lil tugged the elevator gates closed.

"Don't bring the lady flowers."

The elevator jerked into motion and Lil let out her "Phew," but this time Ella wasn't sure if the sound effect was for the lift or for rescuing her from a flower faux pas.

Ella turned to see Morgan at the kitchen counter separating their mail. "What's that?"

"Two letters for Ms. Ella Eastman." Morgan held them up. "I went to the PO Box this afternoon, and these were in there."

Ella flipped the first letter around. "Wonder who." She was drawing a blank of the last name Kelling in the return address corner as she slipped her finger through the flap to tear it open. Inside was a sketch in a rainbow array of crayon colors.

Morgan peered over her shoulder and admired the child's drawing of two people. One was clearly a little girl wearing rubber boots and a blue cape, and the other was a much taller firefighter in yellow pants with a bright red hat. "It's you and a little girl?"

"Addie. She's the one I told you about. She signed Seb's calendar." Ella flipped the envelope over. "They must have gotten the address from my social media. This is so adorable." She stepped to hang it on the refrigerator beside the calendar.

"Fan mail from children is very different than fan mail from adults," Morgan said.

"You are not wrong." Ella checked the return on the second letter. "Station Eight-Eighteen. This could be the opposite of adorable if they sent it to the post office box." She tore the top of the envelope to find a very different card inside.

"It's from Seb." It was a thank you card for the gift they'd sent to celebrate the pregnancy announcement. On the cover was an image of an ultrasound with 'baby Wilson' printed in perfect block letters. Inside the card, Seb shared his gratitude for Ella and the support she'd always shown.

Ella hung the card on the front of the refrigerator so she could see it every time she went into the kitchen. "What a great way to end the day."

Morgan held her close. "What an extraordinary way to live your life."

23.

The Wall

In her daily life, Lil was surrounded by noise. Hammer to nail, an engine rev, heavy metal or grunge blaring from a site crew radio—these were her comfort sounds, and their absence was almost physically impossible to endure. There was something about silence that put her off, creating not diminishing an anxious state.

She'd never pushed herself through the discomfort, never given herself the chance to be silent in the company of another, and until now that was fine. She wanted to ignore Ella and Morgan's prodding about taking a leap and abandon her pursuit of romance with the flower-shop owner. There was no text response, no email or voice message from her service, and it hit Lil like a punch to the gut.

Toni was silent, and silence was outside Lil's comfort zone.

"But you like her," Lil whispered as she stared through the truck windshield with the flower shop in her line of sight. It took twenty-three steps to reach the sidewalk. She counted each of them.

She cupped her hand to block the reflection as she peeked through the shop window. The lights were dimmed and the closed sign was displayed. She hadn't expected to miss Toni at two o'clock, when the hours of operation listed opening times from noon until seven pm. She knocked on the door and was surprised when it popped open.

"Toni?" she called. She could hear the trickle of water coming from the fountain display near the door. She knocked hard on the service countertop a little louder than she'd done on the door. "Toni, are you here?" The entrance had been repainted with a bright shade of blue and the short tables displayed folded paper flowers in stenciled clay pots. The presentation was inviting, and she recognized the technique from the presentation on the final night of the convention .

She was startled when a man wearing a damp canvas apron came through the archway leading from the back room.

"She's not here." He stood at the service counter, blocking her from moving into the greenhouse space.

"Do you know when she'll be back?" she asked.

"I do."

He didn't share any additional information, and Lil was hesitant to stay, and at the same time a little worried the man didn't belong in the shop either.

"I'm the contractor who repaired the wall after the fire," she explained.

He scratched his head. "Stacey Builders?"

"Stacey Construction," she corrected.

"The job's done."

Lil chuckled. The interaction was awkward, and as much as she didn't belong in the space she was also questioning the presence of this strange guy in Toni's flower shop. "Yes, the job is done, but I wanted to double-check that Toni was happy with the final product."

"Seems fine," he said. "She hasn't complained to me."

Lil stretched a hand to him, hoping for an introduction. "Lil Stacey, I don't think we've met."

"Nope, we haven't." His answer was icy, dismissive and really confusing.

"Dad," Toni scolded. "What are you doing?"

"Protecting the shop. This person showed up, barged right in and who knows what kind of trouble they—"

"Dad, this is Lil and—"

"She shouldn't have barged in."

Lil defended her presence. "The door was open and I knocked." She held up her fingers. "Twice."

"Rude, if you ask me."

"Ricky, you making trouble?" Cove bumped into the man as they scooted backward into the room. They were pulling a pile of boxes labeled 'flower pots' on a teetering, well-aged cart.

"Protecting the assets," he said, moving aside until Cove passed.

"Dad, I told you Lil is a friend."

"Oh, hey Lil." Cove wiped their hand clean before stretching it out. "What's going on?"

She was feeling very put on the spot as all eyes turned to her. She'd come to talk to Toni, not about the wall or satisfaction with repairs, but about the uncomfortable silence and maybe going out on another date. She wanted to clear whatever obstacle was preventing Toni from continuing their friendship or whatever else was forming after their night at the river.

"She came to check the wall," Ricky said.

Cove laughed. "Is that what we're calling it?"

"Stop it, you two." Toni's glare shifted from her best friend to her father. "I'll unload this cart. Why don't the two of you get the rest of the supplies." Although it sounded like a request, the two of them moved as if ordered.

Lil was trying to be cool but it lasted less than ten seconds. "Have I offended you?"

Toni pulled the cart closer to the empty display rack and sliced the packing tape on the first case. She seemed to be focused on the task, maybe too focused, as she unfolded the flaps. "I don't think you've offended me." She unwrapped the first clay pot, inspecting the edges before placing it on the shelf. "Why do you ask?"

Lil leaned against the service counter. "I called and you didn't answer."

Toni tipped her head toward the desk behind Lil. "I don't see any blinking lights on the machine."

"I didn't leave a message."

Toni stuffed the paper wrap inside the waste bag she'd tied to the cart. "Maybe I should be the one who's offended."

Lil stepped closer. "I wanted to talk to you, not your machine."

Toni continued the job of unwrapping the first case of clay pots. "I'm not a magician, Lil. I've been running around for the last few days trying to restock everything I lost in the fire, and with the horrible phone reception out west I forwarded my cell to the shop's machine."

"Oh."Lil didn't know what to say.

Toni tipped the empty case and punched the bottom to flatten the box. "Why were you calling?"

Lil recognized the folded paper flower lying on the counter. She rolled the short stem, recognizing the technique from the conference. "I wondered if you'd like to go out."

"So not about the repairs?"

Lil chuckled. "No, I... your dad freaked me out. I said that because I didn't know who he was and why—"

"You were going to be my protector?"

"I'm not sure what I was going to do." Lil shrugged. The confrontation could have been dangerous, now that Toni was pointing it out.

Toni cut another box open. "That's very sweet."

"Or stupid," Lil added.

"Well maybe if you help me unbox this inventory we can go get some coffee?" Toni suggested.

"I'd like that."

"I would, too." Toni inspected the pot. "I meant it, though. If you have a question, you should just ask. I promise to answer."

"Good to know." Lil took the pot and stacked it inside the others. "You have nice pots." She closed her eyes, immediately embarrassed by the comment. She was being awkward and blurting out ridiculous things.

"Thank you." Toni chuckled. "They better be, since I had to return the last shipment."

"Really?"

Toni unpacked another box and flattened it. "Two hundred pots arrived sounding like a box of rattling rocks. That's why I was gone for so long and why my dad is here. He's the only guy with a big enough truck to carry all these." She fanned over the cart of boxes.

"Technically, he's not the only one with a big truck." Lil grinned.

"Yes, but I didn't know if it was an overstep to ask." She passed a pot to Lil.

Lil held her hands sandwiched against the pot. "You know what, Toni?"

"What?" Toni liked the warmth of Lil's hands on hers.

"If you have a question, you should just ask."

Toni looked up into earnest eyes. "Touché."

Lil took the pot and set it on the display. "You do know that means touch?"

Toni knew exactly what it meant.

"I have a question," Lil said.

"Ask it."

"Will you go out on a date with me?"

24.

The Sleuth

The station house was never completely still. There was always the sound of preparation; checklists for gear in the right places, equipment safety inspections and the never-ending job of maintaining Station Eight-Eighteen's vehicle fleet.

The important component for Ella was filling her time away from Morgan. "Twenty-four more hours," she said as she adjusted the single earbud while the second dangled from her breast pocket. She was sitting on the floor, her shoulders propped against the incline bench in the department weight room. She didn't call Morgan every time she had a four-day schedule, but in recent weeks, after a fairly quiet shift, the down times made her miss her girlfriend more.

Morgan was sitting in the Sage Lounge, sketching a piece of artwork commissioned during the convention. She liked to fill her too quiet moments in the loft by escaping to the restaurant's second-floor dining area. It was almost always the perfect escape. "Tell me about your shift?" Morgan asked, trying to judge how her partner might return the following day.

Ella didn't hesitate, knowing after so many years together that Morgan could read every flavor of response. "Oddly consistent."

"That's new," Morgan quipped. "Care to define that for me?" She scooped a pile of eraser crumbs onto her plate.

Ella chuckled. "Let's just say the Blacktree Senior citizen community kept me busy." The station house had received three non-critical calls over three days from the same long-term care center. A lover's spat that turned into scooter rage in a grossly-carpeted hallway. One medication mishap, leading to irritable bowels, and a confused resident who'd knocked her head on the cabinet in her en suite bathroom. After eight years, Ella didn't need to share all those details.

Morgan knew it was code for a rather slow stretch of activity. "That means you'll be ready to stock the shelves."

Ella could picture the smile on her partner's face. "I'm so excited to move everything into one place."

"Speaking of moving books, I've got a new one for you to read," Morgan shared. "And we finally decided on our first novel for book club."

Ella found the news exciting. "What tropes?" she asked.

Morgan could picture the excited smile Ella was wearing . "Oh no, it's a surprise," Morgan teased.

The station alarm sounded before Ella could protest. "Gotta go, honey."

"Be careful out there," Morgan whispered, certain Ella wouldn't hear her.

Ella blew a kiss into the phone. "I love you."

~~~~~~~~~~~

Morgan's next twenty-four hours were the opposite of Ella's. She'd set and reset all eight rage rooms throughout the day. She was tired but excited to have Ella off-duty for close to a week. After the previous day's phone call, she'd received
~~~~~~~~~~~

several messages from Ella with precise strategies for organizing the shelves. The plan had taken many forms and even as she waited for the firefighter to return, she wondered if there was another iteration of shelf stocking in their future.

She wheeled a cart full of books toward the elevator, surprised when she pushed the call button that the elevator was resting on the second floor.

Beatrice was gone for the day and she wasn't expecting Ella for a few more hours, so she pressed the button impatiently before the motor engaged.

"Hello," she called through the safety gate but no one responded. She watched the floor of the loft pass slowly as familiar ankle socks came into view, followed by bare legs, loose-fitting shorts, a Briick Briicktacular convention t-shirt, and finally a dazzling smile.

"Hi there." Ella raised the safety gate to open the elevator for Morgan.

Morgan stepped around her book cart. "What are you doing home already?"

Ella shrugged. "Surprising you."

"I like it." Morgan fell into her arms, holding tight as her girlfriend swooped her up for a kiss.

"Everything alright?"

"Yes." Morgan nodded against Ella's chest. "I'm very happy to see you."

"I'm very happy to be seen." Ella grabbed the cart and held tight to Morgan's hand as she maneuvered the books into the loft. "What have you been up to with these?"

There were three stacks piled atop the cart, but Ella was distracted by the artwork on one. "*Remember Not to Die.*" Ella read the title on the spine. "This is the book club choice?"

"It is," Morgan said. "The main character is a spy and she's fighting to save a—"

"A spy romance?" Ella interrupted, her nose crinkling with disapproval of the subject choice.

"It's very good."

Ella wasn't convinced. "I wanted a meet cute or maybe even a second-chance romance."

"Are you joining book club?" Morgan asked as she slid a crate of books from the bottom shelf of the cart. "You're really getting into the genre."

"Maybe," Ella said. She collected a pile of books.

"I'll take a maybe."

"Did you read my shelving plan?" Ella asked.

One after the other, Morgan checked the title of the book as she moved it from Ella's arms to one of the many shelves. "I did read your plan. And then I read another plan and another."

"But you aren't using any of my suggestions." Ella attempted to sort what was stacked on the floor.

Morgan grinned. "I'm unboxing first."

"But you're putting them on the shelf."

"Trust the process, my love." She touched her girlfriend's cheek before giving her a kiss. "The first plan you sent was the best."

"Oh, you really thought so?" They worked through the novels on the cart until they'd made small piles alphabetically by author and then by title.

"I liked this one." Ella flipped the book over to skim through the blurb. "'Fated love' seems like a hokey plot but the characters were so sweet in this one."

Morgan shrugged. "It's not my favorite trope."

Ella stopped. "You don't like fated love?"

"It's almost as cliché as 'never felt fulfilled before I met you' or 'never had better sex'," Morgan mocked. "Like this main character." She tapped the cover. "She's almost thirty and never had an orgasm?" She tucked the book on the shelf. "Every woman should know how to find pleasure."

Ella stared, flabbergasted by Morgan's opinion. "Did you just suggest that every woman should have a vibrator?"

"Well, not specifically, but that works too," she said unapologetically. "We shouldn't have to rely on someone to find pleasure."

"How is it that we've been together for eight years and you can still surprise me."

"I don't know." Morgan put the book club copies in an empty box so she could bring more boxes from the bedroom.

Ella didn't move. She couldn't move.

"You're gonna catch flies, lover." Morgan used the spine of a book to close Ella's mouth.

"You don't believe in fate?" Ella backtracked to the novel trope.

Morgan shrugged. She wasn't jaded about life. She was a fighter. The scars on her legs ran deeper than flesh; they burned to her soul as she fought to regain mobility. "I don't believe in waiting around for life to happen to you."

Ella considered the idea. Is that what fate was? She hadn't been waiting for Morgan to come into her life; she'd been living pretty happily before meeting her. "Can we roll back to your list of clichés?"

Morgan knew as soon as she'd shared them that Ella's romantic heart would stumble to process them. "Which? The first one or the second."

"Yes."

Morgan chuckled. Communication was where she felt secure in their relationship. If Ella wanted to know, she'd ask, and the same went for Morgan. "El, sweetheart. You are the love of my life."

"I know."

"But—" she took the books from Ella.

Ella didn't like the use of the word, "But?"

"But we *became* lovers."

"I wasn't your best ever?" Ella's frown was more powerful than the question.

Morgan nodded. "You are my best ever. Not because of a single act, but because of every single act."

"Oh."

Morgan kissed her. "So, you see. Love isn't a stand-alone novel, baby. It's an epic series that we keep experiencing."

"I like that."

She sidestepped to add a book to the shelf. "I thought you would."

Ella flipped the copy of *Remember Not to Die* so she could read the blurb. "Alright, this spy thing, is it a stand alone or part of an epic series?" she asked.

"You'll have to read it and see."

"No spoilers for me?" Ella unlatched the side cabinet to pull out the hidden ladder.

"Nope." Morgan opened the tote of Briick sets. "The way Lil designed that ladder cabinet is so smooth." Morgan waited for Ella to climb before passing a Briick flower set to her.

"I'm so happy she let me help her."

"You made a great team."

"We did, didn't we?"

They continued their unpacking. "So I have an idea for the business," Morgan said.

"What's that?"

Morgan passed another Briick set to Ella. "How would you feel about throwing axes?"

25.

The Axe

Lil was nervous about the date as she approached the door of the restaurant and bar. She'd chosen a cut-off flannel that fit loose on her shoulders but showed off the tribal design of her tattoo sleeve. She was going for comfortable clothing as an axe-throwing bar wasn't an atmosphere she was accustomed to. Ella of all people had chosen the location, calling it a fact-finding mission to determine if the rage room should add axe-throwing targets to their venue.

Lil had invited Toni and wanted to pick her up at the flower shop but Toni insisted that arriving separately was a better choice while she waited for her florist, Penny, to finish a last-minute special order.

Toni was standing outside the door, reading the advertisements taped to the venue's windows. She snapped a picture of an indie band's poster.

"Have you ever heard their music?" Lil asked as she approached. Her hands were jammed deep in her jean pockets.

Toni shook her head. "I've never heard of them, but I like their art style."

"It's colorful." Lil looked closer, and read the band's title aloud. "The Radiant Tears."

"I wonder what they play." Toni slid her phone into her back pocket.

"We could go next Saturday, maybe check them out."

"Sounds like it might be fun," Toni said.

Lil opened the door to the bar. "It's a date." She grinned as she waited for Toni to pass through. It was a good sign to have plans for another date before the current date began, right? She was going with a yes.

"Hey, slowpoke." Ella stepped out from behind the high-top table. "We were wondering if the two of you were ever going to come inside." She was dressed to compete with loose-fitting jeans and a RATS rage room logo t-shirt beneath her favorite red flannel button-up.

"We just got here," Lil defended. Toni followed behind, still feeling a little anxious to be so casual in front of the couple.

"She's very impatient," Morgan said as she slid from the barstool to hug her friend. Her skirt was loose-fitting, and Lil thought it an odd choice for the evening's event, even though Morgan almost always showed up in a dress.

"We've been watching those two guys throw for the last ten minutes, and I'm ready for some fun." Ella was enthusiastic.

"Hello, again," Morgan greeted Toni, sizing her up to determine if she was a hugger. Taking a chance, she opened her arms.

Toni hugged her back, surprised when Morgan gave a very intentional and heart-warming embrace.

"We booked an hour, so let's get the party started." Ella handed a clipboard to each of the women. "Fill these out and get your ID ready because the dude will card you."

"I thought this was an alcohol-free bar."

Morgan set a cup of pens on the table. "It is, but you have to be twenty-one to throw some of the weapons on the wall." She pointed at the display behind the metal cage.

"Hell yeah," Lil cheered. "I didn't know we could throw hurlbats." She approached the display to admire the menacing weapons.

"That thing looks hard to throw," Toni said.

"Nah, it's actually easier once you figure out your throwing style," Lil explained. "The blade is super light but it also has spikes on the top and backside, so your odds of it sticking in the wall are very good."

"That's right," the attendant said as he came to greet the new arrivals. "I'm Peter, part owner, and it looks like you're all here."

"We are," Ella said. "And we are ready to throw."

They heard the loud thump of the felling axe hitting the wall behind them. It was the robust sound of someone using a lot of might.

"That's the one I want to throw." Morgan grinned, showing the first signs of her competitive side. The usually cool member of the relationship, she was ready to launch at the center target.

Peter collected their waiver forms and began going through the brief but intense rules of the bar. "There are three weapons out for you to start. I suggest the short-handled axe for beginners. It's lightweight and well-balanced." He continued explaining techniques for throwing all three weapons, and Lil was excited when he demonstrated the hurlbat. "The bar is open. Everything on the menu is alcohol free, and we have our local brew on tap." He pointed to the laminated menu on the hightop table. "Jillian, the brewmaster, is quite the character."

"It's so supportive to have a sober venue like this." Lil read through the advertisement. "She shares space in this building?"

"Yep, Jill is the reason the place is alcohol-free. She talks a lot about how hard it is to socialize in recovery. She found her purpose in 'alcohol free malt brewing'." He tapped the colorful ad on the table. "She also happens to be my business partner."

"Super smart and inspiring. We'll take a pitcher of Jillian's house brew," Ella said.

"Coming up." He walked away, leaving them to sort out their throwing order.

Lil scooted around the caged barricade wall. "I think you and Morgan should go first. With the rage rooms and all I'm sure you'll be better."

"Ella has an unfair advantage."

The firefighter shook her head. "We never throw axes. We break through barriers and such but I've never thrown an axe on the job. I'll probably be terrible."

"That's what all the ringers say," Lil teased. She was feeling comfortable in the company of her friends but was also aware that Toni was standing back from the group.

Ella picked up the felling axe. "I'm going for the two-handed throw."

"I'm going to try the little hatchet." Morgan picked it up. "I think this one is for me."

"Do you have a preference?" Lil stepped back to ask Toni.

Toni was eyeing up the hurlbat. "I think I like the one you like."

"A lady after my own heart." Lil grinned.

"Something else we have in common."

The pitcher of beer arrived with a stack of glasses. "Can I get you anything else?"

Lil called out, "Eastman, beer's here. Need anything else?"

Ella paused with the axe over her head, two hands loosely gripping the long handle. "I'm good. Morgan?" she asked her girlfriend.

"Just the beer is great for me." Morgan didn't pause or look away as the short-handled hatchet over-rotated and bounced to the rubber mat on the floor.

Lil looked at Toni. "You good?"

Toni nodded. "I think we're good." She flinched at the sound of the felling axe sinking hard.

Ella hit the target wall, missing the rings. "It stuck. That's good for the first try." She retrieved her weapon at the same time Morgan picked up hers.

"Don't worry, Morg. There's always a learning curve." Lil squawked.

Toni was very quiet, anxious as she experienced the playful nature of the trio and doubly insecure about her ability to hit any circle on the wall. She was questioning her choice to come on this double date.

"Would you like some?" Lil asked as she began pouring drinks.

Toni nodded.

Noticing her fidgeting hands, Lil asked, "Are you okay?"

"Just nervous," Toni confessed.

The sound of an axe hitting the wall startled Toni and they all looked over to see the men having a physical and competitive session.

"That's intense," Ella said as she slid close to Lil to grab a beer.

"I'm surprised they can get the axes out after their throws." Morgan tipped her glass against Ella's and Lil and Toni joined in.

"Cheers all," Ella said. "To a great night out with friends."

An enthusiastic round of cheers followed.

"You're up, Lily Flower," Ella patted her friend on the back, nearly spilling the glass at her lips.

"Eastman, your move from sentimental to taunting is enough to give me whiplash."

"Let's see what ya got," Ella challenged. She picked an empty chair opposite the wall and flipped it around to watch. She felt for the drawstring bag holding Morgan's engagement ring. The pocket of her pants was shallow, so she'd switched it to the button-closed flannel shirt pocket she wore. Since the mishap of leaving it in Charlotte's glovebox, Ella had decided to take it everywhere, forcing her to place it in the more discreet velvet drawstring bag. She wasn't expecting to propose at their axe-throwing outing, but she hadn't ruled it out completely.

"Don't embarrass Lil," Morgan whispered. "She's already nervous enough."

"You think *she's* nervous?" Ella nodded toward Toni. "I think her date is about to puke."

Toni picked up the felling axe, testing the weight and determining it was too heavy for her first round. She liked the hatchet's size but she was particularly fond of the hurlbat and that it gave her four different ways to stick it in the target.

"Try that one," Lil encouraged. "I think it's the easiest."

Toni watched as Lil stepped up to the line. The markings on the floor indicated the span of fourteen feet. Surely she could hit it from that distance. She repeated the technique in her head. Step with your throwing hand, don't wind up, throw from your shoulders and torso, not just your arm. Keep your wrist straight. The last rule made her chuckle. Straight wasn't something she aspired to do or be. She released the axe, sticking it off-center but in the two-point ring.

"Woo hoo!" Lil cheered. "Hell yeah, that's my date right there."

Toni smiled. As nervous as she was minutes before, she noticed she was the only one who made their axe stick in the target. Lil's hurlbat was lying on the rubber mat.

"Ringer!" Ella leveraged herself to stand on the edge of her chair.

"Can it, Eastman." Lil grinned as she retrieved her axe. "Don't listen to her, Toni. She's too competitive for her own good."

"It's fun." Toni needed to use a little force to wiggle the axe free, and her next two throws, also off-center, stuck solidly in the target.

~~~~~~~~~~~

It was more than fun for the foursome. They spent their slotted hour taking turns throwing close to a dozen different weapons. Lil and Morgan were most comfortable with the one-handed tomahawk while Toni favored the hurlbat and its multiple points of contact. Ella remained loyal to the two-handed style of throw with the weighted double-bit axe.

"One more throw." Toni didn't want their night to end. She'd managed to turn her nervous energy into only slight discomfort, but getting to know Ella had been a huge turning point. Lil had insisted the firefighter was a regular person, and she was right.

"I think we've created a monster." Ella hooked her arm with Toni's and the two entered the throwing lanes. "Give us all you got."

"Bruce—hey, man. What the hell are you doing?" The yell was loud and Ella watched through the chain-link partition as the man she assumed was Bruce fell face forward into the target wall. "Dude!" He grabbed for his friend but wasn't strong or fast enough to hold him. "Bruce!"

Ella didn't hesitate as she ducked from her lane to where the men had been all night. She shouldered the second guy
~~~~~~~~~~~

aside so she could assess the situation. The man was down and her first thought was a heart attack. She used great care to roll him over. If it was a heart attack, she could see another issue; when Bruce had fallen, he'd landed against the spike of his hurlbat. Blood was pouring from the puncture in his shoulder. "Get me something to apply pressure; a bar towel or anything," she ordered Bruce's friend, who stood frozen at the sight of blood.

Ella checked for a pulse. It was faint but still there.

"Here." Lil held out the bar towel but Ella grabbed her hand and tugged her down. "Put pressure on this. Don't let up."

The owner arrived with an overstuffed red canvas bag. "There's an AED in here."

Ella ripped at the velcro enclosure. The first aid kit was fully equipped for a wound and for Bruce's obvious cardiac arrest. She slashed his t-shirt open with the shears to find that Bruce was a particularly hairy guy.

"I need the duct tape," Ella barked but the owner looked confused. "There's always something for hair removal with the kit. The pads don't adhere well to hair." Ella found the roll and drew out two lengths, applying each to the location on his chest where she was about to place the AED pads.

It all happened in a blink. Ella was in charge; what she said is what everyone in the room did. The man's face went purple and Ella checked again for a pulse. It was gone.

"Starting compressions," she yelled, and with palms down, fingers laced together, she started pumping his chest. She knew the rhythm; she'd done this hundreds of times in her career, so her sights were laser focused.

"Did someone call 911?" She didn't pause.

Peter, the bar owner, had the phone against his ear. "I'm on with them now."

Ella felt Bruce's ribs crack with each compression, but she kept going. "Come on, Bruce."

Lil was stunned by the scene—frozen in place, afraid to lift the wad of towels, but also worried about getting in Ella's way. She scooted herself above his head.

"You're fine, Lil. If his heart isn't pumping, neither is his blood." The flaps of the fabric impeding her leverage, Ella paused to pull off her flannel shirt, tossing it behind her. Bruce wasn't a large man but it was taking all Ella had to compress his chest, and she wished for a second set of experienced hands.

"You know how to do this?" she asked Lil.

Lil nodded.

"I need to get the AED attached. Follow my rhythm so we can switch."

It was a clumsy maneuver as Lil scooted to the man's right side while Ella worked from the left.

"Don't stop." Ella looked into her friend's eyes. "Keep going, no matter what you feel beneath your hands."

"Okay." Lil choked out the word. Seconds later, she understood what Ella meant when she felt the movement of ribs with her first compression. She remembered the lecture from her first aid class. The instructor was insistent when he told them compressions would break ribs. The dummies they learned on were soft but firm. They were nothing like the reaction of a real person.

"Stop compressions, Lil. It needs to take a reading." Ella had the leads attached and when she activated the defibrillator a recorded voice began barking commands.

"Shock advised," the machine's mechanical voice said, and Ella held Lil in place.

"Stay clear. You don't want to be touching him when the machine goes off." Ella waited for the orange light to indicate a full charge. She pressed the glowing button.

"Shock delivered," the mechanical voice said, followed by the command, "Start CPR."

The entire incident played out in less than two minutes but it felt like hours to Lil. She was out of breath and her forehead was sweating, but she was relieved when Ella guided her hands back to the bleeding wound.

Ella hovered over him, continuing to pump his chest. She noticed the time on her watch, making mental notes for the EMS team when they took over.

The arrival of the ambulance and the unit inside was a blur to Lil. Unlike Toni, she'd never experienced Ella in action and she was humbled by the firefighter's command of the scene.

Ella never stopped doing compressions as they loaded her along with Bruce into the ambulance. "Where are we taking him?" she asked the driver.

"BMC," he answered without pause.

"Follow me to Blacktree Medical Center," she said to Morgan as they exited the building. "That's where we're headed." Emergency lights flashed red and white across the wall of the bar, casting a strange glow on the women left behind.

Lil's clothes were covered in blood.

"Let's go wash your hands." Toni led her to the first bathroom.

Lil was trembling, disoriented by what she'd experienced and clearly a little shocked.

Toni turned on the water, checking it was the right temperature. "I'm going to put your hands under here." She was gentle as she helped wash the blood away.

"Do you need anything?" Morgan asked from the doorway.

"I've got her, if you need to go after Ella."

Morgan didn't hesitate. "I'll call and check on both of you later."

26.

The Toll

The ambulance was parked in the emergency-room bay at Blacktree Medical Center. "Eastman, we need to shock." The paramedic touched Ella's shoulder to pause compressions as they activated the defibrillator.

Ella's hands were up in the air. "This guy is all over the place." She wasn't only talking about his blood on her jeans. He hadn't stabilized at any point of their transport.

The paramedic entered notes on the computer. "Good thing you were there when it happened."

"Having an AED saves lives." She was about to share the story about the kit hanging in the hallway at Morgan's rage rooms when the rear doors of the ambulance flew open, and the gowned team of doctors started asking questions. Ella stayed to the side, allowing the on-duty crew to take charge of Bruce's care. Ella exited through the side-access door, hopping down to the concrete floor to stay clear of the activity.

As her feet hit the pavement, her life with Morgan and her life as an emergency services team member, which rarely overlapped, felt like the collision of two worlds. It wasn't only Ella who'd reacted. It was Morgan and Toni, and the most involved was Lil.

Ella washed her hands in the sink of the patient transfer bay, doing the first full inspection of her clothes. She had blood on her shirt and pants and patted her chest, realizing she'd left her flannel on the floor at the bar. "Shit," she cursed. She knew Morgan was sitting outside waiting in Charlene, and there was no way she could go back tonight, not discretely. She was beginning to think there was a curse on her and the plan for a perfect proposal.

"I brought you some scrubs." The EMS driver set them on the cart along with a red plastic bag.

"Thanks," Ella said. The transfer bay wasn't terribly busy, but she also didn't care who saw as she tugged off her shirt and pants to slip into well-worn scrubs. She stuffed her clothes into the red biohazard bag, and heard her phone buzz through the plastic. It was still in her pants pocket. In the twenty minutes it had taken to arrive at the hospital, the phone had missed three calls from Morgan and two from an unknown number she assumed would be Toni with information about Lil.

She called Morgan first. "Hi baby."

"Hi," Morgan answered, unsurprised to hear the fatigue in Ella's voice. "I'm in the ER parking lot. I'll be here when you come out."

Ella was already headed toward the exit. "I'll be there in a minute." When she pushed through the door, she saw Morgan. The artist was leaning against the car, hand resting on Charlene's hood as if nothing traumatic had happened in the last hour. She was perfect standing there, and in every way what Ella needed. "You're exactly who I need right now." She locked eyes with her lover, continuing the phone conversation as she approached.

"The only place I'd ever be," Morgan said. She noticed the bright red biohazard bag, understanding that if Ella was wearing scrubs, things must have worsened in the back of that ambulance.

"That's why I love you." Ella ended the call and the bag fell from her hands as she wrapped her arms around her lover, holding tightly. She kissed the top of Morgan's head. "Thanks for following us."

Morgan could feel Ella's heartbeat against her cheek and had a thousand questions. She asked the most important one. "Are you okay?"

"Yeah, I'm fine, but Bruce isn't doing as well." Her arm fell over Morgan's shoulder as she walked them to the passenger side door.

"I brought his cousin Ted with me. He's probably in the waiting room." Morgan leaned against the door, preventing Ella from opening it. "I called someone to come and meet him here. Bruce's sister is on the way, too. You can learn a lot about someone in a short car ride."

Ella shrugged. "My ride was definitely different than yours." She tried to lift the door handle but Morgan squeezed her fingers around Ella's. "You need to let me drive."

"Do I?"

Morgan stood her ground. "I know you. As much as I understand this is what you do, I also understand you're about to crash from what we've just been through and I'd rather be behind the wheel when you do."

"Very smart."

Morgan opened the door and waited for Ella to sit before walking around to the driver's side. She picked up the bag and tossed it behind her seat.

Ella's phone buzzed. "I think this might be Toni." She showed the display to Morgan.

"Possibly. You want me to answer it, just in case?" Morgan offered. Charlene's key ring dangled in the ignition but she waited to start the engine.

Ella answered. "Ella Eastman." She knew she sounded gruff, but if it wasn't Toni or Lil she didn't want to talk to the mystery caller at that moment. The line was silent. Ella checked the display. "There's no one there."

Morgan started the car. "If it's important, they'll call again."

~~~~~~~~~~

The shell-shocked duo sat parked outside Lil's duplex in Toni's ancient Toyota pickup truck. Lil was numb and she couldn't wrap her thoughts around the events of the evening.

"Can I walk you in?" Toni asked, trying to break the silence that had settled during the drive.

Lil nodded but reconsidered quickly. "Nah, I've got this." She opened the car and didn't say a word as she walked to her front door. She stopped, staring at the lock as if she couldn't remember what should happen next.

Toni was there, taking the key from Lil's hand to open the door. "What can I do?" she asked, but Lil was already moving down the long hallway. Lil stepped out of her shoes, pulled open her button-up shirt and kicked off her pants. "I need a shower" was all she said as she turned into what Toni could only guess was the bathroom.

Toni worked her way down the hall, picking up the discarded clothing. She'd never been inside Lil's place, and as she walked through on her quest to find the washing machine she was aware of how tidy the duplex was. There were no discarded take-out containers on any surface or piles of clutter to be found. The trail of clothing was an obvious anomaly, which made her worry about Lil being in shock.
~~~~~~~~~~

She tried to call Ella again, but there was no answer. "She's probably still at the hospital," she whispered to herself as she located the washer and dryer just off the kitchen. She emptied the pockets of Lil's pants and thought it was a very personal act, but necessary to clean the bloodied clothes. She listened for the shower but couldn't hear any running water.

She knocked on the bathroom door. "Lil," she called to her but there was no answer. "Lil," she said again as she pushed the door open. The woman stood in front of the shower, completely naked but making no move to turn the water on.

Toni couldn't help but stare at a body so different from her own. Lil's build was thick, fully clothed, but naked she looked different. Her shoulders were powerful but not defined by muscle. Her back told a story with scars Toni couldn't identify. Lil had a history she kept hidden well.

"Lil." Toni leaned close to her ear, afraid to startle her from behind. "Lil, you need to get in." She kept repeating her name, hoping it would break her from the haze.

Lil turned her palms up. "There's so much blood on me," she said, barely above a whisper.

Toni kicked off her shoes and stripped out of her own clothes. She wasn't thinking about anything other than helping this woman through the task of a simple shower. She stepped beneath the spray, deflecting the shock from the water contacting Lil directly.

She grabbed a washcloth off the towel bar and pumped soap on it. "I'm going to wipe your hands, honey." She touched Lil with the towel and the woman didn't react. She moved slowly, explaining each touch before it happened as she carefully cleaned the blood away. She noticed it then: the two jagged lines, long-healed wounds. Bigger, stitched stripes mirroring those on her back. "What happened to you?" she whispered. But Lil just stood in the spray.

Toni was trying not to look at Lil's body as she washed away the damage of the evening, but it was impossible to miss the tattoo on Lil's thigh. The artwork was lifelike and detailed even if she couldn't identify the furry creature. The date above it was more than twenty years ago. Toni tried to decipher the tattoo but also couldn't ignore the beautiful art was covering marks made from self harm.

Looking at Toni, Lil knew that a part of her past was no longer private. Lil closed her eyes, hoping to shut out Toni's stare. Very few people in her life knew about the origin of her scars: Cove, her therapist, and the tattoo artist, but not Morgan or Ella. Until this moment, she had been able to keep them a secret.

Toni was there. She didn't care about Lil's physical differences, she only cared about the hurt behind those closed eyes. "Hey, it's okay," Toni whispered. "It'll be alright. I've got you."

Lil stepped into her arms, needing the contact of another. Her tears came, falling with the pulsing stream of the shower's spray. She'd seen death up close more than twenty years before and experienced the act of dying. It was like the twenty-year gap was gone and she didn't know where to put the emotions bombarding her.

Toni held her. It was all she could do until the spray began to cool. "We should get out." She turned the water off and helped Lil out. She dried their bodies, took hold of Lil's hands and led her down the hall to the bedroom. It felt intrusive to go through her chest of drawers, but the air was cool, and without night clothes, a chill was sure to follow.

Toni helped her into a pair of sweatpants and a t-shirt, and she borrowed some for herself. There was nothing left to do but pull back the covers and guide Lil beneath the blanket. She tried one more time to phone Ella, but with no answer again, she decided sleep might be their best option.

She walked through the duplex, turning off all the lights and locking the front door. She paused in front of the second bedroom's open doorway. The walls were filled from floor to ceiling with built-in shelves. There was very little space for anything but the numerous Briick building sets on them. Lil was not as casual about her collection as Toni had been led to believe. The drawstring contraption in the corner was a curious thing, and she couldn't wait to ask Lil about it and so many other things.

Tomorrow she would offer the opportunity to talk about the accident and maybe get a few answers about those scars. She also was slightly curious to know why Lil downplayed her obvious passion for the Briickhead world. For now, she was tired and wanted nothing more than Lil's warm body beside her while she slept.

~~~~~~~~~~

Lil listened to the light squeaky snore coming from the woman next to her and was pleased Toni had stayed. The noise hadn't woken her, and it was a welcome sound after the nightmare she'd experienced seconds before. She recognized her clothes were different from when she'd arrived home, and smiled at the sight of Toni in her favorite pride Briick figure comic sleep shirt.

She didn't want to wake Toni. It was only half past four in the morning and she needed to stay in this quiet space for the entire day. She'd call her therapist in a few hours. There was too much to unpack from the incident last night.

Toni adjusted, rotating her head to get closer to Lil.

Lil remembered the shower, the dreadful walk as she stripped down the hall. She would have been embarrassed by it but all she could think about was that the sleeping woman must have seen all the scars.

Lil brushed the hair from Toni's face. "Good morning."
~~~~~~~~~~

Toni buried her cheek against Lil's body and chuckled at the awkwardness of it. "Hi." She rested her chin on her chest. "How are you feeling?"

Lil tried to get up, but Toni's body kept her from escaping to avoid answering the question. She didn't know how to express what she was feeling, because she wasn't sure herself. Anything she might share was weakness, and that wasn't going to make a great impression. Not after last night's zombie-like behavior.

"It's okay if you aren't okay," Toni whispered.

Lil chuckled. "Yeah?"

Toni nodded, pushing up to look into Lil's eyes. "Yeah."

"I suppose you saw my stuff?"

Toni nodded again. "It must have been hard for you?"

"It was, until I got help."

"It's important to ask for what you need," Toni whispered. "And get help."

"Thanks for being here this morning and for everything last night."

Toni held her tighter. "I'm glad you let me."

"I'm not sure I could have done anything for myself last night." Lil rolled onto her back.

Toni lay beside her, afraid to look into her eyes. "Do you want to talk about it?" she asked.

"Nah, I don't think I do right now." She coupled their hands.

"Will you talk to me when you're ready?" She squeezed Lil's hand.

"Yeah, I promise I will."

Toni rolled to lay against Lil. "That's good enough for now. You seem like the kind of woman who keeps her promises.

"I try."

"So can we talk about your spare bedroom, instead?"

Lil turned so they were face to face, her cheeks blushing. "You saw it?"

"I wasn't snooping. The door was open."

"And?"

"There's a lot going on in there?" Toni chuckled. "Like, a lot, and you've got a weird rack or something hanging in the corner."

"It's a drawstring shape sorter," Lil explained, but the look on Toni's face was an obvious indicator that the woman did not understand. "Come with me and I'll show you."

"You're going to let me play with your toys?"

Lil chuckled. "Yes, I think I am."

The walk through the room was slow, and Toni asked many questions about the history of what she deemed Lil's 'toys'. The contractor was slightly offended by the reductive use of the word 'toy', but once she explained the history behind the older sets, Toni seemed to understand why the sun-faded mini brick buildings and vehicles were under dust proof acrylic domes.

Lil was replacing her mini replica of the sphynx when Toni left the room to take a call.

"That was Penny." She waved at her phone. "She needs to run out to restock supplies for a wedding. I really should go and keep the shop open."

"I'm glad you could stay and see all this."

Toni stepped into the Briick room. "I never expected the big tough builder who fixed my shop was also a builder of little things too," she teased as she leaned in the doorway.

"That's not the only surprise you'll find if you go out with me again," Lil said.

"Are you asking me out on another date?"

Lil nodded. "Yes, and this time we can keep it less dangerous."

Toni leaned in for a kiss. "I think I'd kinda like that."

The kiss was slow, promising more to come. "Then it's a date."

"It very definitely is."

27.

The Hunt

Ella sat parked outside Lil's building at well past nine in the morning. The contractor's truck wasn't in its designated space, but a small pickup was. She walked down the path, hoping Lil hadn't been left alone and that Toni had stayed through the night.

She knocked twice and waited.

The curtain over the door's etched-glass window moved and Toni's face peeked out. "Hi," she whispered as she opened the door.

"Hi," Ella said a little louder. "Is she awake?"

Toni shook her head. "She's—"

"She's awake," Lil said from the hallway. She was barefoot and still wearing the clothes Toni had dressed her in the night before.

"Hey," Ella said.

Lil gave her a quick wave. "Come in." She stepped toward the kitchen. "Sit." She pointed at the bar stool tucked beneath the eat-in kitchen counter.

"I made coffee," Toni said as she followed Lil. She'd been awake for hours, never resting completely after Lil kicked her awake after a dream.

Ella snickered as she watched Lil watching Toni navigate her kitchen, knowing how territorial the single woman was. "Thanks."

"You sit, too." Toni pulled the bar stool out for Lil. "How do you take your coffee?" she asked.

"Exactly as it comes from the pot," Lil said.

"Same," Ella said.

"Easy enough." Toni began opening the kitchen cabinets looking for the mugs.

"Left of the sink," Lil instructed.

"Over the coffee pot." Toni smiled as she poured three cups. "Genius location," she mumbled as she set the coffee in front of the women.

"Lil is handy like that," Ella said as she blew across the top of her mug. This was not a moment for their usual banter or teasing. She needed to help her friend through the events of last night.

The energy in the kitchen was weird. Toni felt like the odd one out as she watched the two strong butch personalities struggle with expressing vulnerability. She wondered if her presence was part of the problem. "I'm going to grab the laundry and change out of these borrowed clothes," She tugged at the hem of the oversized t-shirt.

"Okay," Lil said, disappointed that Toni would probably leave without a proper thanks for everything she'd done through the night and into the morning.

Ella waited until Toni closed the bedroom door before asking, "How are you doing?"

Lil shrugged. "Okay, I guess. Last night was a lot for me."

Ella nodded. "I know."

Lil interrupted. "I don't get how you watch people dying day after day." She squeezed the mug with both hands, clearly uncomfortable with how she was feeling. "He was dead. I don't think I could see what you do and..."

"Yeah, it isn't easy," Ella said. She sipped her coffee and listened, knowing that the most important thing right now was Lil expressing how she felt.

"I couldn't do it, man. I just couldn't."

"Not everyone can."

Lil blew across the top of the mug. "I was kinda out of it last night."

"To be expected," Ella said.

Lil wasn't ready to talk seriously about the sight of blood and the traumatic memories it brought up. "If Toni had nefarious plans, she could have robbed me blind last night."

"It's a good thing she's not a bad seed."

The bedroom door opened and Toni moved noisily, making it obvious she was returning to the kitchen.

"I left the clothes on the bed," she explained. "I think I'm going to head out." She pointed to the door. "My florist is in to open for me, but I hate leaving her there to run the whole shop."

Ella set her mug in the sink. "I'm gonna go." She nodded at Lil. "You call me if and when you need to talk." She pulled a card from her wallet. "This is a friend of mine. He runs a support group for EMS team members and works with trauma survivors. You might not think it now, but tomorrow you'll feel different and if it's hard... don't be brave, call him if you don't want to call me." She set the card on the counter beside Lil's mug. She rolled her hand into a fist and Lil gave it a little bump. It was as close to a hug either of them would get from the other.

"Thanks, Ella." Lil stood to walk her out.

"Don't get up." Ella stepped backward as she addressed Toni. "Thanks for staying with her. I was glad to see she didn't drive last night."

"I was glad to stay."

Ella was out the door without another word.

Lil leaned against the counter. "I don't suppose you could stay for breakfast?" she asked.

Toni set her mug in the sink and collected Ella's. She wanted to stay but she was also feeling like she'd crossed about a hundred boundaries in the last twelve hours. Before last night, they were casual friends but now she had more information about this woman's vulnerabilities than she'd had throughout her two-year relationship with Mandy.

"I've been in your fridge; what you've got to offer isn't terribly impressive," Toni mocked.

Lil walked around the kitchen counter, approaching Toni where she stood. She leaned in, her body close as she reached over to pour another cup of coffee. Toni didn't move away and Lil grinned. "Those are called ingredients. And if you stay, I will impress you with how well I can put them together."

"Yeah?"

"Yeah, but with an Italian name like Antionette I'd have guessed you could cook," Lil teased.

"Who said I couldn't cook?"

"Your assessment of my refrigerator was a big clue."

"Can I, can't I. I guess it'll remain a mystery." Toni grinned. "At least for now."

"I can live with that." Lil wanted to kiss her, and felt the heat of their bodies and the closeness from the trauma bonding them together. "I'd kinda like to thank you for last night."

"You don't need to." Toni's voice was breathy, anticipatory, as she was drawn to Lil.

"I think I do, but right now I'd really like to kiss you."

"Yeah?" Toni whispered, and Lil nodded, one hand on the counter and the other drawn away so as to not spill the coffee. She was so focused on the hot liquid that the touch of Toni's lips were a welcome surprise.

The kiss was brief, it wasn't smoldering, but Lil felt energized by the newness of the touch.

"That was nice," Toni whispered as they parted.

Lil didn't move. "Oh yeah, it was, and you should do it again."

Toni took the steaming mug from Lil's hand and placed it on the counter.

"Getting serious," Lil joked before Toni's lips pressed against hers. The gentleness of their lips touching made Lil want to stay in her kitchen forever. She opened her eyes.

Toni was staring, pleased with herself. "You're a good kisser."

"Stick around and you'll find out what else I'm good at."

Toni raised a curious brow.

"I meant, stick around for breakfast."

Toni returned the mug to Lil and sat at the kitchen counter. "Since I've already seen you naked, I guess you'll have to wow me with your culinary talents."

Lil spat the coffee back into her cup. "Oh, ouch." There were a dozen thoughts filling her head because Toni had seen her naked, which meant she'd seen the scars and the tattoo on her thigh and so many other reminders of her high school trauma. She didn't know what to say.

Toni saw her panicked expression. "I didn't mean to bring up—"

"You didn't," Lil interrupted. She wiped her mouth on a towel and dumped her cup in the sink, realizing she had a choice to make: trust Toni with her most private memory or shut her out along with the past. She wasn't about to waste twenty years of therapy because she liked Toni more than a little.

"I went to Saturn League High," she said, certain that was enough to explain everything.

"Is that local? I'm not sure where that is."

"It isn't local." Lil continued, "It's not anywhere close to Blacktree, and that's kinda why I live here." She opened the refrigerator and removed the ingredients to make french toast or omelets. Knowing what she was about to share from her past, she didn't have an appetite for either. "Pancakes or eggs?" she asked.

"Whichever is easiest," Toni said.

"I'll make eggs."

Toni didn't care about eggs or pancakes; she only wanted to understand Lil and whatever had left the marks all over her body.

"Last night wasn't the first time I've held my hands on the wound of a dying person." Lil avoided Toni's reaction by rinsing the frying pan and placing it on the stovetop. "More than twenty years ago, Saturn League High was the site of a mass shooting. I was there. My buddy Cove was there, and we…" She paused to clear her throat. "We were in the cafeteria eating lunch when it happened."

"Those wounds are from being shot?" Toni asked.

Lil nodded.

"And Cove?"

"They were lucky, they weren't shot. They went down to help the person beside me. I covered both of them and that's when I got hit. We dragged May to the access elevator and stopped it between floors. She bled to death, and if it wasn't for Cove, I would have, too." Lil didn't stop. Once the memories started to spill out, the details were like a film playing in her mind's eye. "The shooter was a student. A dumb, spoiled kid with too much freedom. Emphasis on the dumb." She added, "It came out later that he was called by God to kill. I'm not sure how that makes sense." She began chopping tomatoes to make omelets.

"And the stuff on your leg?"

Lil paused her knife. "Stuff." She snickered at the understatement. "The honey badger ink or the scars that it's covering?"

"You cut yourself?" Toni asked.

Lil nodded, thinking it ironic that they were discussing her self-harm while she was slicing the ingredients for their breakfast.

"I can't imagine how hard it was," Toni said.

"Honestly, I'm glad you can't imagine it," Lil replied. "I had a lot of emotions after. I hid in my room and I got lost in the silence. May was gone. Cove and I didn't talk for a long time. I wanted to go away to college, but I was drifting. Cutting made me feel something besides all the nothing. Does that make sense?"

Toni nodded. "It does."

"It better." Lil opened the carton of eggs. "Because I've spent about a thousand hours discussing it with my therapist."

Toni was curious about the cover-up. "Why did you get the tattoo of a honey badger?"

Lil cracked the eggs. "The badger was our school mascot but it means more than that to me. I isolated myself from people, from going out in public, and then there was the numbness…" She paused to collect her thoughts. "Numbness makes feeling anything… it's just nothing. During a session, my therapist made an observation comparing me to the fearlessness of the animal on our school's logo. I argued that I didn't feel fearless and she insisted that taking the step to ask for help took courage. Going to therapy and feeling all the emotions that came after took courage, too. So when I stopped cutting, I wanted to cover those scars."

"With a badger?"

Lil looked up from her task. "Have you ever seen a real one? They're fierce."

"The ink looks fierce." Toni agreed. "But what about the scars on your back and side?" she asked.

"Wounds from the gunshot and shrapnel." Lil beat the eggs and poured them into the hot pan. "I don't know why I haven't covered them. I think about it sometimes, but those scars are different. I didn't cause them; they're what's left of Lilith before she had to survive. I don't want to erase her."

Toni didn't understand and she wondered if she ever could.

Lil was so focused on cooking that she didn't notice Toni get up from her seat and move behind her until a hand stilled hers.

"Thank you for telling me."

"You're welcome." Lil added, "I've never told Ella and Morgan about it."

"Why?" Toni asked.

"It'll change our friendship and I don't want that." Lil folded the eggs. "I'm kinda worried it'll change the way you see me."

"I promise it hasn't and it won't." Toni took the spatula and the task of cooking. "Let me wow you with my ability to burn breakfast."

"I didn't mean to get so serious." Lil leaned against the counter, afraid to abandon the contents of the frying pan.

"I asked, and I'm glad you trusted me with a very complicated part of your past."

Lil didn't know what to say or how to explain why she'd shared so much with Toni, but she was glad she had. "Thank you for listening and for staying last night." Lil set two plates beside the cooktop.

Toni flopped an omelet onto each plate. "You're welcome."

28.

The Breakthrough

Ella wasn't convinced that Lil would reach out for help, but she was glad to see that she hadn't been alone after the way their evening had ended. Ella was on a new mission to retrieve her flannel shirt and recover the ring she'd left buttoned in the pocket.

She was listening to Morgan's book club selection while she drove. This one had a twist she didn't expect and she liked where it was going. A great romance needs a great story arc, and the main character's scavenger-hunt plan to find true love was silly but at the same time quite entertaining. A personal love note leading to the next love note was genius, Ella thought. It was perfect; blasting all of her previous plans to the side, this would be it. Morgan would think she was being romantic, acting out the book.

As she drove to the Axe bar, she was glad her previous attempts had failed. Leading Morgan to all their favorite places, revisiting each with a special message, and one leading to the other, would be more than perfect.

She parked outside the bar, hoping it wasn't too early for anyone to be there. The closed sign was up and as she peeked through their window the bar was dark and there wasn't a person in sight.

She dialed the number on the front door and reached their voicemail. Leaving a message was her only option. "Hi, My name is Ella Eastman and I was in your shop last night when the ambulance was called. I left my shirt there and I'm wondering if you'd hold on to it so I can come by and pick it up?" She didn't leave a number as she ended the call. Her three-day shift started tomorrow so she'd make time to come back later in the day.

Taking off her shirt and leaving the ring behind was an absolute blunder. "Why can't I get this right?"

~~~~~~~~~~

Ella returned to the Axe bar twice, finding the doors locked and the building empty. She'd left her name and number during her most recent phone message and asked anyone who heard it to please call her back. A few hours into her three-day shift, the owner confirmed that if the shirt was there when they locked the doors, the shirt was there now.

"Are you sure it's still there?" Ella asked.

"The bar hasn't opened and won't reopen until the biohazard is addressed," he explained. "Since we couldn't get an appointment with a professional team for a few days, we're out of town to pick up some equipment for the brewery."

"No one's going in without you there?" Ella sighed, feeling relieved that the shirt was secured in the building.

"You'll be the first person, aside from the cleaning crew," he assured Ella.

"I appreciate that," she said. "Thanks for the help." She knew the ring was safe, but she didn't want to wait another
~~~~~~~~~~

week to execute her new plan. She had two days to think about it, to create a map of their relationship, one perfect location at a time. This was it. This was finally Operation PP.

~~~~~~~~~~~

Ella sat in the parking lot of the gym, the darkness outside her car window creating the perfect vibe as she listened to the end of the current chapter of the book club choice. It was romantic but not without the excruciating heat of the main characters' smoldering slow burn and she didn't want to stop listening and break the poetically written spell.

She jerked, startled, when Marsh knocked on the glass of her car door's window. "You coming in, or you taking a nap?"

She pressed pause. "I'll be right in." She hit double-speed, and although it wasn't as poetic, she got through the chapter. She knew her head was somewhere else as she pushed through the gym door.

She was distracted as they worked through their arm-day routine. Thoughts of losing Morgan's ring were making her more than a little uptight, but coming up with the perfect proposal tipped the scales in the opposite direction.

Marsh was on his back, a full bar of weights above him as he focused on his bench-press lift.

"I've got it," Ella said as she leaned in to spot him.

"You better," he grunted as he raised the weights toward Ella's face.

"Not the weights, dummy. The proposal."

She cupped her hands beneath the bar as Marsh pressed it up and down to complete his final set. She didn't take the seriousness of their workout lightly, and held her explanation until he pushed through the final rep.

He ducked from under the bar. "You have a new plan for Operation PP?" He was almost more excited than she was.
~~~~~~~~~~~

"I do, and I think it might be my best one yet."

He waved, encouraging her to continue. "Do tell."

"The first thing I've got to do is get a temporary ring." Ella unclipped the plate on the bar to adjust for her set.

"You lost the ring?" He paused as she slid a twenty-five pound weight on top of the plate he'd just racked.

"I didn't lose it. I just left it behind and I haven't been able to go back and get it," she explained.

"I swear you and that ring are gonna give me a heart attack."

"Funny you'd say that." She chuckled and began the long story of their night out, the Axe bar, and the trauma her foursome had experienced. Marshal listened and was still a little disappointed by the choices Ella had made.

"You put it in your shirt pocket?" he scolded.

"After that entire story, that's what you ask me?"

"Well, yeah," he scoffed. "What were you thinking?"

"Under any other circumstances, it would have been safe with me."

He unwound his wrist wraps and stuffed them in his gym bag. "Maybe you should give the ring to someone who won't lose it."

"You mean someone like Morgan?" She grinned.

"Exactly!"

"And this is where the scavenger hunt plan comes into play." She wiped down their bench and tossed the paper towels in the trash as they exited.

"Did you consider it'll be dangerous to recruit our mutual friends for this scavenger hunt plan?" Marsh shouldered his bag as they left the gym.

"None of you have leaked Operation PP yet, so I think it can work."

"And you got the idea from a romance novel?"

Ella shook her head. "Yes and no. The scavenger hunt, for sure, but revisiting our love story came from all the romance novels and from my life with her."

He was skeptical. "You are aware there are a few gossips in our crowd of friends."

"I know." She glared as she made a zipping motion across his lips.

Clearly offended, he insisted, "I can keep a secret."

"Mm-hmm." She explained her plan in detail, running through how she would tie together some of her favorite first experiences with Morgan to the places they'd been.

"I like it," Marshal said. "It's not very original, but it's extremely memorable."

"It's original for us," she insisted. "And romantic."

He nodded his agreement. "What's my role? Do I get a part in this installment of Operation PP?"

"The Sage plays a big part in the story of us. It was technically our first date, and you were there. So yes, you definitely have a role."

"You're a good egg, Ella." He smiled. "I think this might be your best plan yet."

She nodded. "Hopefully it'll be my last."

~~~~~~~~~~~

Ella grabbed the bell over the door as she entered the rage room, surprised and delighted to see Beatrice watching the monitors when she entered.

"Hey, hot stuff."

"How do you always know it's me?"

Beatrice didn't bother to turn around. "You are the only person who walks in here and grabs that ridiculous bell."

Ella released it. "Really?"

"Predictably so." She was focused on the monitors. "Morgan isn't here. Not in the rage rooms and not upstairs."
~~~~~~~~~~~

It was the first time Beatrice had been so forthcoming with Morgan's whereabouts.

"I know," Ella said. "I came to talk to you."

Beatrice spun around in her chair. "Really?"

"I need some help—"

"And you're coming to me for it?" Beatrice interrupted. "You must be desperate."

Ella pulled the step stool over so she could sit while she shared the details of Beatrice's role in her new plan.

~~~~~~~~~~

Ella stood outside the Axe bar in the pouring rain, wishing she could reach through the glass and find her shirt somewhere inside. The number rang and rang. "Empty your damn voicemail," she muttered. There was a sign taped to the door explaining why the shop was closed and that the owners would re-open in another week.

"Another week." She pressed her forehead to the window. "At least I'll have a funny story to tell Morgan."

~~~~~~~~~~

Ella checked her watch. She'd purposely chosen to stop by the flower shop a few minutes before closing time, hoping for a chance to talk one-on-one with Toni about a special request. She wasn't surprised to see Lil's truck parked out front.

"Two birds with one stone," she whispered as she pushed through the unlocked door.

Toni looked up from her desk. The sight of Ella in person still made her nervous, but after the night they'd had at the Axe bar a few days prior, the idol had become more human, although no less impressive.

"Hello, Toni." Ella leaned over the counter. It was the first time she'd been in the shop since the day of the fire. "Lil did a great job. I can't even tell there was damage."

"Hi Ella." Toni grinned. "Yes, I'm so happy with the work and very happy to have met Lil in the process." She pushed the stack of invoices to the side, clearing off space to work. "Are you here for a fire inspection or something else?"

"This visit is definitely something else, very personal, and I'm hoping you can help me solve a problem."

"You have a flower problem?" Toni suppressed a half-laugh. It wasn't the usual request from a customer, but Ella wasn't a usual customer.

"I have a ring problem."

"I don't sell jewelry," she said. "Not even made with Briicks."

"But you could make one from paper, yeah?"

Toni smiled a grin so big it lit up her face. "I definitely can."

"What are the two of you scheming?" Lil asked as she pushed through the greenhouse door carrying an armful of boxes.

Ella waved her closer. "Your new friend here is going to save me and save Operation PP."

"My friend?" Lil chuckled. "And how is my friend doing this?"

"Wait, I didn't mean to offend," Ella said.

Toni reached across the counter. "No offense taken." She held Lil's hand. "We are friends and more, and I'm honored to be part of this plan, but Operation PP?"

"It's a very long story and involves a very gay man who is also a big part of why I'm here."

"You've met Marshal. He's the manager from the Sage," Lil added.

"I have."

Lil bumped Ella's shoulder, playfully asking, "So what's my role in this chapter of Op PP?"

"Your role involves that truck out there and a temporary build at the end of a hiking trail at Spring Falls."

29.

The Third-Degree

Morgan pulled in beside Lil's truck on the construction site, trying to figure out what the extra noise was as she drove Charlene. She had a back seat full of plastic totes, each holding damaged light fixtures from an apartment remodel. She'd left room in the massive trunk to hold the dozens of glass bricks she was receiving from Lil's brickmason, and she didn't have time to take Charlene to their mechanic.

Lil waved at her to stop, and slid into the passenger seat, thinking it weird that Morgan was driving to see her in the huge car. "Hey, what's going on?"

"I was on my way to pick up some scrap from that demo on Fifth," Morgan explained, "and I hit a pretty deep pothole. Now I've got a funky sound when I'm driving."

"Funky sound," Lil teased. "Very technical jargon. I'm not sure I have the mechanical skills required to fix a funky sound."

"Oh, sass. Great, that's exactly what I need." Morgan nudged her shoulder. "You and Ella are so much alike."

"That's a compliment coming from you," Lil said as she made a hand gesture to steer. "Let's go for a ride."

Morgan drove around the block and it wasn't long before Lil heard the funky sound that was coming from Charlene's front tire.

"Pull into that parking lot over there," Lil directed. "I'm pretty sure you've thrown a few wheel weights. These old cars are heavy and can be finicky. If we were at the house, I'd be able to fix the tire. Let's put on the spare, just to be safe, and you can take it to a tire shop to rebalance the old one."

Charlene was Ella's baby, and Morgan was relieved to hear it was only a tire issue. When she found a level spot to stop, she engaged the parking brake and pressed the button inside the glovebox to open the trunk.

Lil walked around the car, checking the rest of the tires before she raised the trunk lid. She spotted some red flannel and pushed the trunk lid down so she could question Morgan about it. "Uh, Morgan?"

Morgan leaned out the door. "Yep?"

"In the trunk, the—"

"Is there not a jack? Oh shoot… no spare? But Ella would never drive Charlene without a spare." Morgan stepped around the car and raised the trunk lid. "They're both right here," she said. She attempted to remove the jack but it was heavier than she expected. The ancient Buick was built to last, and so was the jack.

Lil picked up the bundle of fabric, ignoring Morgan's struggle to remove the jack. She recognized the red flannel from the Axe bar and knew immediately it was the one Ella was desperate to recover.

"Where did you get this shirt?"

Morgan was confused. "It's Ella's."

"I know it's Ella's, but how did it get in Charlene's trunk?"

"I put it in there." Morgan leaned on the bumper, the jack resting against her leg as she tried to unscramble the puzzling questions about Ella's flannel shirt. "Why do you ask?"

"It's nothing." Lil was trying her best to pat the pocket discreetly but Morgan saw the odd behavior and called her out.

"What's in the pocket, Lil?"

At that moment, Lil questioned her whole existence in the universe. She should have played it cool, could have pretended anything other than practically shining a spotlight on the buttoned tight pocket of Ella's favorite flannel shirt.

"Nothing's in the pocket." She wadded it up in a ball and shoved it in the corner of the trunk. "Shit. Shit. Shit," she whispered to herself.

"Lil, you are the worst liar." Morgan uncrumpled the shirt. "What's the big secret about Ella's shirt?"

Lil shook her head. "She's going to kill me."

Morgan felt the breast pocket, unbuttoned it and held the drawstring bag in her hand, wondering and knowing at the same time what would be inside. "Spill!"

The tale of Ella's dream of perfection didn't take long to share. Lil avoided Morgan's reactions by focusing on raising Charlene and switching out the wobbly tire.

"So she's been planning this for months?" Morgan asked. She'd sat on the sidewall of the damaged tire, half in awe and half in frustration that Ella was working so hard to give her perfection when the woman was already that and so much more. "And you're all in on it?"

Lil grunted as she torqued the final lug nut, securing the tire on the car. "Yes. It's been me, Lester Feller from the station, Marshal, and she even asked Toni to help with a part."

Morgan was rubbing the textured jewelry bag, thumbing the embossed letters that read Gem's by Jem on the fabric. She wanted to look inside, but knew that if she did, it would spoil whatever dream Ella had of presenting it to her. She wouldn't take that beautiful moment away, but she was stunned that a marriage proposal was happening in the background of her life. Ella was always full of surprises.

"When is the execution of Operation PP supposed to happen?" Morgan chuckled at the name.

"Do you have to say execution?" Lil groaned. "It sounds like Ella kicking my ass for spoiling months of planning."

"Your ass is safe, I promise." Morgan smiled as she stood to help load the tire back into the trunk. "Tell me what day."

Lil was destroyed, feeling the full weight of spilling the beans on the plan. "Saturday night," she said. "My part is setting up the romantic picnic site at Spring Falls."

"And Les?"

Lil shrugged. "I only know what she asked me to do. You'll have to check with the others." She smacked her head. "She really is going to be so mad."

Morgan held the flannel shirt, folding it neatly after returning the ring to the pocket. She had plans for it and she had plans for every member of their friend group, too.

"I promise you, she will not be mad once we pull off this little switcheroo." She closed the trunk. "Operation PP, though? What the hell is the PP all about?"

"You'll have to ask Marshal to clarify that one." Lil climbed into the passenger seat. "From what I understand, he came up with the name. I think he wanted to keep things very covert and mysterious."

"And Ella let it…"

"Oh no, I think the PP was a serious no-go for Ella from the beginning."

Morgan started the car. "Maybe you should tell me a little more about what's been going on."

30.

The Switcheroo

Morgan sat at the rage room reception desk still a bit stunned. She cherished the home she'd made with Ella. After eight years as a couple, Morgan was content and in her heart they were already committed for life.

"I can't believe you," she whispered to the photo of Ella on her desk as she noted the finishing touches on her version of Operation PP. It felt more covert than devious, but once she'd grilled Beatrice, Marsh and Toni, Ella's plan was revealed in full detail. Morgan had a few ideas of her own.

~~~~~~~~~~

"Call for you." Lester nudged Ella. She was almost finished with the book club's romance, and the climax was not disappointing. She flipped the open book over to hold her page.

"Morgan?" she asked.

"Nah, some guy named Peter."
~~~~~~~~~~

Ella's chuckle was bitter. "Of course he calls now." She picked up the phone near the reception desk. "Ella Eastman," she said.

"Hi, this is Peter from the Axe bar. Sorry it's taken so long but—"

"Tell me I can come get my shirt?" she asked, cutting off his chance to continue an apology.

"We still can't let anyone inside."

Ella appreciated the call. "Are you re-opening?"

"We have to stay closed until we decontaminate." His frustration seemed insensitive to the medical emergency they'd experienced, but she understood how important it was to run a business that was so like the rage rooms. "That guy bled everywhere and there's only one company to call."

"I understand the protocols," she said, fiddling with a paperclip. "When will you reopen?"

"Tomorrow afternoon."

She smiled, knowing the ring would be in her hand tomorrow. "Do you mind if I stop by to grab the shirt?"

"I'll be here any time after two."

Ella hung up the phone. It didn't seem real that she'd finally have the ring in her hand and she could execute the new version of her proposal in twenty-four hours. She opened the group chat on her phone. The 'Op PP' title displayed at the top of the group text, and after weeks of mishaps the nickname wasn't quite as annoying. She messaged the group:

> Ella: Okay team. I'll have the ring tomorrow. Op PP is a go to start at 1700!
>
> Lil: great!
>
> Marsh: Yay, you finally got Peter!
>
> Lil: You did what with a Peter?
>
> Lester: Peter? I thought you were proposing to Morgan

Ella: @ Lester (middle finger emoji)
Beatrice: good one Les
Lil: 10/10 Les!
Ella: @group (middle finger emoji)
Les: (high five emoji)
Marsh: What is 1700 again?
Ella: 5pm
Beatrice: 5pm
Les: 5pm
Lil: 5pm
Marsh: thanks EVERYONE (brain explosion emoji)
Ella: thanks team, I think

Ella looked up when she heard Lester snickering on the other side of the room. "Fucker." She flipped the middle finger at him for real.

He yelled from across the room, "Watch it, Cinder, or I'll have to write you up."

~~~~~~~~~~

Ella climbed the stairs to the loft, expecting to find Morgan cozy on their couch with a book in her lap. The loft was quiet but she found a note on the kitchen counter.

Hi sweetie,

Missed you. Peter from the Axe bar called and he said you left a shirt at the bar. I'm running errands. I told him someone would swing by at four to pick it up.

Love you, see you at 4:30

S.W.A.K.

Sealed with a kiss. Ella cherished the sentiment as she checked her watch. If she left now she could get to the bar in
~~~~~~~~~~

time to intercept the shirt and prevent Morgan from finding the ring. She would also have time to send Morgan to point A of the scavenger hunt plan. She dropped her bag by the chair and didn't notice how many stairs she skipped on the way to the door. She raced by Beatrice.

"What's the hurry, Fire Babe?"

Ella paused in the doorway. "I'm intercepting Morgan."

"Sounds kinky," she teased as she pretended to look at her watch. "Hope you're done by 1700."

"I will be, don't you worry."

The bell jingled and Beatrice picked up the phone to send a text.

Beatrice: She just dashed out the door.

~~~~~~~~~~

Ella parked on the street in front of the bar. The sign on the building said 'open', and the relief was like having a truckload of rocks hoisted from her shoulder. She pushed through the door and found Peter wiping down the tables in the bar area.

"Can I help you?" he asked but recognized her quickly. "Oh, hey."

"Hey." She didn't waste any time as she knew Morgan would arrive soon. "I came to pick up that red-flannel shirt I left here."

He looked confused. "Someone came about a half hour ago."

Morgan checked her watch. "It's not four yet."

"They were early," he said. "Got time for a drink? I kinda owe you one or a dozen."

"Nah." She was trying to sort out the time overlap or underlap. "Weird, my girlfriend said four."
~~~~~~~~~~

"Oh, it wasn't the lady you came with. It was the other couple who picked it up." He stepped around the bar. "Here, one of them left this behind."

It was Lil's business card with a note scribbled on the back.

Got your shirt. Come grab it from me at Toni's shop. Don't worry, Op PP is in safe hands.

Ella chuckled. She had no idea how Lil knew about the shirt, and that Morgan was on the way to pick it up, or how Toni's role in Opp PP had grown again, but she was glad the ring was in safe hands. "Thanks, Peter. I can't stay right now but we will be back."

"Cool, thanks and glad you got the shirt."

She was out the door without looking back. Technically, she didn't have the shirt yet, but she had plenty of time to get the ring from Lil and still drive to the falls for Operation PP. It was difficult to move through afternoon traffic and not feel the pressure of her plan. This was it, finally.

She arrived at the flower shop twenty-five minutes after four and Lil's truck was parked out front. She wondered if the woman worked anymore.

Toni wasn't at the counter, and Ella wandered through the aisles looking for either of the women. "Can I help you?"

Ella was startled by the voice. "I'm looking for Toni?"

Cove paused with the cart of flowers positioned between them. "You just missed her."

Ella was more confused than ever. "Did she leave something for me?"

They grabbed the bundled paper. "Yep."

Ella had to unwrap the artfully folded square to read the message inside.

We got hungry waiting. I know you're nervous and haven't eaten all day. Come to the Sage and grab a snack and your shirt.

"Thanks for the help, Cove. Sorry I have to be rude and take off." Ella was not amused by the miscommunication and she was running out of time. "Come on, Lil." She dialed the number but her friend didn't answer. "Probably downstairs where the reception is bad," she mumbled as she pushed out the door.

> Cove: She just left the shop
> Toni: 10-4
> Cove: 10-4?
> Toni: I got caught up in the covert-y-ness.
> Cove: 10-4
> Toni : smartass

The caller ID on Ella's phone displayed Morgan's name. The current version of Operation PP seemed to be crumbling around her.

"Hi honey," Ella answered.

"Hi, I just got home and you aren't here. Everything okay?"

Ella wasn't physically out of breath but she was out of sorts. She should have waited at the loft and executed Operation PP without the physical ring, using the origami ring as planned. "Everything's fine. I'm just running errands myself," she explained. "I have one more stop and I'll see you later."

"Sounds good," she said. "I have a surprise for you."

Ella stopped beside Charlene, taking a moment to slow down and enjoy the woman she loved. "You know how much I enjoy surprises."

"I do," Morgan said. "See you soon."

"Bye, love." Ella felt a sense of calm as she ended the call, realizing that in that moment, Morgan's voice was exactly what she needed.

Ella made the short drive to the Sage Lounge to find Marsh working the front of the house. "Man, what are you doing here today?"

He didn't look up as he messaged.

Marshal: She's here

He put the phone in his pocket, shrugging the question off. "The real question is what are you doing here today?" He whispered through his teeth, "Operation PP was supposed to start at seventeen-hundred." He tapped his watch face sarcastically.

"Les has phase one under control, so we're good." She leaned around him, looking for Toni and Lil. "Is Lil here?"

"She's not, but she left something for you." He stepped around the bar and returned with a paper gift bag.

Ella thought it was weird, but the logo on the bag was from Toni's shop. They were probably trying to keep the ring from falling out of the pocket by putting it in the bag. She tugged the paper from the top but the shirt wasn't in there; instead a small Briick box was in its place.

Marsh handed her a notecard.

For Morgan, when you see her.

The card was bold block-style lettering in the way that only a few people she knew would write. "Are all of you out of your minds today?" She tucked the card in the bag. "This is not how Operation PP is supposed to go. At this point I'm not changing anything."

"What do you mean?" Marsh asked, working hard to keep Operation PP/ Switcheroo on track.

"It doesn't matter," she said as she felt her phone vibrate in her pocket. "Now what?" she answered without checking the screen. "Ella Eastman."

"Cinder, we've got a little problem with your plan."

She raised the paper bag in her hand as a wave to say goodbye to Marsh while she stepped outside to answer the call.

Marshal: she just left the building, bag in hand

"Soot, I'm beginning to think I've failed again." Ella opened the car door and slid in behind the steering wheel. She took the Briick box from the bag and began fiddling with it like a puzzle cube. She saw the hinged Briicks on one edge and the bar on the opposite side. The bar slid out easily and the top opened revealing an origami ring wedged between two thin rows of Briicks. A note fell out onto her lap.

For your sweetheart's finger.

"It's not that big of a problem, Cinder. I just need you to come over here and pick up a box. There was a mixup and Lil forgot one she was supposed to take to the falls."

Ella had made all the arrangements for Toni to help assemble the Briick potted flower sets the manufacturer had just released. Perfect timing to add to the proposal decor. All Lil had to do was pick them up and deliver them to the picnic spot set-up at Spring Falls. The plan wouldn't be difficult to fix but she wasn't sure why Les hadn't called Lil.

"I need to get to the falls," she explained. "Did you call Lil?"

"Lil isn't answering. Maybe she's already there."

"She was just at the Sage," Ella explained. "Blaah," she growled into the phone.

"Breathe, Cinder," Les soothed.

"I'm fucking breathing, Soot." Ella was second guessing her decision to get so many of their friends involved.

"Can you come get the stuff?" he asked.

Ella closed the lid on the Briick ring box creation and tucked it back inside the bag. It was a cute ring box, and as she drove the few blocks to Station Eight-Eighteen she decided to use it until she could track down the flannel shirt holding the morganite engagement ring.

Lester met Ella at her car. "Don't get out," he said. "Open the trunk and I'll put this in there."

Ella frowned. The box was bigger than expected and certainly held more than the set of Briick flowers she had asked Toni to build. "What's in that?"

He shrugged. "Whatever Lil was getting."

"Dude, if you're punking me with a fucking toaster oven today, I swear I'll wrap that cord around your neck and—"

"Cool down." He reached through her open car window. "No punking. I promise I wouldn't do that to you today."

"Alright." She started the engine. "If anyone needs anything now, we're screwed."

"It'll be fine," he assured her.

"I'm heading to the falls."

31.

Op P P

Ella settled in the driver's seat as she listened to the epilogue of the book club romance. It was setting the mood, and as each mile passed, so did a bit of anxiety from the chaos of the last few hours. As she approached her destination, she noticed immediately that the Spring Falls parking lot only had one vehicle in it, and it wasn't Lil's.

An accessible van was parked near the trail head sign-in, and Ella remembered choosing this place all those years ago for the paved paths that created safe walking for Morgan.

Her girlfriend was stronger now. With the help of braces and physical therapy, their safe walks had become hikes. This was the right place to continue their forever.

A person in a wheelchair was under the canopy, looking at the trail map.

Ella walked around her car to remove the box from her trunk, and squinted to get a closer look at the person coming toward her.

"Probie?" she asked. Of all the people in her life, he was the last one she expected to see there.

His chair coasted as he raised a hand from the wheel to wave. "Hey, Cinder."

"What the hell are you doing here, man?" She was thrown, her world tilting a little off balance. She hadn't heard from him since he told her about the baby, and although she'd sent a gift, she had yet to congratulate him in person.

"You should ask Morgan why I'm here."

Ella was confused. "What do you mean?"

"Come with me."

She followed him to the canopy where he'd been when she arrived. A collapsible canvas wagon was nestled behind a bush.

"Put your stuff in there."

Ella complied, teasing, "You're kinda bossy for a Probie."

He chuckled. "I'm not a Probie anymore, but I sure will grab any and every chance I get to boss you around."

"It's good to see you, Seb." Her heart felt full and somehow he quelled the sporadic energies of the day.

He pushed forward. "It's been too long."

"It has," she agreed. "So, you going to tell me what's going on?"

His smile was wide. "Nah, this is where I leave you."

She stopped.

"Follow the path to the falls," he said as he handed an envelope to her.

"You're not coming along?"

He shook his head and turned to go back to the parking lot. "You're on your own now, Cinder. I hope you can handle what's up there."

Ella stood in the middle of the path watching him go. The canvas wagon held her box, and for the first time, she noticed it was taped in an obvious manner to prevent any accidental or intentional peeking. She tucked her foot behind the wagon wheel to keep it from following Seb down the hill.

Sebastian: She's on her way

Four letters, S.W.A.K., were written on the flap of the envelope, and no one but Morgan would write them. "Sealed with a kiss," Ella read as she made cautious tears around the letters to open the envelope. Morgan's beautiful penmanship was on the card.

Meet me at our spot.

The reality of those words hit Ella straight through the heart. Her lover had pulled off one of the greatest double-crossing switcheroos in their romantic history.

She hardly felt the drag of the wagon as she ascended the hill. She wasn't following a trail of breadcrumbs, but as she approached the signs marking the way to the falls, she found folded origami hearts and cranes, each with a distinct dangling Briick attached.

Ella knew who was waiting for her and she was eager to arrive, so she paused just long enough to toss each collected piece in the wagon. After thirty, she'd lost count, as Morgan had tied the pieces to tree limbs when there weren't enough signs along the route.

She was near a light jog when she heard the rushing sound of water dashing against a wall of stone. She saw her then and it felt like the very first time. Ella was captivated, telling herself to draw this image of Morgan in the back of her mind. The way she stood, confident, never thinking for a moment that Ella wouldn't appear. Her dress was speckled with a rainbow of color that eventually turned to flowers as Ella drew closer. The faded denim jacket she wore over the top protected her shoulders from the day's sun. She was everything Ella dreamed a partner of being.

The handle of the wagon clunked to the surface of the pathway. Ella was done towing whatever Lil had left behind.

"Hello, there." Ella choked out the greeting, wanting more than anything to drop to one knee and ask for their future.

"Fancy meeting you here." Morgan held out her hand. "Come with me."

Ella moved to step forward.

"You should bring that." Morgan waved toward the wagon. "I've got plans for it."

Ella dragged the wagon, grasping Morgan's hand as they walked.

"Where are you taking me?"

Morgan teased. "Somewhere perfect, I think."

"Really?" Ella asked.

"It's come to my attention that my girlfriend has been trying to pull off the perfect proposal."

"You don't say."

Morgan stopped. "I do say, and it has also come to my attention that my girlfriend believes that in some alternate reality there is a way to imperfectly propose to me."

"Someone told me it was cheesy."

Morgan took hold of Ella's hands. "If you recall, I happen to be a very big fan of cheese."

Ella smiled. "You're making me feel like a teenage girl on a date with her very unattainable crush."

"Unattainable crush, huh?" Morgan guided their palms together, rotating them behind Ella's back. "That's pretty good street-cred for me after eight years."

"Very hot."

Morgan smiled. "So let's say I didn't know you were luring me to our spot, what was your plan?"

Ella liked this playful side of Morgan. The part where she was comfortable with every word and emotion between them. She had no idea on the day they'd met that this compact human could change her world. She released a hand to open the box in the cart. Lil was in charge of delivering the

Spring Falls elements of Operation PP. She patted her front and back pockets, remembering she never found time to change her clothes. "I don't have a kn—"

"Knife." Morgan held the box cutter in her free hand.

"Does your dress have pockets?"

Morgan chuckled as she dipped her hand inside one. "It does."

"Baby, that is so fucking hot." Ella was careful to slice the tape and not cut into the package. She was surprised when she opened the box. "What the hell?"

"You should put it on," Morgan whispered. "There's something very special in the pocket."

It was *the* red flannel shirt from the Axe bar. The one she'd chased all over town to find for this moment. "Lil had it?"

Morgan held the shirt like a jacket so Ella could slip it on. She brushed her fingers over the pocket. "Lil didn't have it. I did."

"What?" Ella was stunned. "When?"

Morgan slid her fingers through the collar to adjust the fit. "Honey, it was in Charlene's trunk the whole time."

Ella didn't know what to say. She was in shock, feeling betrayed and euphoric at the same time. "I think I need to sit down."

Morgan reached into the cart, hooking the looped handle of the little bag with her finger. "I was pretty sure you'd need to sit." She giggled as she abandoned the cart to lead Ella down the forest trail to the base of Spring Falls.

The picnic blanket was laid on the ground, the one Ella borrowed from Toni as part of her plan, and it looked perfect.

"Sit here." Morgan guided Ella.

"Are you going to—"

"Shh," Morgan touched Ella's lips with hers. "The rest of Operation PP is all yours."

Ella held Morgan's hand. Now that the moment was here, she didn't know what to say. "You realize, from the second I met you, my life went in ways I didn't know I needed it to."

Morgan smiled, slightly confused by the jumbled thought. "Good ways, I hope."

Ella nodded. "The very best ways, and I can't imagine living any of them without you." She rolled to her knees, feeling inside her shirt pocket for the drawstring bag. "Morgan."

"Yes."

Ella frowned. "You have to let me ask before you say yes."

Morgan was still standing, one hand in her pocket while Ella squeezed the other. She wondered for a second, if she let go, whether Ella would fall or fly, as the firefighter's nerves were the most out of character she'd ever seen.

Ella struggled to open the bag and Morgan helped, neither wanting to let go of the other's hand.

Morgan chuckled. "We make a great team."

"I'm pretty sure that's why we are here." Ella pinched the ring between her fingers, presenting it to her partner. "Morgan." She paused, waiting for a reaction to the stone.

"El."

"Yeah, baby. You mean everything to me and… will you be with me forever? Will you be my wife?"

Morgan fanned her hand, offering her finger. "Yes, I'll be your wife." The ring fit perfectly. Morgan admired the setting and the stone, which felt more than right. "Where did you find this?"

"I didn't find it. I had it made and you can't imagine the story behind me in a jewelry shop."

"I can't wait to hear it later," Morgan said through happy tears. "I'd really like to kiss you now."

"Funny, I'd really like to be kissed by you right now."

"Wait." Morgan turned away, quick to retrieve the small Briick box from Toni's flower shop. "Before I kiss my fiancée for the first time, I have to give her this." She opened the box and held the origami ring to Ella. "I think I already know the answer…" The ring was made from pink and white printed paper, with raised pointed angles folded to stand out like a diamond. "I know you won't wear a ring all the time, but I wanted to ask you with this one."

"Yes." Ella was on her feet, standing in front of Morgan with a smile she didn't think she'd ever tire of wearing.

"I didn't ask you yet," Morgan scolded.

Ella held out her hand and Morgan slipped the paper ring over her hearty knuckle. The overlap of the paper loop expanded to fit her finger. "Yes."

"Ms Impatient, are you going to let me ask?"

"Yes." Ella touched the ring and held Morgan's hand, steepling them to admire both rings at the same time.

"Ella Lane Eastman, will you marry me?"

Ella didn't want to cry, hadn't expected she would, but here they were with the waterfall in the background, and all she could see was their life ahead. "Yes, Morgan Elise Hail, love of my life, I will marry you."

The rest happened in slow motion as their arms came around one another, fingers tangled in hair and a passion-filled kiss sealed the promise of together and forever.

~~~~~~~~~~

"It's getting kinda cold." Morgan snuggled closer.

The sun had set hours before, and in the remote darkness, the billions of stars were shining so brightly Ella could hardly find a constellation amongst them.

Ella took off her flannel and wrapped it around Morgan.

"Your body is very hot."

"Thanks, baby." Ella fanned herself.
~~~~~~~~~~

"Not like that..." Morgan glanced at her. "Okay, like that, but also you got this shirt very warm for me."

"I'd do anything for you." Ella opened her legs and Morgan scooted between them, letting Ella cuddle tight.

"You've proven that a thousand times over." Morgan held the ring up to the moonlight.

Ella loved the way it fit. "I learned a few things about you while getting that stone."

Morgan twisted to look at Ella. "Really? Like what?"

Ella fiddled with the ring much like the way she thought Morgan had done with her granny's. "You're my rock."

"Sexy," Morgan teased.

"Wait, it gets better," Ella said. "You're also this rock. Morganite represents healing, inner peace and love, and you're all those things to me."

"I never thought about it that way."

"I've thought a lot about it," Ella shared. "When we met at that convention and we walked out together, I was already falling."

"I know." Morgan smiled. "You are easy to read. Well, easy for me because you let me in."

"Your love let me in, gave me a place to heal and find peace."

"That's a lot of responsibility," Morgan said.

Ella stood, holding a hand to help Morgan up. "My rock, my morganite, my divine love."

"I like that."

Ella scooped her into her arms. "I like it too."

32.

The Win

"Ooh, you smell so good," Morgan whispered into Ella's ear as they hugged.

"A shower can do that, you know," Ella teased.

"It's more than your shower; it's you." Morgan kissed the water droplet on Ella's neck.

"Should that turn me on? Because it seriously does."

Morgan tipped onto her toes. "It can do whatever you want." They turned from the bedroom doorway when the elevator cables squealed their awakening.

Beatrice barked as she stopped at the loft floor, "Get a room."

"Okay." Ella grabbed Morgan's hand, attempting to take her away.

"Not so fast." Morgan spun around, staying in the circle of Ella's arms as she attempted to greet her friend.

"Welcome to the party, Judas." Ella glared.

Beatrice pointed to herself with the bottle of sparkling cider. "I'm the betrayer?"

"One of many in this chosen family of ours." Ella wasn't serious; in fact, she was delighted by the way the proposal unfolded.

"Who's the betrayer?" Lester stepped aside as Lil and Toni entered.

"All of you jerks." Ella peeked around looking for someone else. "Where's Marshy Plum?"

"Phew," Lil mumbled as she shut the elevator gate, sending it back to the floor level.

"Lil's sound effects were making him nervous. He's coming up now," Les said.

"Perfect." Morgan set out a combination of glasses to celebrate their engagement with a sparkling cider toast.

The elevator returned a minute later and Marsh was there with an unexpected couple of guests.

"Seb." Ella sidestepped the rest of the group to get to him. "Twice in two days, man. Thanks for being here. Hi Sally." She hugged his wife. She was similar in height to Morgan, and the baby bump was starting to show.

"We couldn't be anywhere else; not tonight," she said.

Morgan hugged them both. "It's good to see you, and congratulations."

"Congratulations back to you." Sally smiled. "Thanks for including us and for making Seb a part of your special day."

"Morgan knew." Ella gave her fiancée's hand a little squeeze. "She's very smart like that."

"How does it feel?" Seb asked.

Although the switcheroo was unsettling in the moment, the outcome was all that mattered. "It feels like a new beginning, and ending, and whatever fits in between," Ella said. "I think moving forward, there will only be partnership in big moments, because this one here," she kissed the back of Morgan's hand, "she's too clever for the rest of us."

"You got outplayed, Cinder." Les patted her shoulder. "And by this tiny powerhouse of a woman."

"Never would have expected it," Marsh teased, tugging the hand of the tall, equally muscular man standing beside him.

Morgan was offended. "Did you call me tiny?" Even tipped up onto her toes she was eight inches shorter than everyone but Toni.

"Tiny *powerhouse*," he corrected.

"And don't you dare forget it." Morgan eyed the man with Marsh. "Is this your breast man?" she asked with a devilish grin.

Ella gasped. "Baby, that was not..."

"Shut up! You're him?" Lil squawked. "Do you still have the signature?"

"It was months ago," Marsh said. "Do you really think I could hold this man and stare at the signature of my lesbian best friend's big scrawling E on his pectoral muscle?"

"Don't know. That's why I asked."

"That's Mr. Breast Man to all of you," his boyfriend joked.

"Do not encourage them." Marsh patted his boyfriend's shoulder. "Ivan, this is my family. Family, this is Ivan."

"You've come on a great day." Morgan opened her arms for a hug.

Ivan hugged her. "That's what Marshal said, and I was nervous to invade."

"No invasion," Ella said as she offered a handshake. "It's nice to meet you with your shirt on."

"I got a lot of miles out of that signature."

Lester teased, "I'll bet you did."

~~~~~~~~~~

Ella lay in the lounge chair on their rooftop patio, with Morgan snuggled between her legs. The couple were transfixed by their hands, admiring the way their rings looked together.
~~~~~~~~~~

"I think I'm always going to love the way we proposed," Ella said.

"No regrets?"

Ella thought about the question, really looking in her heart for a truthful answer. "I don't think I want to change any of it."

"You aren't upset that I deconstructed your perfect scavenger hunt to Spring Falls?"

Ella sighed. "It was hardly a deconstruction, more like a reorganization of the actors."

"The element of surprise was pretty good," Morgan joked. "You never saw me coming."

"I didn't," Ella agreed. "Let me ask you this. Before Lil spilled the beans, did you have any clue I was going to propose?"

Morgan shook her head. "I didn't. I never expected a proposal."

Ella leaned forward to see Morgan's face. "Never?"

"In my heart, I've been committed to you since you told me about Kay. I know what it meant when you let down that wall and let me into that dark place. I'm with you, El. There isn't anyone else for me, and I figured eventually we'd decide together."

"You do want to be married, don't you?"

"To you." Morgan smiled. "I do."

They sat for a long moment before Ella asked, "Would you have proposed to me?"

"I think I would have." Morgan stood. "Maybe one day. We have so much together already. Why change?" She helped Ella to her feet. "Dance with me."

"There's no music." Ella wrapped her arms around her fiancée's waist.

Morgan shook her head. "Ella, Ella, Ella, sweetie, there has always been music right here." She patted her heart.

~~~~~~~~~~

Morgan shivered.

"Getting cold?" Ella asked.

"Something like that." Morgan kissed Ella's neck. "Let's go to bed." She led Ella down the rooftop stairs into the loft.

"Do you have thoughts about when you might want a ceremony?" Ella asked.

"I was thinking I'd like a February date, maybe close to the most romantic day of the year."

Ella chuckled. "Valentine's day? How very predictable."

Morgan slipped out of her dress and dropped it in the laundry basket. "No way. I'm no cliché. I was thinking about another holiday."

"There's another holiday in February?"

"Another?" Morgan pulled a sleep shirt over her head. "There are many."

"Many for a wedding?"

"There's February fifth, World Nutella Day. And February tenth, National Umbrella Day, and don't forget the ever-important February sixteenth, National Do a Grouch a Favor Day."

The last suggestion made Ella laugh. "You're joking."

Morgan wrapped Ella in a hug. "I'm joking. I really want to get married on National Muffin Day."

"You do?" Ella kissed Morgan before asking, "What day is that?"

"February twentieth."

"Okay," Ella agreed.

"Okay?"

"If you want to get married on National Muffin Day, who am I to deny that pleasure? Plus, muffins are just about the most delicious and versatile sweet treat."

"Did we just set a wedding date?" Morgan asked.

"I think we just did."
~~~~~~~~~~

"We're really going to do this." Morgan walked them to the bed.

"Yes, my love, we really are."

DE
CON
STRUCTED

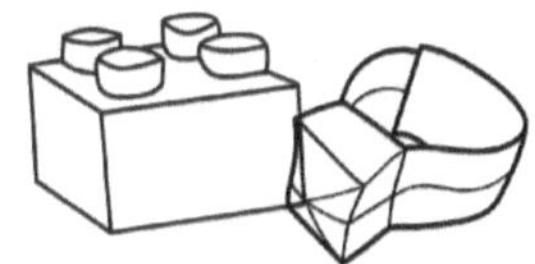

MORE BOOKS BY SHARON K. ANGELICI

<u>Rage Room Romance Series</u>
Book 1
CONNED

For Ella Eastman, firefighting is life. She's devoted her body to being the best, but everyone needs a break from reality once in a while. For Morgan Hail, art is life, but she has to make a living. Their lives collide when television fandoms intersect at The Blacktree Comic Palooza.

Morgan's captivating fanart leads to a heated misunderstanding, and a cosplay contest brings these two women together–though only one of them knows the truth. This unlikely pair heats up when their real-world lives collide, but what will happen to their budding romance when Ella reveals her secret identity? And can they find a way to make things work when Ella's job hits a little too close to home? Conned is a story of love, loss, new beginnings, and fandom.

Book 2:
DECONSTRUCTED

After eight years, Ella Eastman has a plan to create the perfect marriage proposal for her partner, Morgan. Inspired by Morgan's to-be-read pile, Ella struggles to incorporate her favorite romance tropes while asking the big question. The ideas pile up, as do the failed attempts to create their once-in-a-lifetime memory. How do you give the perfect partner the perfect memory of a perfect proposal? For Ella, it all seems to come together quite imperfectly. Revisit the Rage Room Romance's chosen family as they unite for Operation Perfect Proposal.

ORIGIN OF THE MAKER
(BOOK 3 OF THE MAKER SERIES)

Wildwood and her girlfriend Shay have uncovered Brigid's secret hidden deep in the earth.

Who is the stranger in the carriage house? How are they there? What do they know about the secret and the power it holds? Can Wildwood and Shay find the answers and keep fighting the monsters hunting them night and day?

LEGACY OF THE MAKER
(BOOK 4 OF THE MAKER SERIES)

In a secret world filled with magick, Wildwood Blackstone has encountered unbelievable mysteries. As the blacksmith in her new hometown, she's survived and endured the call to wield the hammer of the goddess Brigid, but to what end?

Celebrating a year with her girlfriend, Shay, the two continue their search for answers. What lived inside Andrea Peters? How did the entity survive for hundreds of years? Who controlled her all this time?

Their call to be The Magick and The Maker of Bannock comes with more questions than ever, but it might also come with answers to their past. Wildwood and Shay are drawn into endless realms, all of which lead to the Legacy of the Maker.

BEHIND THE EYES

Theirs was a love story for the ages: Rasabel, the captain of the guard, and Isolde, the woman of the territory. In a world of swords and arrows, love could not defend against a cruel curse. For years, they searched for an end.

When the alarm bells of Acadia ring, Rasabel goes home, but she is not welcome. Her path collides with Bylyn, a young thief on the run from the executioner's axe. Their lives are forever entangled.

Can Rasabel and Isolde find hope in the hands of a girl who will do anything to keep her freedom?

DEAR KANE;
WHAT I WISH WE WOULD HAVE SAID

Do the words that we say in front of our children build them up or tear them down? This short story explores the consequences of hatred and bigotry when it applies, unknowingly, to someone that you love. There's a time in every relationship when a parent must let go of the dreams they have for their child, so the child can chase what they dream to become.

IMMORTAL HUMAN TRUTH

Immortal Human Truth is a collection of poetry written by the author as she traveled to promote her first book
Dear Kane; What I wish we would have said.
Each section explores experiences with love, injustice, loss, and triumph of the spirit.

SHE BELIEVED SHE COULD

What can you do in a single day? Why haven't you done it yet? Jump out of your comfort zone and dive into life as you follow the author on her journey to achieve 365 new experiences in 365 days.

ABOUT THE AUTHOR

Sharon K. Angelici, she/her, was born in the American Midwest, but her heart and soul belong to the mountains of Colorado.

She began writing as a child, using words to recover from trauma-induced depression. As a member of the LGBTQ+ community, she's an advocate for depression awareness and suicide prevention. In 2016, she published her first book dealing with both subjects, *Dear Kane; what I wish we would have said.*

Sharon is a full-time lover of life and all things Pagan and Magick. She's an artist and blacksmith, which inspired her to create her Maker series.